B.L. OVERMAN

LIZZY'S FLOWER GLIZZY

THE PRIMEVAL ONES UNIVERSE

Primeval Ones: Parasites of Pleasure Series:

The Amazonian Uteroboscis (Book 1)
Uteroboscis: **Outbreak** (Book 2)

Primeval Ones: Plants of Pleasure & Horror Series:

The Yoni Flower (Book 1)
Lizzy's Flower Glizzy (A Tie-in Novella) (Book 1.5)
Blight of The Yoni Flower (Book 2) *(The Uteroboscis & Yoni Flower* Crossover **1***)*
Flesh Forest (A Tie-in Novella) (Book 2.5)

Primeval Ones: Deities of Lust Series:
The Horned One (Book 1) (The Uteroboscis & Yoni Flower Crossover **2***)*
The Flowered Goddess (Book 2)

And there will be more pleasure organisms & gods of lust to *come!*

B.L. OVERMAN

LIZZY'S FLOWER GLIZZY

SCIROTIC
BOOKS
Scirotic.com

**SCIROTIC
BOOKS**
An Imprint of Masterless Press

Scirotic.com

Lizzy's Flower Glizzy
Copyright © 2022 by B.L. Overman
Cover design by Thea Magerand

First Scirotic Books print edition: March 2022

Printed in the United States of America

ISBN: 979-8-9856127-2-1 (print)
ISBN: 979-8-9856127-3-8 (ebook)

FOREWORD & *CONTENT WARNING*

If you're a reader from Literotica, or if you're coming here from *The Amazonian Uteroboscis* or *The Yoni Flower*, hello again! If you're new, welcome, dear reader, to the Primeval Ones Universe—a universe where phallic organisms who evolved to deliver pleasure and lustful beings who want nothing more than to mate are slowly beginning to be discovered in uncharted regions of our current world by adventurers and scientists alike. *Lizzy's Flower Glizzy* is the 3rd book in the Primeval Ones series so far. If you like erotic and weirdly fascinating tales with epically bizarre and naughty crossovers, **sign up** at **Scirotic.com** for updates & *FREE* reads from **The Primeval Ones Universe**! Speaking of **freebies**, everyone who signs up at www.scirotic.com/scirotic-freebies will receive an email with **4 exclusive bonus chapters**—chapters that will shed light on why one of Lizzy's friends isn't responding to calls or texts at the end of the story…

This book is a spin-off sequel to *The Yoni Flower* that begins a few days before the last chapter of *The Yoni Flower* closes, and this book will tie in with/significantly affect *The Yoni Flower* Book 2. If you haven't read *The Yoni Flower*, **don't worry**, you can read this story independent of it, then you can double back if you want to. *The Yoni Flower* covers more of the flower's origin and the science of it all, but you don't need to know the science to enjoy the naughty fun and mystery-solving Lizzy and her friends get into.

Lizzy's Flower Glizzy [as well as the other books to *come*] is an erotic horror/sci-fi, splatterpunk story intended for adults who are into tentacle stuff, monster erotica, and Lovecraftian tales of titillation. As such, the text ahead will contain *very* graphic descriptions of Lizzy and her friends doing naughty things with a phallic flower that oozes sap and splooges all sorts of hot cream. Girl-on-plant fun aside, there will also be explicit details of freaky sex scenes with F/M & F/F partners as well as solo play, and strong language. Fair warning, gross things happen to the girls after the gooey fun is over (***cough, cough*** Chapter 7). So, if you're not into splatterpunk, there are quite a few chapters ahead that may be disturbing for those who are uncomfortable with imagery intended to elicit a certain gross-out factor. Because of that, *Lizzy's Flower Glizzy* may not be suitable for all readers.

All characters are over 18 years of age and any sexual acts described in the pages ahead are for entertainment purposes and not as a resource for sex-ed.

Enjoy the read! And prepare to be left feeling entertained and uncomfortable in the best way!

CHAPTER 1
JUST THE [FLOWER'S] TIP...

LIZZY RUTHERFORD | 18
Wednesday, July 20th, late afternoon

It's just another cloudy, summer's day here in rural Olympia, Washington. As my beautiful Palomino stallion named Sundance gallops swiftly towards the fence at the western end of our ranch's property line, warm wind wooshes past my ears and whips through my curtain of wavy, dirty blonde hair, making my locks dance behind me. I imagine it's flowing as elegantly as this horse's mane is. With each thunderous clomp of his hooves against the soil, my tender lady parts smash into and grind against the saddle horn.

Ugh, I have no idea why guys assume girls get off from riding horses, I think, pulling on Sundance's reigns to steer him left so this show jumping trained horse doesn't try bounding over the rail fence again. *There's nothing pleasurable about bucking into this hard pommel over and over. Not for me, anyway.*

With two clicks of my teeth, I lean forward then whip the reigns, sending the stallion into a sprint alongside the western fence towards the southern end of the property. In the corner of my eye, the lush greenery of the woods beyond the fence blurs by.

Rutherford Ranch—our family's home and business that's located here at 10043 Evergreen Valley Road—rests on a 55-acre patch of open land that's surrounded by dense woods. It's nothing special, just a two-story house with four bedrooms, a big red barn, a smaller run-in shed, and a big ole paddock for our horses to roam. The only other house on our woodsy, desolate road is about a mile north of us and just around the bend—another home business called Sheepdog Farms where people take their dogs for cattle herding lessons. On the other side of the fence to the northeast of our ranch, over at 7941 Johnson Rd SE, is the second closest home to us, and that's where my best guy friend Jake Landau lives. To the west, there's about a mile of woods separating us from a few isolated homes.

Other than that, there's nothing but dense woods beyond our ranch's fence to the east and south—woods that go on for nearly two miles in any direction before you hit another house or even a road. I know this because me, my brother Eli, and Jake spent much of our middle school and high school years exploring out there. Also, my friends and I used to hike a mile southeast through the woods to Fiander Lake, our place to drink from time to time when we had nowhere else to go. Or we'd go to the smaller Yelm Lake, a crappy little body of water to the southwest-ish where kids from school also throw secret parties.

My folks raise and breed horses at our ranch for a living, and they offer equestrian lessons from time to time on the side. Since I've taken after my professional equestrian of a mother, I've been riding all my life. As a result, teaching kids how to ride has been my part-time job on weekends during the school year and usually all summer long. But that's not what I'm doing today though.

Since I'm leaving for college in about four weeks, today's all about bonding with Sundance by riding around the property the way I do when there's nothing else going on. Because there ain't shit else to do around here, not when you're 18 with an old car that's been in the shop for weeks thanks to a backordered part.

A few yards from the southwestern corner of the fence, this heavenly, sweet, and floral aroma titillates my nostrils. *Literally* a second after smelling it, I swear I start feeling high or something. It's not like weed high, more like getting hopped up on caffeine then taking three shots of vodka on an empty stomach. Less than five seconds later, my skin legit gets all tingly like I'm passing through spiderwebs, and it sends a pleasant shiver down my spine.

What is that delicious smell? I've never smelled anything that good around here before, I think, pulling on the reigns.

The second Sundance slows to a trot, he starts sniffing all hard and fast, turning his head towards the woods to our right.

"Is it coming from the woods, boy?" I ask, petting his neck.

The further he walks along the fence, the more intense the smell becomes. And the more intense the fragrance grows, the more intoxicated by it I become. Suddenly, I'm dizzy in the best way, and the body-wide tingling for some reason has concentrated between my legs, making my pussy throb with a need the likes of which I've never felt before. The next thing I know, dampness soaks my panties, like this smell has my cooter drooling instead of my mouth. Not only that but my clit and labia feel super-sensitive to the point that, contrary to my earlier thoughts, grinding against the saddle horn feels amazing in a way it normally doesn't when I ride. It feels so good, I can't help but buck into the saddle in the most inappropriate way, undulating my torso to grind into it like I used to do to my pillow.

Fuck hell, what am I doing? Why am I so horny?

After a hard, slow grind into the saddle horn, a little "Oh-mm" of a groan slips out of my mouth.

That's when Sundance abruptly turns to the fence and neighs, rearing up on his back legs a bit like he wants to get over the fence.

"Whoa, boy," I say, patting him. "Is that where the smell is coming from?" With my right foot dug into the stirrup, I swing my other leg over his back then jump down. Now I take the lead rope and bring him to the fence so I can tie him up.

Right as I'm about to loop the rope around the fence, Sundance rears again and, as his front legs raise above my head, my gaze falls onto his erection.

"Holy shit!" I yelp, jumping back right before he comes down on me. "This smell has you all aroused too, huh, Sunny?" I tie him up to the fence before he does rears again. "You stay here and I'll go find out what's doing this to us, okay?"

Sundance licks at me then lets out a purr-like huff through his nose as I climb over the fence.

Branches rustle and twigs snap beneath my feet as I mindlessly wander through the dense brush in the direction the scent is the strongest. I'm in such a trance, it almost feels like I'm in a waking dream and my body is being guided by a migratory instinct or some shit. I can tell I'm getting close because now I'm started to pick up specific notes in the fragrance.

It smells like… I sniff in rapid puffs like a dog. *Smells like sugar cookies… sweet mango, and flowers.* With every sniff, it gets damper and damper between my legs. *Never have I ever been this wet before,* I think as my hand wanders between my thighs.

"Ugh-mm," I moan the second I rub myself over my jean shorts. Just as I'm rounding this tree, I see something in the small clearing ahead that makes my breath hitch and makes my pussy throb so hard that it clenches like a fist. "Holy fuckity-fuck!"

Sticking out of this bulge in the soil ahead is a pale plant-thingy the likes of which I've never seen. The white stalk of the thing is 6-inches long and as thick as a cornstalk, maybe just under 2-inches in diameter. Growing from the top of the stalk is something that can only be described as an erect, skinny, cream-colored, dildo—a dildo that has five hand-sized petals shaped like starfish arms that are growing out and down from the base of the dick-like shaft, dangling around the stalk like a skirt. And I call it a dildo because this plant's fleshy *appendage* looks *exactly* like a rubbery dick—not that I own a dildo or have actually seen a real penis in person, but I've seen many of them on the internet, so… yeah.

I mean, I once gave this boy from my summer camp named Andy Jankowski a hand job once, but it was dark so I didn't actually *see* it…

But, anyways, yeah, I say this flower's *protrusion* looks like a dildo because it's beige, maybe 7-inches long, appears to have a rubbery texture, and the shaft is webbed with an appropriate number of bulging veins. Also, the head of it is bulbous, smooth, and curved with rounded edges just like the head of a circumcised penis down to the very last detail. The damn thing even has a tiny urethra-like opening in the center of the mushroom cap of a head.

"There's no way there's a glizzy flower growing behind my house…" I whisper in awe, kneeling on the soil before this glorious, phallic plant. A *glizzy* is, like, Washington DC slang for hotdog, a term my generation hijacked and started using on TikTok as a euphemism for dick so that we could talk about them without getting flagged. Out of habit now, I always call dicks glizzies when I speak about them out loud.

This has to be a prank, I think, leaning in to better examine the plant. As I'm closing in, I notice that the undersides of the five petals aren't beige like the outside, they're vibrant red and glistening wet. Also, they aren't paper-thin like normal petals. Each one is as thick as my hand. *One of my friends surely must've 3D printed a stalk and stuck a dildo to it to fuck with me.* My eyes wander to the brown leaves on the ground around me, then I look up to the tree behind the flower that has several bare branches. *Since when do evergreens shed this much?*

It's only now that my face is inches from the flower's glizzy that I realize that the sweet, fruity, flowery fragrance that lured me here—the scent that made both me and my horse horny—is more potent than it's ever been because it's coming from this flower. Like, the aroma is so overpowering now that I can't smell the woodsy, earthy smells around me anymore.

I smack my lips. *Holy hell, I can taste the faint sweetness on my tongue.*

Now that I'm this close, the floaty, horniness I've been feeling since I first caught a whiff of this plant is now dialed up to 110%.

I've gone from dizzy to completely loop and giggly like that time I ate too many weed brownies, body high included.

I can't for the life of me stop my vagina from clenching and relaxing over and over—I can't shake the feeling that it wants to be filled with this long, carrot-thin dong.

My chest heaves from slow, deep breaths just like the first and last time a boy touched me between my legs—that was right in the middle of me giving Andy a handy out by the lake seconds before the camp counselors almost caught us and stopped me from potentially losing my virginity.

I feel like an animal in heat who needs to be bred right the fuck now and, while I've been very horny many times in my teen years, I've *never* felt this way in my life.

As I reach for the flower's glizzy, my lips part and this uneven, shaky breath floats through my lips like I'm cold and shivering. My pointer and middle finger press gently into the leathery shaft, tracing a path up the thing's soft *skin* to its cockhead.

Holy fuck, I think, curling all of my fingers around the shaft like I'm about to beat it off. Not only does it feel as firm as a boner, but it's also the temperature of a human body.

"Eek!" I squeal, snatching my hand away. "It's warm! Why the fuck is it warm if it's in the shade?"

Plants shouldn't be body temperature, right? I curl my fingers back around it more firmly this time and give it a stroke.

As if being warm to the touch wasn't enough, the second I stoke my way from the head to the middle of the shaft, it throbs ever so gently in my hand, then a bead of thick golden liquid oozes out of the glizzy's tip like precum.

I snatch my hand away again. "What the fuck…" Hesitantly, I dip my finger in the secretion and pull it away, staring in awe at the glistening string stretching away with my digit like snot. "It's sap… It's got to be sap…" I lick up the goo from my finger. As I swish it in my mouth with a bit of spit, this insanely sweet, slightly fruity honey excites my taste buds.

More, I think, stroking the shaft again. *I want to taste more.*

Two strokes later, it spurts more sap than last time. I waste no time wrapping my lips around the glizzy's head, sucking it like a lollipop so I can drink the deliciousness right from the hole.

"Mmm!" I moan.

Each stroke makes the flower's glizzy throb and spurt more sap. Each throb feels harder than the last. The sap that comes out with each pulse is more and more voluminous than the last. I waste no time slurping it off before it drips down. Eventually, I stop using my hand and just start bobbing my head on it the way I've seen women do in porn, only engulfing it to a few inches below the tip because I know I can't deepthroat like my bestie Piper.

I can't believe I'm blowing a weird-ass flower, I think, sucking noisily with desperation in an attempt to keep sap from pouring out with my drool.

The more slickness I gulp down, the more intoxicated and aroused I become. The longer I go on, the more my jaw starts to hurt and the more breathless I become.

A gasp escapes me as soon as I pull the glizzy out of my mouth, then I just kneel there panting for air. "What. The. Fuck. What am I even doing?" I giggle to myself, wiping away the slime running down the corners of my mouth, smearing the slickness across my chin.

Things heterosexual virgin girls do:

1.   *Give a hand job to a plant because it looks like a dick…*

2.   *Blowing said dick-shaped flower because it cums syrup…*

What next? You gonna fuck it? The silly thought makes me snicker, but my vagina throbs like it wants that to not be a joke.

For whatever reason, this stupid TikTok sound pops into my head and, like the brainwashed Gen-Z teen that I am, I start reciting it aloud. "At first, I was, like, mmm… feet… as a joke," I mutter as my hand slips into my panties. "But, *bro*… I don't think it's a joke anymore…" My sap-glazed finger glides between my already slick folds before plunging deep into my tightness with a gushing sound. "Ugh… fuck…"

You know what? That'd be a pretty funny video… Wait… this is it! This is how I go viral. Make a TikTok with the 'mmm feet as a joke' sound, then make it seem like I actually fucked it… Raunchy shit like gets the most views. If I blow up, I can say fuck college and just be an influencer, I think, pulling my phone out from my back pocket with my clean hand.

It doesn't take long to find the sound through the app's search function. Once I have it cued up, I use my shirt to wipe the saliva and sap off of the skinny dong. Now that it's clean, I scoot back, point the camera at the glizzy flower, and hit record.

'*At first, I was, like, mmm… feet… as a joke,*' the girl's voice says in that weird moan of a tone. That's when I pause the recording and switch it to the front-facing camera, doing a naughty lip-bite-thing before hitting record again. Now I lip-sync the '*but, bro… I don't think it's a joke anymore*' part. That's when I stop recording again. All I have to do now is stroke the flower's glizzy to make it look like it's covered in my wetness, then I can record a clip of the plant before turning the camera back on me as I'm pulling my hand out of my shorts as though I actually fucked the flower.

Just like before, I jerk off the plant nice and slow, watching as sap spurts from its hole with each pulse. It takes all my willpower to resist sucking it clean. Pretty soon, the head of the glizzy is coated in a glistening, golden sheen that starts dribbling down the shaft, glazing it in this viscous slime the texture of raw egg whites. Now that the glizzy is all lubed up, my hand glides up and down the carrot-thin phallus with a bit more speed. Feeling how slippery it is against my skin makes me imagine what this throbbing rod that's the perfect size for my virgin pussy would feel slipping in and out of me.

"But what if I *actually* fuck the flower first," I moan out, visualizing myself squatting onto the glizzy and bouncing on it like it's a dildo suction cupped to the floor. My pussy aches so bad for the fantasy to be real that it flutters hard—hard enough to make my core spasm.

The next thing I know, my free hand is back in my pants and I'm fingering myself to the thought. I'm so fucking wet that the schlicking and squelching down below sounds like someone is playing spitty, ASMR mouth sounds at max volume in my pants.

I really, really want to feel it inside of me. Because I'm an 18-year-old virgin who's weeks from college and I don't know what it's like to have a cock in me. But now… I moan loudly. *Now I can experience that pleasure without any of the risks or drama or emotional attachment…*

I don't know if it's because I've been inhaling this aroma for an extended period of time or if the sap that I guzzled has me even more aroused than before, but I'm so fucking horny that I'm anxious to the point that I want to scream. I legit feel like I might actually lose my mind if I don't get penetrated until I climax right the fuck now.

Fuck it, I think, removing my hand from the glizzy while rising with haste. *Maybe I'll just try the flower's tip.*

My hands tremble as I feverishly unbutton my shorts, then I tug them and my panties down in one go, kicking them off over to the tree behind the glizzy flower afterward.

The anticipation of what I'm about to do has my heart racing and my legs all shaky. *Just the tip, Lizzy,* I think while squatting over the glizzy flower. *Just take it nice and slow.*

The second that the warm, slimy head of the phallus presses against my folds, I moan out a breathy "oh." Reflexively, my hips involuntarily rock back and forth in rhythmic undulations, dragging my slit back and forth against its slick, mushroom cap of a cockhead. Over and over, I tease myself from clit to hole, using the phallus to paint my pussy lips with its lube-sap. The entire time, I'm moaning like I've never moaned before from fingering myself or toying myself cunt with the handle of a hairbrush. With each grind, the sweet agony grows more intense, like I'm a pressure cooker that's about to explode from overflowing, liquid pleasure.

As the glizzy's narrow head once again slides up against my oh-so-sensitive clit, the unbearable ecstasy makes me grind into it harder—so hard that the slick crown quickly glides south of my clitoris only to part my folds and slip right into my tight entrance. The glorious pleasure of the surprise penetration makes legs go weak—so weak that I squat lower onto the sap-lubed glizzy quicker than intended, accidentally forcing the smooth head to bulge through my tight entrance before it bores a few inches into me.

"OHH!" I cry as even more of the glizzy than I was ready for impales me, filling me as deep as my cavity will allow. "AHH!" I whimper from the sweet pain of its head smashing into my cervix.

Being stretched this deep for the first time makes by something undisguisable from a penis me quiver. *So much for just the tip,* I think, looking down and staring in awe at how much of the glizzy my pussy swallowed. All seven or so inches of the shaft are inside of me, leaving the five petals dangling out of me like I'm birthing a deformed squid with flat, wide tentacles.

Slowly, I rise off of the skinny ramrod, trembling from how incredible it feels having the slickest phallus gliding back out of me. Right as the tip wedges in my hymen—right as it's about to leave my tight hole, I slowly lower myself back onto it, driving it back in. That's when the carrot-thick rod pulses gently inside me, releasing a gush of warm honey right up against my cervix. "Mmmmm," I groan, rubbing my clit. "Fuck, this feels so good!"

I keep the pace at which I bounce on the flower's glizzy nice and slow so I don't break the stalk. The longer I go at it, the quicker it throbs, the more sap it oozes, and the slicker the thing becomes. The more I bounce on this cock-like organism, the better it feels and the loopier I become.

Wait, why is it starting to feel thicker? Is it swelling? And why is there this weird, stretching sensation in what feels like my cervix? Am I… dilating?

Like a flash of lightning, something way too intense to be an orgasm strikes, shooting sparks of pleasure down my legs, filling my vision with stars, making my pussy contract rhythmically around the phallus that's gone from carrot-thin to nearly as thick as a bratwurst. I don't care why it's swelling or why a flower's glizzy-like organ is throbbing hard and fast inside my cavity like a racing heart, all I know is that coming around it feels amazing. The combination of my orgasm and the swollen thing pulsating inside of me is too much stimulation for me to handle, so much so that it feels like my vagina is about to seize into a cramp—it feels like I'm about to black out.

A cry of sweet agony and pleasure sears my throat as I rise off of the thing, and the glizzy's head slides out my hole with a sticky-sounding *plop*. Somehow, my weak knees hold out long enough for me to stumble back and fall ass-first onto the soil instead of collapsing back onto the schlong.

The orgasm still rippling through me has me too dizzy to stand, too weak to move a muscle. So, I lay back on the ground, my limbs sprawled out in a limp mess across the dirt as though I'm a ragdoll some little girl dropped. I'm so breathless that I'm panting like an overheating dog. With each rolling contraction, my pussy spurts hot, thick sap that leaks down to my butthole and crack.

"Wow… Just… wow…" I smile, writhing restlessly while staring at the still pulsating glizzy flower. "That was the best experience of my life!" I whisper to the plant I just made love to.

Only you'd have your best sexual experience would be with a freaky flower you found in the woods… Because you're pathetic, Lizzy…

You know what? I don't care, a voice that sounds like mine argues back in my mind. *I'm glad that just happened because I feel like I've gone and died to heaven, and who knows if any guy will ever make me cum like this!*

My entire body feels flushed, and a bit sedated in the best way. Even though I'm lying on the hard, lumpy ground, I feel like I'm floating on a cloud high on something more amazing than weed. I've orgasmed a few times before from experimenting the same way all young girls do. I've achieved one by humping my pillow, by using my fingers, toying myself with a hairbrush while rubbing my clit, and, of course, using my showerhead.

Before today, the best orgasm I've ever experienced is when I borrowed my dad's neck massager while he and mom were out and about for the day. I pressed that thing against my clit while I pumped my hairbrush handle in and out of me. It only took a few minutes for me to climax. And it felt so good that I laid in bed moaning and trembling with that vibrator between my legs for, like, four hours, or however long it was before I heard my parents pull into the garage.

But even orgasming for hours on end with that massager didn't make me cum the way that flower just did. And none of those back-to-back climaxes left me feeling like this afterward.

Maybe it's because I'm high off this aroma. Or maybe the sap has narcotics in it like opium plants do. That's gotta be it. Because I didn't start feeling drunk like this until after I was fucking it for a while.

Around the time the glizzy stops throbbing and oozing sap is when I come down from the orgasm and muster the strength to sit up. After taking a nice, deep breath, I maneuver onto my hands and knees then rise from the dirt, my legs still trembling beneath me. My legs still feel so noodly that I almost fall over three times before finally getting my shorts and undies back on.

Time to finish this TikTok and get back to the house before my parents wonder my horse is tied up on this side of the property, I think, using the inside of my shirt to wipe my hands off.

I open the app, tap on my draft, then I point the camera at the sap-glazed glizzy before hitting record. After slipping my free hand into my shorts, I zoom in on the phallus, I zoom back out, then I flip the camera back onto me just as I'm pulling my hand out of my shorts. Now I give the camera a naughty smile while I show the sap-coated fingers I've just pulled out of my pussy to the camera. That's how I end it.

"This is *so* getting taken down," I mutter to myself, giggling as I tap the **'POST'** option. Good thing that this is my secret spam account that one I know follows…

After slipping my phone into my back pocket, I give the glizzy flower one last longing look. *God, I really want to fuck that thing again,* I think, sighing. It takes everything in me to start walking back towards where I left Sundance. *It's okay, you've got the rest of the summer to practice riding dick with the flower glizzy. I'll just come back tomorrow. Or tonight, if I can't wait that long…*

Hmm, maybe I should invite the girls over to show them what I found. I wonder if it'll have the same effect on them as it did on me… My parents are leaving tomorrow for that destination wedding in Jamaica, so maybe I should host a little girl's night and find out…

CHAPTER 2
DOUBLE DARE: *SEGGSY* EDITION

LIZZY RUTHERFORD | 18
Friday evening

It's almost 6:00 P.M. My parents barely left five minutes ago and my walls are already vibrating again from a different car that's pulling up to the garage—vibrating from both the engine and from the loud-ass rap music coming from its speakers. Before I even have a chance to get out of bed, a horn blares three times.

"Lizzy!" Piper screams from down below. "Get up!" When I look outside, I find her with her head out the passenger's side window. "It's party time, betch!"

"WOOOOO!" she and Whitney scream in unison as they climb out of the red Subaru Legacy. As soon as they're out, they start twerking.

Savanna just climbs out of the driver's seat shaking her head.

"You're lucky I don't have neighbors!" I shout. "Door's open! I'll be down in a sec!"

By the time I get downstairs, the girls are just walking in.

First through the door holding a box of pizza is the slender, beautiful, strawberry blonde with hazel eyes, Whitney Emmerich. "Hey girl!" she greets, looking around the house. "Where's this surprise you have for us?"

I smirk. "No surprise until we're appropriately fucked up…"

"If we have to be drunk first, it's got to be really good," Whitney says.

"If we have to be drunk first, it probably means it's something we won't like," Savanna Lockhart, the curly-haired brunette with bangs and a case of resting bitch-face mutters.

Whitney shoots her a look. "Let's be real, Sav. If Lizzy wants us to get drunk beforehand, it's because she secretly just wants to get your uptight-ass to relax since you never like anything fun."

You hit the nail on the head, I think, keeping my facial expression neutral. *Because I'm sure if Savanna the prude sees a dick-shaped flower, she'll just get her panties all in a bunch and complain about how inappropriate it is or something.*

Savanna glares at Whitney over her cat-eye glasses.

"No!" I say before they start to argue. "I just want us all to be turnt the fuck up because I want tonight to be the crazy, pre-college sendoff we deserve!"

"That's my girl," Piper, my raven-haired bestie, says as she finally walks in with a heavy tote bag in hand.

Savanna is dressed modestly per usual, sporting a teal shirt and high-waisted jeans. She's not even wearing makeup. Whitney has on a bit of makeup with eyeshadow that matches her pink sundress. However, Piper Cummings, the former sex goddess of Yelm High School, has her face all done up and she's dressed in a skimpy skirt with a lowcut tank top that showcases her perky C-cups. Something tells me she's expecting to see some boys tonight. Then again, I'm sure at some point she'll sneak off to see Jake Landau the way she always does when she comes over.

Piper is seduction incarnate, the girl every guy wants to be with—the exact opposite of my plain-Jane-ass. There's a reason why every boy from our high school couldn't help but cover their crotches with textbooks whenever Piper Cummings walked past them down the hall. That reason is also why Jake didn't hesitate to make a move on her in ninth grade even though I've been by his side since we were toddlers. Hell, he's known Whitney and Savanna since I introduced them to him in kindergarten and he's never once expressed interest in them either, not even after they hit puberty, and they're both prettier than most girls from Yelm.

There's a reason why Jake keeps pursuing her even though *literally* everyone knows she's hoed her way through school.

"I stole a bunch of White Claws from my sister," Piper says, giving me a naughty look as she hands me the heavy tote bag.

That naughty look isn't her flirting with me. Even though she's straight, it always feels like she's flirting with us whenever she stares at us. Some girls, like Savanna, have resting bitchface. Then there are girls like me who always look bored and sort of sad. But Piper has resting fuck-me-eyes—topaz irises that always seem to pop in an almost unnatural way because of how they contrast against the dark eyeshadow she always wears. It also doesn't help that her default expression is this pouty look where her plump lips are slightly parted like a French model who's using sex to sell perfume—parted like she's just always seconds away from getting on her knees to suck dick.

Maybe that's because she *is* always seconds away from giving someone a BJ. I mean, there's a reason everyone at Yelm High called her the Cummings Dumpster, a nickname that she was proud of...

Because she pretty much blew all the hot guys from our school...

And she's been barebacked and creamed quite a few times since going on birth control...

"Good," I say, smiling at her before turning and walking the drinks to the fridge, "because we're going to need chasers for the Captain Morgan."

After White Claw number two and shot number four, I dump some ice in the cooler, put the rum and a few Claws inside, then I hand the bag off to Whitney. Now I head to the garage to grab a few battery-powered lanterns.

When I walk back into the kitchen and place a lantern into my backpack, Savanna looks at me with an arched brow. "Why the fuck are we going to need lanterns?" she asks in a bit of a slur.

"Because it's going to be dark soon, and the surprise is in the woods."

"We heading to Fiander Lake?" Whitney asks.

"Ooh, please tell me you have four hot guys waiting for us out there," Piper says, dancing to the song that's bumping on the speakers. "I'd very much like to get dicked-down tonight!"

"What else is new?" Savanna groans with a roll of her eyes.

"Nope. And *nope*," I answer. "The surprise is much closer than the lake." I turn and smile naughtily at Piper. "I promise you won't be disappointed though."

On the hike over to the southwestern corner of the fence, none of us are walking in a straight line, and all of us are basically yelling and cackling like we're half a mile away from each other.

Right as we're about to hit the fence, right as that heavenly aroma excites my nostrils, Piper inhales once really hard, pauses for a moment, then sniffs again in short, rapid puffs. "Yooo!" she moans out. "What the fuck is that delicious smell?"

"Oof, fuck…" Whitney moans next. "It's heavenly."

"Seriously," Savanna says, closing her eyes and inhaling deeply.

"Smells like sugar, sex, and flowers…" Piper adds.

Giggling, I climb over the fence. It's only after the horniness makes me squeeze my thighs together that I realize how damp my panties are already. "How do you all feel?" I ask with a smirk.

Piper's chest heaves as she straddles the fence. "Horny as fuck."

"Umm… same," Whitney whispers shamefully as she climbs over the wooden rail alongside her.

Savanna nods. Right as she's about to climb the fence, she freezes. "Wait… What did you put in our drinks, Lizzy?"

I laugh. "Nothing! That smell in the air? That's what's making you feel like that."

"What?" Whitney mutters. "How?"

"Yeah. How?" Piper adds. "Like, what flower can make you wet just by smelling it?"

Whitney's head snaps toward Pipes. "Okay, so I'm not the only one who's dripping down there?"

The three of us shake our heads no with shy smiles on our faces.

"Lizzy," Whitney says, half-smiling, half-wincing, "seriously, what's going on?"

I grin naughtily. "Follow me and I'll show you…"

I lead them a few yards through the brush and, the closer we get, the loopier and more turned on I feel. The plant-induced high seems more intense than it did last time, probably because I'm drunk this time around.

As we round the massive tree blocking our view of the surprise, I hold up the lantern and gesture to the flower with a broad, sweeping pass. "Tada!" I singsong.

The moment it's illuminated, their jaws drop and their eyes go wide.

"What. *The fuck*. Is *that*, Lizzy?" Whitney says in awe, unable to tear her wide eyes away from the sight.

"The surprise!" I cheer.

Piper approaches it slowly, reaching for it before she's even close enough to touch it. "Looks like a dildo growing out of the ground to me," she says, curling her fingers around it and caressing it lightly. "Oh my fuck…"

"What?" Whitney yelps.

"It feels like…" Piper's words trail off as she gives it a gentle squeeze. "Flesh… Waxy flesh that's… warm…" She turns to me with squinted eyes and the naughtiest of smiles.

"Yo," Whitney says, caressing it with a finger, "she's right…" She turns to me. "You're telling me that this *isn't* a dildo you stuck to a pole in the ground and glued some petals to?"

I shake my head.

A shit-eating grin stretches across Piper's face. "Is there a guy buried alive down here with his freakishly long dick sticking out of the ground, waiting for us to pleasure him?"

I crack up. "Nope!"

"So… what is it?" Savanna asks, finally poking the beige dong.

I shrug. "As far as I can tell? It's some kind of plant… Obviously, I named it the glizzy flower." I cackle.

Savanna arches her brow. "If it's a flower, how the hell does it have a *body* temperature?"

I snicker. "What am I, a fucking biologist or some shit? All I know is that it jizzes some kind of delicious honey if you stroke it."

"You're shitting me," Piper says in awe, grinning at me.

"I shit you not," I respond. "Jack it off nice and slow. And keep your eye on the hole at the top."

When Savanna and Whitney remove their hands, Piper grips it and strokes it with a slow twist. "Yo! It just throbbed in my hand!"

"Holy shit, look!" Whitney chirps. "The sap or whatever is beading up on the tip like precum!"

"Mm-hm!" I hum. "It's delicious too!"

"You did *not* lick sap from a freaky flower's penis growth…" Savanna says in disgust, squeezing her legs together like she's desperately trying to suppress the urge I know we're all having.

"I did. And then I blew the thing and guzzled its honey in a way that'd make Piper proud," I say, smiling at Piper just as she's licking the sap from the glizzy.

"Oh. Mmmmm!" Piper moans, wrapping her lips around the phallus's crown. In one fluid motion, she swallows the rod deeper than I ever could. Her throat makes a glurping-gawk sound as she bobs her head on it, then she pulls it out of her mouth. "That's… the best thing I've ever tasted."

"I wanna try!" Whitney cheers, turning to me. "It's not going to make me sick, is it?"

"Nope!" I say with a smile. "I've ingested copious amounts of the stuff and it just made me feel hornier and sort of drunk."

"Look how much is coming out now," Piper says, still stroking the glizzy that's getting nice and lubed up.

Whitney sucks the head of the phallus like a lollipop then slurps up the syrup. "Mmm… Mmm! Fuck, that's delicious! Sav, try it."

"I don't know…" Savanna says, folding her arms and looking away shyly.

"You prude!" Whitney teases. "See, *this* is why Lizzy wanted to get you drunk. Because you're no fun till you're shitfaced."

The schlicking, sticky sound of Piper jerking off the drenched glizzy fills the silence. "Fuck… it's getting so nice and slippery…" she moans… "Listen, I'm going to say what we're probably all thinking…" She glances over at us. "This fragrance or pheromones or whatever has got me horny as fuck—hornier than I've ever been in my life, and it's unbearable, so I really wanna fuck this glizzy flower so I can get off…"

Whitney winces. "Umm… same!" She giggles, slapping her palm onto her mouth like she didn't mean to say it out loud.

I smirk. "Then do it… I fucking double dare you…"

Piper smiles knowingly at me. "Wait a sec… this was your plan all along… You wanted to get us drunk before getting us to play a game of double dare sexy edition with this intoxicating-ass glizzy flower…"

She's referring to when we used to get hammered and dare each other to do naughty, borderline-lesbian things in front of and with each other. Sexy double dare, as we called it, included challenges like: humping pillows, scissoring each other with pants on, pressing our crotches against Piper's parent's hot tub jets, and sitting on individual back massagers together to see who'd climax first. Of course, Savanna would refuse to take part in anything until we got her hammered, hence the reason I made her drink so much before we left.

"You figured it out, Sherlock!" I say, winking at her.

"Just because we can ingest the sap, that doesn't mean it's safe for our kitty meow-meows…" Whitney says, squeezing her thighs together and bouncing subtly like she has to pee.

"Don't worry, it's safe," I say.

"How do you know?" Whitney asks.

"Trust me… *It's safe*…" I say more seriously.

Their eyes go wide.

"You didn't…" Piper says, grinning and blushing.

I simply stare at her.

"You *didn't*…" Whitney echoes.

"I did!" I finally say. "I don't know if it was the fragrance or the sap that it spurted into me, but riding this thing gave me the best orgasm of my life!"

Piper's jaw goes slack. "You're not lying, are you?"

Blushing, I shake my head.

"When did you… *do it*?" Whitney asks.

"This past Wednesday…" I mutter.

"Fine. Then you go first, Lizzy," Whitney says.

"Nuh-uh, I dared you two first!" I retort.

Piper holds up a hand. "Hold on, as badly as I'm aching to go first, I feel like if we're going to all fuck a glizzy flower in front of each other, we should ease into it. You know, like foreplay…" She slips her fingers into the hem of her skirt. "I'm going to go on ahead and strip, so I dare all of you bitches to strip down to your undies with me." She tugs her skirt down as she shimmies out of it.

"Sure," I say, pulling my top off the same time Piper does. Normally, I'm hesitant to strip or even wear a bikini around my friends, because I'm self-conscious.

"Well, I picked a bad day to go commando…" Whitney says, pulling off her sundress.

"I can't believe this is happening," Savanna says, subtly glancing over at Whitney's bald pussy.

I follow her gaze, unable to look away from the glistening wetness between her folds and on her thighs. My gaze snaps over to Piper next. She's almost as skinny as me, but she somehow has a dump truck ass, her tits are nearly twice as big, and her ribs aren't protruding through her skin like mine are. She, like the rest of our tight-knit squad, looks like a woman while I look like a borderline anorexic teen, despite eating like crazy. Not to mention that my tits are barely A-cups, and my ass isn't much to gander at.

I *wish* I had Piper's body. I've been told I'm cute, but I wish people called me beautiful and sexy like they always say to her. Hell, I'm even jealous of her eyes even though people have been complimenting my steely blue irises since I was young. My grayish-blues were my favorite feature until that day in ninth grade when we were standing side-by-side and Jake Landau looked past me and told Piper how much he loved her eyes…

My gaze wanders over to Piper's crotch where her panties are so soaked that I can see the outline of her meaty folds through the fabric.

Piper scoffs. "You act like we haven't all changed in front of each other before… Just strip, Sav. Strip then blow the damn flower."

"I don't know…" Savanna says, looking away shyly. I don't know what she's so ashamed of, she's a former lacrosse player so she's the most fit of the group, she has the best ass out of all of us, and her boobs are not too big or too small—perfectly perky.

"Take two shots then fucking woman-up and do it!" Piper snaps. "Come on… We're all going to different colleges in a few weeks. When are we going to have another chance to share a wild-ass experience like this?"

"Fine…" Savanna says, pulling off her top. "But I need to drink more before I take my panties off or do anything else…"

"I'll get the rum!" Whitney says, opening the cooler and rummaging around for it. "Here."

Savanna grabs the Captain Morgan, brings it to her lips, then turns the bottle up and takes two big gulps. After that, she wriggles out of her jeans, removes her top, then kneels before the glizzy flower.

"Suck! Suck! Suck!" Piper chants.

Whitney and I join in on the chant.

Savanna wraps her lips around the tip and sucks on it like a lollipop while stroking it gently. "Mmm…" she moans softly. "Mmm…" She slurps hard then takes it a bit deeper. Our prude friend goes at it like a pro for a few minutes before pulling the skinny dong out of her mouth and gulping hard. "That was a lot of sap…" She starts panting for air. "Whitney, I double dare you to go next.

"The things I resort to when Luke is on vacation," Whitney mutters, kneeling before the glistening phallus. Luke McCarthy has been her on-again, off-again boyfriend since freshman year. A few months before graduation, right after learning they both got into the University of Washington, they decided to get back together despite having just broken up after prom. "This isn't cheating, right?" She genuinely looks concerned.

"Noooo," Piper says, waving her off. "Doesn't count if it's a naturally grown dildo!"

"Good," Whitney says, engulfing the phallus's knob.

She gives the glizzy flower a BJ with a bit more skill than Savanna. And, at one point, she takes it too far back and gags so hard that thick amber sap gushes out of her mouth while her lips are still wrapped around the shaft.

"Rookie, bitch!" Piper teases.

Whitney gasps for air as she pulls the phallus out of her mouth. "Then show me how it's done, gawk-gawk queen…"

"I dare Lizzy to go next before I slobber all over it," Piper says with a devilish smile.

Just like I did the other day, I bob my head up and down the glizzy, stopping right before it hits the back of my throat. Globs and globs of warm sap spurt into my mouth at a quicker pace the longer I suck. There's so much flooding my mouth that it's getting harder and harder to swallow it all. I have to let the stuff run down around the shaft to keep from choking and drowning.

"Mmm," I moan, pulling the throbbing carrot-thick plant dick from my mouth. "You're up, Pipes!"

"Yeah…" Piper says, standing up. "I already sucked that thing off, and I'm too fucking horny to do it again, so I'm going to go on ahead and execute Lizzy's first dare. And, since I'm taking my panties off, I dare the rest of you to too."

I'm too high on this flower's sexy-time fumes and too drunk to care, so I pull down my undies without hesitation.

Whitney looks over at me as she tugs hers down. "Holy shit, you are, like, wet-*wet*…" she says, staring at the glistening strings stretching out between my panties and my coochie.

"So are you, girl!" I say with a shy smile.

When I look up, Piper is standing over the glizzy and reaching down to hold it in place.

"Wait," I blurt out, hurrying over to my backpack. "I stole some condoms from my brother's room."

Piper scowls at me. "I've been tested, Lizzy… I'm clean."

"Yeah, I know. But… we should all be safe just in case."

"But I want it to pump my kitty full of sap while I ride it!" Piper whines in a childish tone.

"Then bite a hole in the tip," I say, handing her a condom.

"Fine," she says, snatching it from me. "But I need to lube up first." She strokes the shaft from the skirt of petals to its head, then she takes the palm-full of sap and rubs it across her folds before fingering it into her. "Ooh fuck yeah…"

"Is this weird for anyone else to watch?" Whitney asks.

I nod.

"Oh, come on, Whit," Piper says. "Don't act like your bisexual-ass isn't enjoying seeing your friends naked and touching themselves."

"No comment…" Whitney replies.

Piper rips open the condom and, after struggling to roll it down onto the slimy shaft, she bites a hole in the rubber's tip. After that, she squats over it, reaches down to hold it in place, and then she slowly impales herself with it. "Ahhh!" she moans. "Yes!" She rises off it then drops back down onto it with more speed than last time. "Can someone hold the stalk for me? I don't want to fucking break it." Her words come out all breathy.

"I mean, the stalk is pretty sturdy, but sure," I say, kneeling before her and wrapping my fingers around the firm, sturdy stalk.

As warm sap drizzles onto my hand, my eyes wander up from the stalk to my best friend's pussy that's right in my face, and I just stare in awe at the naturally grown plant glizzy sliding in and out of her. *I'm so drunk and loopy from this pheromone stuff that I don't even care that I'm basically watching my bestie fuck a dildo…*

"Ugh-ah. Ah-ah," she moans. "Fuck… having warm honey gushing into me feels so fucking good… It's like constantly being cummed in…"

Hearing her moan, listening to the *schlick-schlick* of this thing pumping in and out of her, it drives me wild, so wild that my pussy throbs and aches with desperate need. It's taking everything I've got not to reach between my legs and rub my clit.

If I didn't think it'd be weird, I'd totally do it, I think, looking over at the spectators. My mouth gapes slightly when I see Whitney pumping her middle finger in and out of her while tending to her clit with her thumb. *Clearly, Whitney doesn't think it's weird to pleasure herself to her friend getting off.*

When I glance at Savanna, she's looking off into the woods, subtly bouncing and fidgeting in place. She, like me, is probably so unbearably horny that she can't keep still because she needs to be penetrated immediately.

The longer Piper bounces on the dick-plant, the more sap gushes out around the shaft and drizzles down on my hand, coating it in a glaze. The longer she goes at it, the harder and faster the firm stalk throbs in my hands as it pumps sap up into her from whatever part of it is underground. All I can imagine is some sort of sap-filled taproot pulsating beneath the soil.

"Why does it feel like its swelling inside of me?" Piper asks breathily. "Does it look girthier to you?" She slowly rises off of it until the head is wedged in her opening.

"Oh, it's definitely swelling," I whisper. "It does that after a while. If you keep going, it'll start throbbing really hard."

She drops back down and impales herself with it while writhing her hips. "Oh yeah… It feels like a heart-shaped like a dildo is beating in my snatch," she moans, reaching down to rub her clit.

As I'm watching her pussy swallow the phallus as far as it'll go for the umpteenth time, Piper's leg tremble. "Oh…" she groans in pleasure as her core spams. "AH-OOH!" she cries out, her body convulsing like she's having a seizure. Suddenly, she springs up out of her squat until the girthy, throbbing thing leaves her with a sticky, *BLAP* sound. Just like I did a few days ago, she falls onto her ass and lays on her back, her limbs a limp mess, her still contracting vagina gushing sap with each throb. "Fuck yeah!" She pants for a while. "You were right, Lizzy…" She pauses to breathe again. "That was the most intense orgasm of my life…"

"Told ya!" I say. "You feel all weird and sedated?"

"Oh yeah…" she whispers. "I was just about to say something about that… Feels like I smoked weed and took Nyquil… And my body feels all flushed and tingly."

"If it felt so good, why'd you stop?" Whitney asked.

"The orgasm was so intense that my pussy, like, cramped, and then my legs got too wobbly to keep going…" Her head lolls over towards me. "Probably for the best though, I can tell by the look on Lizzy's face that she was aching for her turn."

Giggling, I nod rapidly. "I think Whitney really needs to go next. She was over there diddling away the entire time."

"Hush up," Whitney says, smirking.

"You know the rules," Piper says. "The person dared last dishes out the next one. And since you were a sweetheart who held the stalk for me, I dare you to get your fuck on next so you don't have to wait anymore…" She touches her finger to her lips. "Actually, wait. I dare Sav to go next. And I dare her to dare Lizzy to go afterwards."

Savanna shakes her head. "I am *not* fucking this random plant thing…"

Piper sighs. "Fine, then I *at least* dare you to scoop the sap off the glizzy and finger it into yourself. It makes you, like, two times hornier, so maybe it'll put you in the mood for later."

Savanna looks at the glizzy flower. "Fine, but I'm *not* doing it in front of you all."

Piper claps. "That's the spirit!"

After peeling off the used condom, Savanna jerks off the phallus until sap gushes from its tip and drizzles into her hand. She then walks a few feet away, turns her back to us, reaches into her panties, and starts fingering herself. Even though she's not right next to us, I can still hear the sticky schlicking going on. It doesn't take long for her to start panting and moaning. "Oh… fuuuuuuuh-uh-k."

"Wooo!" we all cheer, clapping like we're at a concert.

A minute or so later, Savanna's legs begin trembling and she stifles her moans. "Okay…" she says breathily, turning to us looking all flushed as glistening sap strings drip slowly from her vadge. "Lizzy, I dare you to do what Piper said. *Get your fuck on…*"

CHAPTER 3
CREAMPIED BY A FUGGIN PLANT!

LIZZY RUTHERFORD | 18
Friday evening

While I wait for the glizzy to shrink from sausage-thick back to its carrot-thin size, I drink another White Claw with the girls. Around the time Piper is finally able to sit up is when the phallus has stopped throbbing and returned to its normal girth.

"Alright, it shrank! Go, Lizzy go!" Piper cheers.

"Fuck that glizzy, Lizzy!" Whitney chimes in.

"Alright, alright," I say, squatting before the glizzy flower and rolling a fresh, ultra-thin condom onto the phallus. Once it's on, I bite a hole in the tip then stroke it until it coats itself in sap. The instant it's nice and lubed up, I stand over the plant, curl my fingers around it, then squat down onto it. "Ooof…" I moan when the head of the thing slips between my folds and glides into my tightness. "Ah… Oh yeah… Can two of you, like, hold my hands for support so I don't fall over when my legs start to go weak?"

"Sure," Whitney says, standing to my left and taking my hand.

Piper stands on my right and holds my other hand. "Looks like you get to hold the stalk, Savanna…"

Savanna sighs. "Ugh… Fine…"

Just like my first time with the glizzy flower, I take it nice and slow at first, squatting down at a moderate pace to let it fill me gradually until the firm yet squishy head of the phallus batters my cervix. It only takes a few bounces for the shaft to start throbbing and really spurting sap shots deep into me.

How much sap does this thing even have? After we all blew it and after Piper's ride, it should be drained, I think as my legs quiver from the peaking pleasure.

"Damn it, Lizzy!" Piper says, squeezing my hand, "you can fuck it a little harder than that! You saw how I was going at it. Hate fuck that thing! It can take it! Pretend it's Connor!"

"No, pretend it's your bestie, Jake!" Whitney says.

Piper shoots her a look because she's basically dating Jake now even though she thinks I don't know.

As I pick up the pace, my breathing becomes more labored.

"Come on, gyrate those hips more," Piper says. "Grind into it as you slam down on it!"

I do as instructed, working my hips the way I do when I try doing the TikTok belly dancing trend. That's when the plant's fleshy rod really starts to pulsate faster. A second later it swells and spurts a higher volume of sap-lube into me. Just like last time, there's this weird stretching sensation in my cervix. It also sort of feels like something tickling my cervix.

"There you go! That's it!" Pipes cheers. "Now just come down a bit harder when you grind."

I slam down onto it harder than before, battering my cervix against its cockhead. The sweet punishment hurts so good that my core spasms. The second time the glizzy's head pounds that deep, sensitive spot at the end of the line, its shaft throbs *really* fucking hard, blasting honey against my cervix with surprising force.

Actually, it felt like its thick heat shot straight right through the entrance to my womb.

"Oh my fuck," I moan, as my vagina clenches rhythmically around the dong.

After that, the shaft swells inside of me faster than it did last time while pulsating rapidly like a snake having a seizure. *It didn't feel like this last time,* I think, moaning harder than before.

Just as that thought leaves my mind, my eyelids flutter when a sharp, brain-scrambling orgasm comes out of nowhere and ripples down from my womb to my vagina. "I'm. Cumming!" I cry out, my legs trembling violently as I slowly drop back down onto the glizzy despite trying my darndest to rise off of it.

"We got you!" Piper hollers. She and Whitney don't pull me up, they just hold me in place so I can maintain my full squat of a Malasana yoga pose.

In between my vaginal contractions, while I'm grinding on it shallowly, the glizzy throbs crazy hard twice. On that second throb, right as the head of the phallus is pressing against the end of my cavity, it sprays my cervix with an insanely forceful jet of hot sludge that feels *way* thicker than sap. It's so powerful that it reminds me of when my brother Eli sprayed my belly at point-blank range with the high-pressure nozzle of the water hose. So much of it is pumped into me that one shot overflows my pussy to the point it gushes out around the girthy shaft with a bubbly spurt.

What the fuck, I think, watching in awe as something creamy and white the consistency of mayo runs down the shaft and drizzles onto Savanna's hand… That's when my pussy cramps hard around the now cucumber-thick phallus like a hand gripping the lap bar of a rollercoaster for dear life.

"OOH-AH!" I whimper.

"Ewww!" Savanna whines below. "There's white stuff gushing out of her!"

"It's cumming in me!" I cry out, attempting to stand only to have my legs give out. It's like my body is both immobilized from the orgasm and sedated from the sap. As my cervix slams back onto the glizzy's head, a second jet of sludge sprays right up against it. "UGHH-AH! Pull me up!" the cry for help comes out like a moan of pleasure.

Instead of pulling me up, Piper places a hand on my shoulder and presses down. "Nope! Don't let her up, Whit! She needs to know what it feels like to get creampied." An evil giggle follows.

With one hand still holding mine, Whitney presses down on my other shoulder, forcing me down onto the glizzy until the squishy, mushroom-capped head mashes hard against the deepest most sensitive part of my cavity. And what normally feels uncomfortable feels like the most glorious kind of pressure. "Sorry, Lizzy, rules are rules!"

As the rapidly pulsating phallus throbs hard in me again, whatever thickness that doesn't ooze out around the zucchini-thick shaft sprays right the fuck up against my cervix, and I swear there's warmth filling a space in the base of my belly now…

"Ah! Ahhh! Oh! Oh, fuck!" I cry, my eyes rolling into the back of my head as a third jet of liquid head sprays into me. "It legit feels like its spraying into my uterus! AHHH!"

"Does it hurt or does it feel good," Whitney asks, sounding concerned.

"Good! In a weird uncomfortable way," I moan out, wincing and screaming in sweet agony as another blast fires directly into my womb. "Starting to feel full though…" My words come out all fast and shaky.

"Um, her belly is swelling…" Savanna says. "Pull her off!"

My legs are trembling so hard that they're vibrating. "Please! My womb feels like it's about to fucking explode! Please!"

Whit and Pipes hoist me up off the glizzy at the same time. As the cock shaped plant leaves me, it feels like a thin string is being pulled through my cervix, and it tickles so good that my core spasms. The instant that the unbelievably swollen head is launched out of my still clenched vagina with a *bloop*, thickness gushes out of me, splattering noisily on the soil below like that time I spilled paint all over the barn floors.

"Holy fuck!" Piper says, easing me down to the ground with Whitney's help. "Look how much of that creamy plant cum is leaking out of her! That's gotta be more than a cup!"

"So much is wrong with that sentence…" Savanna says.

"Did Lizzy seriously just get creampied by a fuggin' plant?" Whitney asks, staring in disbelief.

"Um," Piper hums. "Unless there's another term to describe a flower going from oozing lube-honey to ejaculating a different type of gooey white stuff after overstimulation, then I guess so…"

Laying on my back with my feet flat against the dirt, my knees bent, and legs spread, I look down at my distended lower abdomen. In my peripheries, I catch a glimpse of these thin, semi-transparent vines sticking out of the glizzy's tip, seemingly wriggling in the air like three or four snake tongues. The moment my eyes snap over to the flower, the *glass noodles* get sucked into the phallus's *urethra* in the blink of an eye.

Hold on, am I seeing things? No, there were definitely clear vines sticking out of that thing… Maybe that's what was tickling my cervix…

"You okay?" Whitney asks when she sees me wincing.

"It feels like I'm pregnant with a big bowl's worth of hot chowder…" I mutter breathlessly, my eyelids fluttering as this intense drowsiness comes over me.

Using whatever strength that I have left, I sit up, press down on my belly while tensing my abs and pelvic floor like I'm trying to give birth. My womb cramps as warm, thick cream erupts out of me and splatters the ground again. The next time I push, I feel the sludge spurting and bubbling out of my cervix before thickness floods my vagina. A moment later, it all comes pouring out like mayo. Funnily enough, what erupts from my birth canal is not only white like mayonnaise, but thick like it too, and there's something like dark amber maple syrup swirled in it.

"Good lord…" Piper says.

"There's way more where that came from…" I say, poking the *baby bump*. "Feel my belly…"

"Oh… it's hard…" Piper says as she and Whitney poke at it.

"Yeah… As soon as I can stand, I'm going to go squat in the bushes and squeeze out as much of that ejaculate as I can…"

For some reason, my vagina is still partially clamped shut so, when I slip a finger into me, it feels way tighter than usual. Eventually, I decide to use both hands and pull my labia open so I can let the white lava just flow out of me.

"Fuck, that's kinda hot," Whitney mutters under her breath.

"Is it weird I want to taste it?" Piper says, staring at the creamy flower while biting her bottom lip naughtily.

"I double dare you to slurp some off the glizzy, Pipes," I say breathlessly.

"Don't gotta ask me twice!" Piper says, kneeling before the plant. She licks it from shaft to tip then sucks the head clean. "Hmm…"

"What's it taste like?" Whitney asks.

"Not sure… I need a second and third opinion," Pier says with a smirk. "Whitney and Savanna, I dare you to taste it and tell me."

"Pass…" Savanna says, I'll take a shot instead.

"You will take a shot… A shot of plant cum…" Piper says sternly.

Whitney looks down at the cream-coated glizzy flower.

"Nope, not from there," Piper says just as Whitney starts to kneel. "Savanna, *you* can taste from the glizzy. But you, Whit? You have to finger it out of Lizzy, suck your finger clean, then lick and suck more straight out of her coochie…"

"Umm, no," Whitney says flatly.

"Come on, you're bi. It'll be fun… Don't act like you weren't basically drooling and licking your lips watching Lizzy finger that cream out just now…"

"Yeah, but… she's my best friend though," Whit says.

"You have to. I dared you. Besides, if there's a girl you should be getting that intimate with for the first time, shouldn't it be one of your best friends?" Piper arches a brow.

Whitney glances over at me, but I'm all sorts of distracted watching Savanna licking cream from the glizzy's shaft like melting ice cream from a cone. 'Bleh," Sav gags.

Smiling at Savanna's reaction, my gaze snaps over to Whitney. "I'm drunk as fuck and high on plant pheromones so why not," I whisper.

"Okay…" Whitney kneels between my spread legs. "You ready?"

I nod.

The second that her middle and ring fingers slide into my tight, cream-filled hole, my pussy flutters around her digits and the pleasure makes my eyes squeeze shut. A shaky moan escapes me as she curls her fingers in a 'come here' motion inside of me. While she rakes the plant's ejaculate out of me, my pussy clenches so hard that more white stuff oozes out of me.

Well, that just happened, I think, opening eyes.

At that moment, Whitney sticks her creamy fingers into her mouth then sucks them clean. "Mmm," she sort of moans.

"Good, right?" Piper asks.

"Actually, yeah. Tastes like—"

"Not yet," Pipes interrupts. "Chow down on the creampie first…"

Sighing, Whitney brings her head down between my legs. "You okay with this, Lizzy?"

"If she does a good enough job, you might cum hard enough to squirt the glizzy flower jizz out of your uterus," Piper says, cackling maniacally afterward.

"Might be worth a try." I giggle. "Since I doubt that I'll ever let a girl go down on me in the future, might as well have my first and last experience on the same night I got creampied by a flower…"

"That's the spirit!" Piper cheers.

Without further delay, Whitney dives in.

"Oh!" I yelp and jump when Whitney's warm, wet tongue meets the base of my folds.

Her tongue parts my labia as she licks her way up my slit. Whit's mouth leaves my southern lips with a smack only for her to surprise me a moment later by plunging her hot, slippery muscle into me, probing me nice and deep. It only takes a few seconds of her tongue-fucking me like a hungry anteater before a core spasming orgasm ripples through me. Each contraction forces a gush of thick goo out of my hole, and Whitney laps it up like a thirsty dog, gulping loudly every other spurt. And when my pussy and womb contract in unison right as she's taking a breather, more thick goo squirts out right into her open mouth.

"Mmm!" she groans as she lifts her head from between my thighs. "That was a lot," she mumbles, giggling as cream spills down the corners of her mouth and runs down her chin.

"So hot…" Piper says.

"*So* gross," Savanna groans.

"So?" Piper says. "What's it taste like, Whit?"

Whitney smacks her lips then swishes the gunk in her mouth. "Mostly bitter, kinda gritty, a bit salty… and it's sort of sweet like the sap…"

During her review, I finger some cream out of me and suck my finger clean. *She's right…*

"Exactly what I thought!" Piper cheers. "Tastier than semen, that's for sure…"

Whitney and I giggle. Savanna shakes her head.

"If you liked it so much," Whitney says to her, "I dare you to give the glizzy flower the gawk-gawk 9000 until it splooges, then chug the plant jizz until you can't anymore…" Gawk-gawk 9000 is a special kind of blowjob where you take it all the way to the back of your throat over and over so it makes a *gawk-gawk* sound, and then you go at it until the guy's dick is all spitty and messy.

"I doubt it'll cum again after it filled Lizzy's womb to the brim," Piper says with a grin.

"Seriously…" I mutter. "It shot like four or five jets into me, and each one felt like half a cup or something…"

"Only one way to find out…" Whitney says, gesturing to the phallic plant.

"Fine," Piper says, kneeling before the glizzy flower. "But when I'm done guzzling—as soon as I pull it out of my mouth—I double dare you to ride it while it's still coming," she says, looking at Whitney… "You know, because you never let Luke jizz in you before… And after it creams in you, do a bukkake with Savanna…"

Whitney arches a brow. "*Boo*-what now?"

"Bu-kahk-kay. It's, like, this Japanese thing where a woman lets a bunch of guys cum all over her," Piper explains. "Since this plant cums more than 100 men combined, I want you to shower in the jizz when you're done riding it." She turns to Savanna. "And you have to let some of it get in your mouth, too, but don't swallow it. Because I want you to spit it all in Sav's mouth so she can gulp it down."

"You're gross," Savanna says. "I'm not letting her spray me with a weird plant's *ejaculate*, and I'm *definitely* not letting Whit spit that shit in my mouth…"

"You will, because I know you're not a lame bitch," Piper says. "While I'm blowing the flower, you have time to take two more shots and a White Claw… Maybe when I'm done, you'll be loosened up enough to *at least* wanna take it in the ass. You know, since you're *sooo* into butt-stuff now…"

"That's supposed to stay between us, *Piper*," Savanna snarls through clenched teeth.

"Wait, what's supposed to stay between you two?" Whitney asks.

Piper grins. "Before prom, she asked me how to prepare for anal—"

"Piper!" Savanna screams.

"So," Pipes continues, "I didn't answer her. I just went to CVS and grabbed an enema, then I went to the sex shop by the IHOP and I bought her a tub of lube and that thirteen-inch, double-ended dildo that you've seen me sword swallow."

"Geez… *thirteen* inches?" Whitney mutters. "The rectum is, like, 6-inches long. What the heck were you preparing her for, one of Lizzy's horses? Because we all know Keith ain't *that* hung!"

Piper cackles. "No! Eww! I just figured a long, double-ended dildo would be a good idea in case she wanted to do both holes at once. Or if she wanted to finally get around to practicing deepthroating. But, *anyway*," she turns to Savanna with a grin, "Sav told me that she liked toying her back door *waaay* more than expected. So much so that she asked me how often could you safely do enemas because she wanted to flush herself out before every date night with Keith, *just in case*…"

Whitney grins. "Oh… Well, since you two broke up after graduation, I guess that means you didn't do an enema today, huh?"

We all laugh.

Savanna shakes her head and rolls her eyes. "Remind me to never come to you again with private stuff…"

Piper hugs her. "Oh, relax! We tell each other everything! And after all the naughty shit we've dared each other to do over the years, you have nothing to be embarrassed about. I mean, you *literally* just fingered yourself with sap, like, two feet away from us and you watched Lizzy get her womb flooded with a cock-flower's splooge."

"Speaking of which," I groan as I finally get myself to sit up, wincing from the quick flare of pain in my uterus. My womb spams and contacts hard again right after. "Pipes? You have fun sword-swallowing that glizzy flower. Sav? Don't stick my glizzy flower in your ass…" I smirk.

"Where you going?" Piper asks.

"My uterus is cramping. Gonna try and birth this white goo baby… Be right back!"

"Ew… Okie dokie!" Piper says, peeling the creamy condom off of the phallus that's no longer swollen. "Good luck!"

On the way over to where my shoes and clothes are, all I can feel is the gunk dripping out of me. Some of it runs down my legs but a lot of it is splashing noisily onto to leaves and soil below. I haven't decided whether or not I want to walk all the way back to the house, so I just put on my shoes, grab my clothes and a lantern, then I start heading towards a more secluded spot where the girls won't be able to hear me moaning and groaning on top of the other gross, spurting sounds my snatch is going to make.

Upon reaching a small patch of soil behind a wall of foliage where I can no longer hear Savanna slurping the glizzy flower, I pull on my shirt, squat and lean back against the tree behind me, then I push. Hard. Despite how full my uterus still feels, only a little bit of white muck pours out of me like cake batter.

Why does it seem so much thicker now? I grab a lantern and inspect the glob that just fell out. *And what are these brown swirls? Doesn't look like the sap… it looks darker…* I pinch the brown stuff floating on top of the cream puddle then rub the fluid between my pointer and thumb. *Not as slippery as the sap, and it's much thinner too…* Now I lick it. *Ugh, so bitter… Definitely not sap…*

It's only after I slip my middle finger into me and feel around that I notice how thick the stuff pooled in my cavity has gotten. The consistence of the gunk in my vagina is less like mayo and more like thick guacamole. While pressing down on the bulge at the base of my belly, I squeeze my abdominal and pelvic floor muscles over and over in an attempt to try and birth more sludge. Slowly but surely, the thickness oozes down into my vagina like toothpaste, then I scoop out what I can. Despite how gross this is, fingering myself has never felt this good. Because everything has been crazy sensitive since I've been around the glizzy flower.

It feels so good that my other hand wanders between my legs and I start rubbing my clit, hoping I can get myself to climax again so I can eject more goo from my womb. It doesn't take much clitoral stimulation and fingering to get me to cum. As my womb contracts along with my vagina, a voluminous glob of warm sludge pours out from that sacred place where babies come from, flooding my cavity. As I spread my lips apart, my vaginal walls and womb contract again, spurting a thinner shot of creamy sludge that shoots out of me like a water gun filled with white mud—white mud streaked with blown swirls.

Fuck, I think staring at what seems to be less than a quarter cup of goo pooled on the soil between my legs. *At this rate, it's going to take all night to purge this stuff from my womb… Or maybe I should just give up wait for it to come out with my next period… Yeah, that's what I'll do. I'll try pushing a few more times and, if nothing happens, I'll just wait for my body to do its thing.*

CHAPTER 4
GLIZZY GOBBLER, JIZZ GUZZLER

PIPER CUMMINGS | 18
Friday night

Glurp-gawk-gawk-glurp-glurp-gah-gah-gawk-glurp—those are the obscene sounds that come from my throat each time I swallow the glizzy past my uvula. There's also lots of squelching and the sound of me slurping up globs and strands of saliva. Like, I'm taking it so deep that I can feel this long, skinny dong bulging behind my vocal cords. Normally, I can't swallow a dick this far, but because this thing is longer than it is wide and attached to a stalk instead of a man's crotch, I can take it deeper than I've ever taken cock.

After pretty much deepthroating this thing nonstop since Lizzy disappeared into the woods minutes ago, I finally lift my head until the glizzy leaves my throat. A gasp escapes me as syrup and saliva stream out of my mouth like a curtain of slime, swinging from my chin like a pendulum before the cold sliminess splats against my tits.

"Gawk-gawk! Gawk-gawk!" Whitney and Savanna chant.

It's good to see Sav's prude-ass finally getting in the spirit. Then again, I'm pretty sure she's just excited to see me choke and suffer...

"Um, is the queen of deepthroats taking a break?" Lizzy teases as she appears from behind the tree ahead, one hand rubbing the bump at the base of her belly.

Without saying a word, I flash her a sinful smile, wrap my lips around the phallus's head, then I resume bobbing my mouth up and down the sweet, sap-coated shaft, driving it deeper and deeper down my throat with each bob. Just as it's sliding past my tonsils, the phallus throbs gently against my lips and teeth, oozing warmth straight down my throat. Damn does it feel good.

How is this thing still gushing sap? I ask myself while gulping the delicious thickness down. With each passing second, I swear I'm getting loopier and dizzier with a euphoric bliss like guzzling sap is making me feel more drugged than inhaling this intoxicating-ass fragrance was. *If I had a plant like this behind my house, I could and would literally do this all day, every day…*

I love deepthroating dick. Like, a lot. And the only thing I love more than sucking cock is having warm jizz shot directly onto my tongue. I legit can't get enough of it. Honestly, I think I'm addicted to it. That's probably what happens when you blow dudes on the daily.

I mean, there's a reason I earned the name Cummings Dumpster…

I fell in love with semen after I gave my first blowjob to Jake Landau. Bitter, salty, cock snot should've been an acquired taste, but something about how it felt on my tongue and how it tasted *immediately* drove me wild. And after realizing each guy's splooge varies in flavor and consistency, sampling as much baby batter as possible became a bit of a life goal. All the different flavors and textures, the way hot semen feels sliding down my throat, having that creaminess pooled on my tongue before I swallow it—it gets me off in the best way. I love the way boys always turn to putty while I suck them off. I also loved the way they all became a pathetic, trembling mess when they felt their cocks poke the back of my throat, so I trained myself with a dildo until I was able to suppress my gag reflex.

It didn't take long to become a gag-free pro. To test my skills, I blew two guys at one party, barely two minutes apart. The second guy had no idea I still had a mouthful of semen when I took him into my mouth. A few weeks later, at one of Brent Dawson's house parties, I had a bunch of my guy friends meet me in Brent's bedroom, then I let them fuck my throat blowbang-style. That night, I guzzled six cum shots back-to-back. When I left the room with red eyes and mascara running down my face while a bunch of grinning guys filed out behind me, everyone in the hallway knew what happened. I wasn't ashamed either, I was proud.

I craved jizz even more after taking six loads back-to-back that night, so I stopped waiting until after school to gobble dongs. Getting face-fucked in school bathrooms, in the parking lot during lunch, or under the bleachers by whatever hot guy I set my sights on that day became a daily routine. And not just once a day either. At one point it was three times during school hours and then one more time outside my house whenever the senior of the day dropped me off. Oh, and then party nights, I summoned my favorites for a blowbang special.

Literally the day I started taking birth control, I let Jake Landau finish in me up in the Rutherford's barn's hayloft. That was the night I discovered I also had a breeding kink. After that first creampie, I started letting the guys who I knew didn't get around *a lot* finish in me. My record was three guys in one night, and that was a few months ago at the graduation party. Before that, it was just one guy any given night, and that was usually Jake, the one guy I actually trust and like.

Even though I enjoy getting plowed and creampied, I actually still prefer blowing my partners to completion. So, while I've been having way more sex, I still tend to finish off guys orally to satisfy my cravings.

When is this glizzy going to cum? It's swelling so much that it's making my jaw hurt, I think, swallowing the flower's schlong all the way down to where the petals begin splitting from the shaft. *And Jake is going to be here soon, so I need to finish up ASAP…*

I tighten my lips around the phallus and quicken my pace. When I feel it pulsating faster and faster in my mouth like a real cock, I know it's about to blow. Suddenly, the glizzy throbs really hard once, swelling to a size I haven't experienced yet. On the next throb, something hotter and thicker than sap shoots right down my throat, filling my stomach with so much heavy cream that it feels like I just downed a big bowl of oatmeal.

I want to taste it, I think, unswallowing the glizzy until its throbbing head is in the middle of my tongue. The second I taste that briny, bitter, semi-sweet cream, I know it's the stuff that gushed out of Lizzy and not sap. As I suck it off with shallower bobs while chugging the stuff as fast as I can, I let a bit of cream ooze out of my mouth, then I give the girls a thumbs-up.

"Yay! Woo!" Lizzy and Whitney cheer, clapping.

"How is it even coming again?" Lizzy says to the girls.

A second later, another jet of piping hot cream blasts the back of my throat with an insane amount of pressure that actually makes me—she who does not gag—choke. I try my darndest to gulp it all down but I still end up cough-gagging to the point that white cream sprays out of my mouth and my nose at the same time.

"EWWWW!" the girls reel in harmony.

I pay them no mind. I try desperately not to laugh. I just focus on not panicking, forcing myself to guzzle it all down as fast as I can before the next spurt—

And here's the third jet of plant cum, I think, gulping the mouthful of thick, gritty gunk down.

At this point, I'm so full it that my belly hurts. My throat legit feels clogged with thick chowder and it's getting harder to gulp.

When my mouth overflows from the impossible to swallow volume, I try pulling the glizzy out of my mouth but it doesn't budge because it's swelled up so much that it's wedged against my teeth and stretching my jaw as wide as it'll go. Right when it feels like I'm about to drown, I panic and use my hand to squeeze the salami thick shaft harder and harder until I can pull it out of my gullet. As the head of it slips past my lips, the cream overflow spills down my chin and I quickly clamp my lips shut to keep from losing any more of the delicious goo.

"MM! MMM!" I hum, bending the glizzy flower that I'm still stroking towards Whitney while writhing my body. That's my way of saying, *'it's time to fuck it before it stops jizzing again.'*

"Ugh," fine, Whit frets. Just as she's rushing over, the phallus I'm still jerking off throbs hard, swelling in my hand as it fires a long, white goo rope with brown streaks right at her. A second after her mouth gapes from the sight, the high-pressure stream sprays right into her mouth while the rest splatters loudly against her face, tits, and belly. "OAHHRGH!" she gurgles, freezing in place before spitting out the creamy sludge.

"Ew! Fucking gross!" Savanna screams behind Whitney, wiping off the white cream from her cheek. That's when she sees the stuff dripping off her hair. "Come on!"

"Whit, hurry!" I mumble since I've yet to choke down the mouthful, my hand still jerking the throbbing glizzy to keep it ejaculating.

Whit snaps out of it then bolts over and quickly squats down over the phallus that I'm holding in place for her. "AH… OH…" she moans as her pussy swallows the rapidly pulsating chode's knob of a head. "Fuck, this thing is way too girthy for my coochie!" Despite her complaints, she wastes no dropping down on it hard and fast, wincing as she drops into a full squat. "OHHH! Oh, shit!"

CHAPTER 5
GOOKAKE

WHITNEY EMMERICH | 18
Friday night

"OHHH! Oh, shit!" I cry out in sweet agony as the creamy, too-wide, salami stick of a plant dildo bores into my tightness, stretching its way to my depths at a pace that's far too quick given the size and my lack of experience with a *cock* this girthy. "AHRGH!" I groan from the impact of the swollen head punching my cervix. "Ah-Ah… Fawk…"

I didn't mean to impale myself on it *this* fast. While I was in a rush to fuck this glizzy flower before it stopped ejaculating, seeing how wide it was made my drunk-ass think I was going to have to squat down onto it hard to force it into my cooter. What I didn't take into account was the fact that this throbbing thing was going to be *this* damn slippery from the mix of sap-lube, Piper's slobber, and the creamy ejaculate coating it. Like, it glided all the way in and bottomed out so quick that I'm squatting here all dazed and confused.

"Don't stop!" Piper orders from between my legs. "Go! Go!"

Taking a deep breath, I rise into a partial squat, my core quivering as the swollen thing's head bulges its way back to my down to my entrance. Right when it wedges into my opening, I follow Piper's instructions to Lizzy and writhe my hips as I grind down back onto it, swallowing the glizzy until my folds bump into where Piper's hand is wrapped around the conjunction point of the shaft's base and the petals. As the phallus's head mashes into my sensitive flesh at the end of my canal, it throbs as it erupts inside of me with the force of a pressure washer, blasting my cervix so hard that I wince and scream bloody murder.

Oh god… is this what we made Lizzy endure when we forced her down onto it?

As the thought leaves my mind, Piper reaches up with both hands, grabs my shoulders, and pulls me down, forcing me to take it all the way in. Right as the swollen, mushroom cap of a head presses even harder into my tender cervix, another hot, thick jet sprays right against me. Suddenly, I start feeling warmth filling me somewhere deeper than my vagina—somewhere behind my bladder…

"AHH!-OOU! FUUGH-KUGH!" I cry out from both the discomfort of having another high-pressure shot of cream being injected into my uterus and the sensation of the glizzy suddenly and rapidly swelling to the girth of a plastic water bottle.

I shrug Piper off of me then rise off of the thing as fast as I can. For some reason, it no longer feels slick as it drags out of my cramping vagina, it feels sticky, tacky, like a dildo coated in drying glue. As soon as the plump rod leaves me, white and brown swirled goo gushes out of me and splashes the pool of slime below like someone just dumped out a bucket of curdled milk onto a pot of watery oatmeal.

"Boo! You only took one load!"

"Actually, I had *two* cumshots injected deep into me! Thank you very much!" I say breathlessly as I kneel before the throbbing glizzy that doesn't seem as swollen as it felt inside me. "I couldn't handle it. It hurt too much!"

"Karma's a bitch, ain't it?" Lizzy says with a wrathful smirk.

"Yeah," I say. "And I'm sorry… That was *not* a good time."

"Whatever," Piper mutters, stroking the plant at its base as she angles it towards me again, "just jerk it off and shower in the slime. Savanna, kneel beside her."

"Fine, I'll do the gookkake or whatever." I curl my fingers around the phallus that's, for some reason, covered in more amber slime than white cream than it was earlier.

As I start beating it off—as Savanna is kneeling beside me with a huff and a groan, I glance down between my legs and watch in confusion as runny amber liquid leaks out of me with only a few thin streaks of the thicker white ejaculate. *Wait… why is it mostly brown now when Lizzy had a potful of cream pouring out of her?*

"Hey…" I say to the girls, still staring all wide-eyed at the mess pooling on the soil beneath me. "Should it be this color? And why is it so runny now?"

Lizzy squats beside me, wincing and holding her belly. "Umm… I had some brown streaks in the chowder that leaked from me, but not *that* much…"

"Should I be worried?" I ask, slightly bending the glizzy towards my face.

At that moment, the shaft throbs hard in my hand and shoots white cream into the air. Somehow, I manage to squint right before the heavy goo rope splashes my forehead and cheek.

"Angle it to your face more and open your mouth!" Piper demands as the rapidly pulsating rod I'm still jerking sprays my face and tits with more hot, white cream.

Almost immediately after opening up nice and wide, briny, bitter sludge fills my mouth. "AHRGH," I groan from the taste before my gag reflex makes me choke and causes me to reflexively swallow a good bit of the thickness.

"Good girl!" Piper says like a proud momma. "Now spit it into Sav's mouth while you both shower in it."

"MM!" I groan at Savanna.

"No!" she says, pressing her lips shut and shaking her head.

"Just open your mouth!" Piper shouts.

"KMM-HMM," I hum, my attempt at saying *come on!*

That's when the phallus balloons and shoots a blast of runny, brown slime that drenches me from the top of my head to my belly. As the hot liquid pours down to my legs and washes over my vagina, I angle the still spurting glizzy flower over towards Savanna. Through a squinted eye, I watch as white sludge creams her face, hair, and tits. A split second later, before she can react, a second eruption of amber slime glazes her entire torso from her clavicle to her crotch. Because she got doused in both types of ejaculates, her top half looks like a frosted donut covered in maple syrup while everything from her belly to her thighs is coated in just syrup.

As thickness and slime drip off of her, Savanna's jaw drops and she just kneels there with her eyes closed, arms dangling limply out in front of her. "Ah… ugh… Eww-waaaah."

Piper points to Savanna's gaped mouth. "Do it." She whispers.

Smirking and shaking my head, I lean over, bring my face to hers, then I spit the cream I've been holding in my mouth right onto her tongue.

"URGHMM!" Savanna groans, spitting out a bit of chowderlike goo before Piper slaps a hand over her mouth.

"Swallow it…" Piper says sternly.

Savanna gulps hard, pauses, then gulps again. That's when Piper removes her hand from her mouth, strings of brown, milky slime stretching between her palm and Sav's lips.

"Fucking disgusting," Savanna groans, panting and wiping the goo strings from her mouth. "Fuck you, Piper!" she says, blindly reaching out to smear brown slime on Pipes only to miss when she leans out of the way.

Piper giggles, naughtily licking up the slime from her palm.

The phallus I'm absentmindedly still jerking ejaculates once again, spurting a stream of brown liquid right at Piper who somehow leans out of the way in time. The slime spatters loudly against the tree that's like, ten feet away. And, when it finally ejaculating stops, I release the glizzy and the flower springs back to its upright, erect position.

"How the fuck is it still ejaculating?" Lizzy says in awe, staring at the glizzy flower with this wide-eyed, glazed-over look.

"Let's keep jerking it and see how long it'll cum for," Piper says with a wicked smile.

"Um, let's not," I mutter, squeezing the slime out of my clumped hair. "Whatever this syrupy stuff is," I say, shaking the gunk off my hand with a hard snap, "it isn't the same ejaculate that first came out…" I give my hand a sniff. "Not only is it brown and runny, but it also smells musty as fuck…"

The girls start sniffing around.

"Ewww, you're right…" Lizzy says, her face all scrunched up. "I can barely smell the flower anymore."

"Bleh," Savanna gags after sniffing herself.

Piper gags too and doubles over, holding her belly. "Okay… yeah…" she groans, walking over to her clothes. "I already felt queasy after guzzling, like, three cups of glizzy cream. Now this smell has me on the verge of puking." She then squats by her belongings and rummages around until she pulls out her phone.

"Yeah…" Lizzy says, pinching her nose while backing away from the flower. "I'm super drowsy and my fucking uterus feels like it has a fever, so I was gonna say that we should clean up and call it a night." She starts getting dressed.

"Good call," Savanna blurts out with a bit of attitude, rising from the ground with her eyes still clamped shut.

"You know what?" I say, standing up. "I'm kind of drowsy too. And my womb is cramping. *Bad.*"

"Welcome to the club…" Lizzy says, rubbing the *baby* bump at the base of her belly. "It just started feeling fizzy in there too a bit ago, like someone injected me with sparkling water…"

"Um," I say, blinking rapidly at her. "*That's* fucking weird… I hope that doesn't happen to me…"

"Glad I didn't get creampied by that thing," Piper says with a wicked smirk as she texts away on her phone.

"Fuck you, Pipes!" Lizzy and I say in harmony.

"Can someone please give me something to wipe my eyes with?" Savanna asks.

"Here you go," Lizzy says, handing Sav her top.

"Alright," Piper says, pulling up her skirt, "let's get hurry back to the house, I'm legit about to puke…"

"So… I guess I'm walking back to the house naked, because I'm not dirtying up my sundress," I say, looking down at the thickening glaze coating my body.

"Uh, yeah," Savanna chimes in. "Lizzy, Eli isn't back yet, is he? I don't need your brother seeing me naked and glazed in goo…"

"Nope. Eli's gone for the weekend."

"Looks like we're streaking tonight," I say to Savanna and the topless Lizzy.

"Well, that's another bucket list item I get to check off tonight," Lizzy mutters, giggling as she picks up a lantern. "Come on, Sav, take my hand and I'll lead you out of the woods."

CHAPTER 6
PUKE-JOB

PIPER CUMMINGS | 18
Friday night

A few feet from the fence, Lizzy cuts off the lantern, then we all take turns climbing over the wooden rails. During our stroll through the cool night air, the girls are gabbing back and forth about the kinky experience we shared in the woods. The only one not contributing to the conversation is me, the straggler who's lagging a few feet behind the pack and barely listening to what they're saying. It's not because I'm extremely queasy, I'm just too busy catching up on texts to focus on them, and I can't talk while texting when I'm this drunk.

"I don't understand how this sludge in my uterus is still so warm," Lizzy says from the front of the pack.

"Yeah, it doesn't make sense because it feels hotter than when it went in," Whitney adds.

"No, yeah, it does feel hotter," Lizzy says.

"You don't think…" Whitney starts to say. "You don't think the ejaculate is some kind of acid or something, do you?"

"Serious question?" Savanna says in a low, annoyed tone. "We all drank some, and me and you are covered in cream and slime, Whit… Don't you think our skin, throats, and stomachs would be burning too if it was acid?"

"Good point…" Whitney mutters. "Pipes, you chugged, like, two or three cups of jizz, is your stomach or throat burning?"

"Huh?" I say, reading the text from Jake Landau that just came in.

Jake: Aye. I'm at the barn. Where you at gorgeous?

"*Burning*," Whitney annunciates. "Is your stomach or throat *burning* from the plant cum?"

At the exact moment that I look up from my phone, my full stomach rumbles and growls as it spasms.

"That was fucking loud," Lizzy says, wincing.

"Uh… no…" I answer. "My stomach's just cramping and I feel super-fucking nauseous, but that's it. No burning… Why, is yours?"

"*No*…" Whitney snaps. "Our uteruses feel hot and we're trying to figure out what's… You know what? Stop texting and pay attention so we don't have to waste our breaths repeating ourselves!" When she's this drunk, Whit tends to get really grumpy and snappy like Savanna on a regular day. I guess now that the plant pheromones no longer have us in a loopy, giddy trance, we're reverting to our regular drunk selves…

"Just give me a fucking second," I say, thumbing a response to Jake's message, "I'm behind on texts."

"High school is over, sweetie, you're not that popular anymore," Savanna sasses.

I pay her no mind, I just finish the text.

Me: On the way, Jakey-Poo… I left the barn door unlocked for you, so just head up to the hayloft and get our bed ready ;) And hurry! Because I don't want Lizzy to see you. Meet you up there in, like, 5.

Right after hitting send, my stomach churns, growling even louder than the last few times. It's so loud that Lizzy glances back over her shoulder at me. A minute later, as we're approaching the back door, my stomach sours so bad that salty mucus rushes up my throat into my mouth the way it does right before I'm about to puke.

"Bleh," I gag, slapping my hand over my mouth like that's supposed to help.

Lizzy and Whitney turn and eye me with concern.

"You okay, Pipes?" Lizzy asks, opening the door for us. "You look pale and sweaty…"

"Looks like you're about to spew…" Whitney says, taking Savanna by the hand and leading her into the kitchen.

I nod, removing my hand from my mouth once the dizzying wave of nausea passes. "I'm fine… I just need some water. And maybe some Tums."

"There's Tums in the pantry," Lizzy says, giving me a concerned look as I shuffle past her. "And I think my mom has some Alka-Seltzers in their bathroom cabinet."

"Okay," I say with a partial smile as I walk over to the kitchen sink. I turn the hot water on full blast and pump some soap into my hand. "Don't hate me, but… I think I'm going to pop some antacids then head to bed early. I feel like shit."

"Karma is a *you*," Savanna says with a grin, somehow facing me even though her slime-coated eyelids are still shut.

"Ha. Ha." I say flatly while drying my hands. "That's the most clever way I've ever been called a bitch."

"By all means, go ahead, Pipes," Lizzy says with a pitiful smile. "I'm drunk as hell, drowsy as fuck, and it feels like I'm having the worst period cramps of all time, so I totally plan on going to bed after I'm done in the bathroom."

"Fucking samesies!" Whitney shouts from the guest bathroom down the hall where she took Savanna to wash her face.

"Ditto," Savanna says.

"Alrighty," I singsong as I grab the Tums from the pantry, wincing when my stomach cramps and sours again. "Guess I'll see y'all in the morning then." My words come out in a groan.

"Kay! Good night!" Lizzy says. "If you need anything, just wake me. My door will be open."

"Okie dokie!" I say, grabbing a water bottle from the fridge before heading to the guest room on the first floor. "Night, ladies! Hope you all had as much fun as I did!"

"To be determined," Whitney grumbles as I'm pulling the bedroom door closed behind me.

I lay in bed clutching a pillow to my belly for a few minutes, waiting for both the antacids to work their magic and for some kind of indication that Lizzy is using the bathroom. My cue to get out of bed comes a minute or so later in the form of the upstairs toilet seat slamming against porcelain. I know it's Lizzy up there because her parent's bathroom is above this room, and she never lets any of us use it when they're not home.

All is quiet outside the room, so I peek out into the hallway. Not only is the half-bathroom unoccupied, but it sounds like the showers in both Lizzy's and Eli's bathrooms running above. *That should give me about five to ten minutes to slip out of the house,* I think as I make my way down the hall, grabbing a washrag and a towel from the linen closet along the way.

As bad as I want to shower, a quick birdbath in the sink will have to suffice. All I really need to do is wipe down my neck, tits, and belly so I don't have to worry about Jake asking me why there's dried sap and white flakes crusted all over my front side.

Once I'm all cleaned up, I return to the guest room then shut and lock the door behind me. Instead of crawling back in bed, I head over to the window, undo the lock, then climb on outside. On the nights I sleepover at the Rutherford's and Jake Landau walks over for a sneaky link, this is what I always do. It's the only way to sneak out of the house since Lizzy and her parents always turn on the alarm after locking up the house. This guestroom being on the ground level is the only reason I stopped sleeping in her room around tenth grade and began treating that boudoir as my personal room.

Somehow, my drunk-ass runs all the way across the yard to the barn without falling, then I slip inside through the rear door that I left open for tonight's hookup—the door I always unlock whenever me and Jake have a *date*. On nights when his parents are gone, which they pretty much always are, I usually just walk the five minutes over to his house. But I prefer getting my cheeks clapped up in the hayloft. Because that's where we first snuck off to make out. And then, a few years later, that's the place where he and I lost our virginities to each other the night of Lizzy's birthday party back in ninth grade…

I still feel bad about that. Hell, I feel bad for always sneaking off to hook up with him. Jake Landau and Lizzy grew up together, and they've been best friends since they were old enough to talk. I moved here from Connecticut in the fifth grade following my parent's divorce, so their relationship predates me and hers by, like, five years. She's had a crush on him for as long as I can remember, but he's been in love with me from the day we met in fifth grade. As for me? Well, I didn't start crushing on him until puberty. In seventh grade, we were each other's first kiss. When high school began, he was the first guy I ever blew. Then, when I started birth control at 16, he was the first guy I ever let finish in me.

Jake desperately wants to be in a relationship, but I can't commit because I refuse to be tied down. Still, no matter how many guys I hook up with, no matter who my latest crush is, I always find myself running back to my Jakey-Poo.

When I reach the top of the steps, I find Jake sitting on the edge of the bed of hay that he's draped our *special* blanket over, his head down in his phone. "You know, I think it's about time we finally wash that blanket," I whisper.

The tall, handsome, muscular boy flashes me that panty-dropping smile of his as he rises, whipping his brown shaggy hair back out of his eyes. "And wash away all our memories and love stains? Nah…"

I giggle. "Now I really want to wash it…"

"What took you so damn long?" he says in a low, raspy voice as he snakes his arms around my waist.

"Sorry," I purr, wrapping my arms behind his neck. "I was waiting for the girls to start getting ready for bed. You know how it is." I tippy-toe and peck him on the lips.

The second that my lips part, his tongue slides into my mouth with hungry desperation and slithers against mine. "I don't get why we have to keep sneaking around like this…" he whispers into my mouth.

"You know why… Lizzy really likes you."

"And she already knows how I feel about you."

"But she doesn't know what we do and how often we do it," I whisper, kissing him deeply as I grab his belt and undo his buckle.

His hands slide down my back to my ass, then he squeezes both cheeks. "You don't wanna talk first?"

"Nope," I whisper against his mouth, sliding my hand into his boxers and curling my fingers around that horse cock of his that I love so much. "Lay down so I can so you how much I've missed you…" I push him back to the blanket-topped haybed and he flops down onto it.

Jake pulls off his shirt before laying back then lifts his ass so I can tug off his jeans for him. "You better stop when I tell you to this time… As much as I love your gawk-gawk 9000, Pipes, I love your pussy even more, and I'd rather not finish before I've had a chance to bury myself in your tight little love pocket."

I giggle as I pull my tank top over my head. "Fine…" I kneel at the foot of the haybed and caress him from balls to crown, smiling when his cock throbs from my touch. "I'll just get you nice and slobbered up before I ride you to oblivion." I slather his tip with my tongue before wrapping my lips around his crown.

"Fuck… yeah…" he groans, his core spasming as I passionately suck his tip.

Unlike with the glizzy flower earlier, I start off slow, sucking his cock's head for a bit while massaging it with my tongue. During my worshiping of his crown, I caress his thigh with one hand while the other scratches lightly at his six-pack. When his belly starts twitching under my palm, I bob my head further down, swallowing about 4 of 8 inches of his dick. His cock isn't carrot-thin like the baseline girth of the glizzy flower either, it's thick as fuck—damn near 3-inches in diameter. Coincidentally, that's the perfect circumference to fit snuggly in my throat.

"Oh… ugh… yeah…" he groans, palming the back of my head and pushing down gently. This is his way of telling me that he *needs* me to take him to the back of my throat. *Now.*

The transition isn't gradual, I go from having 2 or 3-inches of him in my mouth to opening wide and taking all of him in until my lips are clamped around the base of his shaft with my tongue sticking out and pressed against his ball sac.

Glurp is the noise that comes from my throat when he drives himself into me as far as he can go.

Now I really go at it, effortlessly deepthroating him over and over with the speed of a seasoned porn star, not even gagging once.

Glurk-gawk-gawk-glurp-glurp-gah-gah-gawk-glurk.

It doesn't take many bobs for me to make a slimy mess of his cock.

"UWAAUGH!" I gasp after unswallowing him and pulling his rod out of my mouth. While I catch my breath, I jerk his slobbery meat stick with exaggerated twists, and it schlicks nice and loud. "You wanna fuck my face, Jakey-Poo?"

"Yes," he says in a deep, breathy growl. "Please, baby."

I unwrap my hand from around his dick then plant both palms flat on his thighs as I engulf his well-hung penis once again, taking it to the middle of my mouth. Both of his hands cup both sides of my head, his fingers curling tenderly around the back of my skull. Now he bucks up into my face slowly, driving his schlong all the way to the back of my throat.

Glurk. Glack!

"Argh!" he groans, pausing as he holds a few inches of his cock in place behind my tonsils.

He relaxes his back and lifts my head as he pulls his member out nice and slowly. When his crown reaches the middle of my writhing tongue, he bucks back up into my face, pushing all the way back in. He does that over and over, picking up speed with each upward thrust.

Glurp-glurk-gawk-gawk-glurk-glurk-gah-gah-gawk-glurp.

Saliva pours out around his shaft at an alarming rate.

Glurk-glurk-glurk-glurk-gawk-gah-gah-gawk-glurk.

Eventually, he stops bucking up into my face and instead starts driving my head down into his crotch like it's a melon with a hole that he's using as a sex toy. I don't resist, I relax and go with the flow, letting him control me as fast and hard as he wants to—I let him abuse my throat the way I only let him do.

Glurp-gawk-gawk-glurk-glurk-gah-gah-gawk-glurk.

He's going at it crazy fast now—so fast that it's making me dizzy and winded. The speed and ferocity with which he slams my face into his crotch makes me feel like he's trying to hate fuck my skull because I won't be with him. I don't want this sweet torture to ever stop.

Gawk-gawk-gawk-glurp-gah-gah-glurk-glurp.

He's not giving me a break, because he knows I don't need one. Between being on a swim team since I was 5 along with all the deepthroat practice I've had, I can hold my breath for a crazy long time.

Glurk-glurk-glurk-glurk-gawk-gah-gah-gah-gah-glurk.

As a groan escapes him, he bucks up into me while pressing my head down hard against him, then he just freezes with his dick in the middle of my throat. He's not just relishing in the feeling of having his cock that deep or getting off on the fact that I'm choosing his pleasure of oxygen. This is a signal that tells me if he pulls out even an inch, he might cum down my throat.

A second later, he lifts my head a bit only to surprise me by driving me right back down, mashing my nose against his pubic bone.

At that exact moment, my stomach churns and cramps and growls louder than it ever has in my life.

That's when a wave of nausea hits me so hard that I instantly start sweating.

"HURRGH-BLURRG!" is the noise I make as what sounds like a wet burp gurgles in the depths of my esophagus. Then, "BLURRAH!" What rushes up my throat feels thick—thick like cake batter lacking the right amount of milk, not at all like the creamy goo I drank from the plant glizzy. And, despite it being so viscous, it rushes up my throat with the same speed at which regular puke does after drinking too much alcohol.

It all happens so fast that I don't have time to squeeze or slap his thighs to signal him to let me up. Like, thick, warm, bitterness floods my mouth less than a second after the gurgle, and then an insane amount of what looks like batter erupts out around his cock before I even start unswallowing his meat sword.

He and I both stare down in horror at the white sludge that's completely coated his cock, balls, and pelvis.

"What the fuuuck!" he shouts.

Before I have a chance to catch my breath, before I have a chance to rise from the floor and turn my head, I retch and spew an insane amount of white mud all over his dick. So much of it comes out that it splashes against his stomach before the cream tsunami washes up to his chest. It's an obscene amount. Like, I severely miscalculated how much plant cum I guzzled. The crazy thing is, as soon as I try catching my breath a second after the puke stops flowing, I gag, choke, and retch again. This time, I have enough time to react by turning my head towards the railing.

Bad choice.

The white batter geyser that's somehow just as voluminous as the first two expulsions blast the wooden floor beneath the railing and then I watch in horror as the thick sludge wave pours over the edge, falling towards the horse in the stall below the hayloft almost in slow-motion. The filth splatters loudly on Sundance's hind end the way oatmeal would sound being dumped from this height. Lizzy's beloved Palomino stallion neighs louder than I've ever heard a horse neigh in real life, rearing up on his hind legs as he flails his front legs in the air in a panic. As I rest against the rail and try to catch my breath between all the coughing, I watch Sundance rise onto his hind legs over and over. Each time he rears up, the thick sludge I puked on his backend runs down his tail and rump.

"Fucking hell, Pipes," Jake groans from behind me. His hand falls on my back. "You okay?"

Since I'm still gasping for air and coughing up a storm, all I can do is turn and nod while using my shirt to wipe my mouth.

"What happened? You never puke while giving me a throat-job… You finally develop a gag reflex or did I—"

"No…" I manage to croak now that I've finally caught my breath. "That wasn't your fault. I've been feeling nauseous the last half-hour… I took some Tums and my tummy settled down a bit, so I thought I was good to go… Clearly, I was wrong… I'm so sorry."

"It's fine. It wouldn't have happened if I wasn't trying to choke you with my dick…" He glances down at the slimy mess dripping onto the floor and running down his legs. "What the fuck did you even eat today?"

I stare at the mess plastered all over his lower half. "Uhhh…" I pause for a long while, trying to think of something other than *'I drank a buck's-worth of a dick-shaped plant's cum.'*

"Please don't you dare tell me you blew a bunch of guys then guzzled yogurt before I came here." He cracks a nervous smile.

"It's cake batter," I finally blurt out. That's the best thing my drunk-ass could think of because that's exactly what it looks like.

He cocks a brow. "*Cake batter?*" he echoes, snorting after. "Seriously?"

"Yeah… Me and the girls were… uh… playing a game of truth or dare, and I was dared to down a bunch of cake batter. Like, a lot of it."

"Shit… That's a gross-ass dare… Maybe all the raw egg got you sick… Or maybe you drank so much of it that it fucked up the pH of your stomach…" He would bring up something sciencey like *pH* because he's a bit of a nerd despite being a Lacrosse jock.

"Maybe," I whisper. As I glance over at the mess on the blanket and the pool of goo on the floor at the foot of the haybed, my stomach groans and gurgles for, like, seven seconds straight. "Ugh…"

"You don't look so good, Pipes," he says, brushing my hair back and cupping the side of my face.

"And you look like you need a shower," I say, wince-smiling at him as I walk over to where I tossed my clothes. "Go down to the shower stall towards the back of the barn and wash up while I clean up Sundance, okay?"

Jake nods.

"Here," I say, tossing him my tank top. "Use that to scrub yourself off."

"You sure?"

"Mm-hm. I'll throw it in the wash and borrow one of Lizzy's shirts."

On my way to go find a bucket, I stop at the sink to clean up a bit. In the short time between when I puked and when I got down here, the sludge I spewed has thickened into a tacky coating that reminds me of icing now. This stuff is so thick that it takes a good bit of scrubbing to get it off of me. Well, I get most of it off. There're still a few sticky patches of white dried onto my skin like glue that come off when I scratch at them with my nails. And if it's drying on me like that, it means I need to hurry and clean off Sundance ASAP.

I run around like a maniac in search of a bucket. It takes a while, but I finally find one in the tack room along with a scrubbing brush. Now I race over to the shower stall to fill up the container and grab the horse-safe soap that the Rutherfords use— things I know from working here with Lizzy one summer.

Upon entering the shower stall, I find Jake standing right over the drain, one hand holding the hose while he uses the other to vigorously scrub his crotch. Like me, there's still a thin layer of white stuff smeared on his legs and abdomen. But when he moves his hand, I see that there's still a crazy amount of white goo plastered all over his dick, balls, and crotch. And when I say all over, I mean *all* over. Like, I don't see skin, just the thick, off-white coating. It legit looks like he dipped his junk in a tub of buttercream frosting…

"How are you still scrubbing?" I ask, squinting at him. "You had the water going since you got in here…"

"How are *you* so clean already?" he fires back, frustration and panic in his voice. "I started before you!"

I shrug, holding out the bucket so he can fill it with water for me. "You just have to scrub a little harder and it'll come off. That's what worked for me."

Jake hands me the hose. "I *have* been scrubbing hard, Piper!" he snaps through gritted teeth, his face matching the color of the patches of irritated flesh on his belly. "Don't you see how red my skin is?" He takes the soapy, drenched top and scrubs his schlong harder than a person should ever rub their skin with something that abrasive. "You see? It's not coming off!"

I reach down and curl my fingers around his semi-hard, frosted cock. The thick, sticky coating mushes against my fingers like I'm touching a sausage slathered in peanut butter. When I tug him slowly and gently from the middle of his shaft to the crown, the frosting smears but it doesn't come off, like gum stuck to a carpet. And when I look at the palm of my hand, there are only a few speckles of tacky spots on my skin with what looks like little white fibers sticking up from it.

"What the fuck…" I mutter, handing him back the hose.

"Yeah, what the fuck for real, Pipes…" he snaps harshly. "You wanna tell me what you really puked all over me? Because, whatever this shit is, it's not *cake batter*…"

I don't say anything. I just stare blankly at him as a panic attack sets in.

"Do you have some kind of fucked up throat STD?"

"No!" I mewl.

"Then why the hell won't this shit come off, Piper?" he shouts. The horses all start making noises.

"Jake, please calm down, okay? I'm sorry that this happened, and I'm sorry this stuff isn't coming off. But I don't know why. All I know is I don't have an STD."

"Fucking hell… this is so fucked up!"

I rub his arm. "It is fucked up. But now's not the time for freaking out, okay. You should just go home and soak in the tub for a while. Maybe that'll help…"

"Maybe…" he growls, handing me the hose without even looking at me. After that, he storms out of the shower stall and picks up his clothes. With his back to me, he bends over and steps into his boxers

"Everything is going to be fine, Jake," I assure him as I cut off the water.

"It fucking better be." He pulls up his Jeans.

Unsure of what else to say, I just stand there, watching him pull on his shirt while stepping into his sneakers.

"Thanks for the puke-job, Cummings Dumpster," he snarls without looking back at me as he disappears around the corner. Even though everyone calls me that, he never has until just now.

Fuck…

When I finally walk into Sundance's stall, I realize how much of a mess I actually made. Not only are his tail, back end, and his rump all creamed up, but the sludge I puked somehow flowed all the way down to his massive testicles while he was rearing up.

Oh, come on… I'm not cleaning this horse's balls…

If my night wasn't already bad enough, things go from bad to worse when I rinse off the soapy water from the stallion's hind end only to discover that I spent the last five minutes scrubbing him with a brush for nothing. Like, *none* of the gunk came off at all. This shit is stuck to him like plaster.

"Fuck!" I shout, stomping my foot.

Panicking, I lead Sundance to the shower stall and scrub him down for another ten minutes. That doesn't work either…

"Fuck! Fuck! Fuck!" I mutter, leading him back to his stall.

Since nothing is working, I give up and decide to return to the hayloft to try and clean up the floor. As I scrub the wooden boards with soapy water, my stomach growls and another wave of nausea washes over me. It feels like I'm on the verge of barfing again, which makes no sense considering I puked my guts out three times already.

You've got to be shitting me, I think when I see that the goo on the floor is coming up from my vigorous brushing. *Why the fuck is it coming off the wood but not scrubbing off Jake and the horse?*

Once the floor is all clean enough, I grab me and Jake's *special* blanket then head out of the barn, my stomach groaning the entire time. On the way to the house, I stop at the trashcan to throw out the blanket. Pretty much right as I toss it in the bin, my stomach sours and cramps hard, then I retch out of nowhere and puke a cupful of something white and brown right top of it. This time it looks more like regular vomit—a mix of what I ate and drank earlier.

"Ugh," I groan as my stomach cramps and sours again. "It feels like I'm dying…"

You're not dying, I tell myself during the short walk to the guest room window. *The glizzy jizz is probably, like, curdling from all the alcohol in my stomach, that's all… Or maybe I just swallowed too much and it messed up my pH like Jake said…*

Fucking hell… why did I chug so much of the glizzy flower's cum?

CHAPTER 7
FLOWER GLIZZY JIZZ SICKNESS

LIZZY RUTHERFORD | 18
Friday night

A flash of pain throbs in my womb, jarring me out of my sleep like a punch to the gut. I'm so woozy and delirious that I just lay there staring at the clock on the nightstand beside me for a long while, trying to figure out how it's only 11:00 P.M.—trying to figure out why I'm even in bed so early. That's when I remember the events leading up to me crawling into bed at freaking 10:00 P.M. with a womb full of sludge—sludge that has everything *down there* feeling warm and fizzy like hot, thickened vinegar just got mixed with baking soda.

That super-uncomfortable fizzy feeling on top of the intense cramps and the uterine fever made it hard to fall asleep at first. But then, a few minutes into laying down, my whole body got a little feverish and the drowsiness I've been experiencing since the glizzy flower splooged in me pretty much knocked me out around the time I started shivering.

A few minutes after finally falling asleep, loud neighing woke me up. As concerned as I was that something was wrong in the barn, I felt too sedated and cold to force myself out of bed to look out the window. I mean, I did try but, when I rolled over, I blinked and passed right the fuck out.

Now, as the pain dulls into a mild cramp, I realize that my body is trembling and I'm drenched in sweat.

I definitely have a fever, I think to myself, clutching a pillow to my abdomen and curling into fetal position.

The thought crosses my mind to get up and grab Tylenol from the bathroom, but then I remember I drank copious alcohol earlier, which makes me recall Jake Landau's warning to never mix the two if I didn't want my liver to fail.

The fever will break on its own. If it doesn't, I'll take Tylenol in the morning when I'm sober, I think, shutting my eyes.

Consciousness fades to blackness seconds later.

"AHH!" I scream, my eyelids going from shut to wide open in an instant when another uterine cramp wakes me.

The first thing I notice is that I no longer have fever chills. However, I still don't feel warm. Probably because my clothes and sheets are drenched in a cold sweat.

I guess the fever broke, I think, pressing the back of my hand against my cold, clammy neck. As my eyes loll over to the clock that's now displaying 3:33 A.M., I hear a toilet flush down the hall. *I wonder if that's Whitney… I should ask her if she's been going through what I have…*

Now that I finally have the strength to move, I desperately want to get out of these wet clothes. Right when I sit up, something cold and thick squishes between my thighs, making me realize that the wetness I felt down there when I first woke up isn't from sweat-drenched panties.

Ewww, I think, grabbing my phone from the nightstand. *What is that? Did all the womb sludge gush out in my sleep?*

After turning on my Samsung Galaxy's flashlight, I pull the covers off, aim the light at my lap then lift my undies and sweat pants. The second I see what's jiggling in the crotch of my panties, I gag and slap my hand over my mouth.

That's fucking disgusting, I think, staring in horror at this gelatinous mass of what I can only describe as pureed salmon with chunks of cranberry sauce and white, lumpy globs that resemble cottage cheese mixed in. Upon bringing my light closer, I see some amber streaks in the white and pink filth-pudding…

Whatever this crap is, the smell that wafts out of my pants is musky, sort of sweet, and slightly metallic—a combination that makes me wince and gag even harder.

"Oh god… what is that?" I whisper into my hand, trembling from the worsening panic. "And why is it pink and red instead of mostly white?"

Looks sort of like my menstrual flow, but I just had my period, like, a week ago… Is my uterus fucking dissolving or something? The thought makes my heart race even worse.

Staring at the horror show between my legs with unblinking eyes, I try to figure out how to get out of bed without this gelatinous glob spilling all over the floor. During my brainstorming session, another cramp strikes. As I double over in pain, there's this bubbly, squirt noise coming from between my legs that sounds like someone is squeezing mac and cheese through one of those Heinz bottle nozzles. It sounds like a wet queef…

"Ah! Ah! Ah!" I groan each time my vagina rhythmically contracts. It feels good, but it's also hella uncomfortable.

Towards the tail end of the contractions, pink and white gunk oozes out from between my folds with an obscenely loud, bubbly spurt, pouring out of me like a thick fruit smoothie that wasn't fully blended.

"What. The. Fuck." I whisper, watching the grossness clump onto the jam in my panties. "What the fuck! What the fuck!" My words come out in a panic.

Maybe I started my period early. Yeah, that's why it's pink—that's why there are red chunks. The white sludge mixed with period blood, and white and red make pink. That's it…

Not wanting to lay there with my panties full of filth, I release my waistband, reach down and cup my vagina from the outside of my pajama bottoms, climb out of bed carefully, then waddle my way to my bathroom. Somehow, I make it past the sink before cold, globs start running down my leg at a snail's pace.

Only after climbing into my bathtub do I pull my pants and undies down. Right as I'm stepping out of my bottoms, my uterus cramps hard then my vagina starts flexing almost like an orgasm. Chunky jam spurts noisily out of my vagina again then it splatters against the floor of the tub. Once the contractions pass, I reluctantly slip two fingers into me to scoop the remaining stuff out of me. The gunk my digits press into feels like mashed potatoes and filling from a fruit pie, and there's a lot in there. After scooping most of it out, I turn on the water and rinse off my vagina and thighs. Now that I'm somewhat clean, I sit on the toilet and double over, resting my elbows against my thighs in preparation for the next cramp and expulsion. It doesn't take much waiting for it to come.

"GAHH!" I groan as my womb spasms and clenches.

Globs of the stuff pour out of me like my pussy is a froyo dispenser. From the looks of it, it's about another half-a-cup's-worth. Between what I woke up to in my pants, what came out in the tub, and the volume of muck I *birthed* just now, I am extremely alarmed. The only thing stopping me from calling 911—other than the embarrassment of having to explain how this happened—is the fact that I left my phone on the bed and I'm scared that I'll gush all over my carpet if I go get it.

The cramping and subsequent oozing of pink gunk from my womb and vagina come in waves that ripple through me at shorter and shorter intervals. It feels like my uterus is a jelly bottle and there's a hand inside of me desperately trying to squeeze out every last drop.

For about twenty to thirty minutes, gelatinous gunk is repeatedly expelled into the toilet with each wave of cramps. The pain, the fear that something is horribly wrong with me—it leaves me crying quietly on the toilet the entire time.

"AHHRGHH-GAH!" I groan quietly as my womb cramps harder than it has all night. At the tail end of my groan, I transition to sobbing.

Despite that being the hardest cramp ever, only a little bit of the gross womb jam plops down into the toilet water.

The last contractions went from, like, three minutes apart to two minutes apart to around one minute. So, when five minutes pass and nothing happens, I start feeling hopeful—so hopeful that my heart rate finally slows and I stop trembling.

After another twenty minutes or so passes without a cramp, I sigh in relief and decide it's time to get off the toilet and clean up.

It's over, I think, wiping myself with sanitizing wipes. *My fever is gone and the cramps are done, so it's over now, right? Please tell me it's over…*

WHITNEY EMMERICH | 18
Saturday, sometime after 3:00 A.M.

I've been hunched over on the toilet with my elbows propped up on my thighs and my chin resting in my palms for so long waiting for the cramps to resume again that I'm starting to doze off. Just as my heavy eyelids are slowly shutting against my will, I hear a toilet flush down the hall.

That must be Lizzy, I think, sitting upright. I heard her shower running for a bit about thirty or forty minutes ago. My guess is that she probably woke up to a mess in her panties like I did so she washed up quick, like I did, before sitting on the toilet to ride out the cramps and the violent discharge of sludge. *If she's flushing, that means she's done. And if she's done, it should mean I'm done. Because she had way more glizzy jizz injected into her womb than I did…*

It's been about fifteen minutes since my last expulsion, and since I'm feeling mostly back to normal and my womb doesn't feel full and hot anymore, I figure it's safe to leave the potty.

It's finally over, I think, wiping myself clean before rising. I reluctantly gaze down at the gelatinous mass of pink jelly that's horrifically decorated with clumps of what looks like scrambled egg whites and congealed red chunks—the mound of filth sitting in a layer of the dense amber slime that sank to the bottom of the water. The sight of it and the dank odor makes me dry heave. *If I hadn't thrown up before I went to bed, I'd probably be puking right now.*

I reach down to flush it but I decide to take a picture of it first, just in case I need to show a doctor. Problem is, I passed out without plugging in my phone to charge, so I'm gonna have to grab my charger and come back. For now, I just close the lid.

As I stand before the sink, I stare at the reflection of the naked sweaty, exhausted-looking strawberry blonde before me, scanning her from head to belly, looking at all the slightly red blotches all over her skin.

Wow, the bumps are already gone! I've never had a rash clear up that fast before.

Not long after getting out of the shower and curling up on the living room couch across from where Savanna was sleeping, I got feverish and super itchy all over. That's about when the nausea came on. Eventually, I got so itchy that I had no choice but to rush to the bathroom and find out what was wrong. And since Piper was still puking her guts out in the first-floor bathroom, I checked to see if she was okay before heading all the way back upstairs.

Getting up those stairs was a struggle because I felt too weak and achy to stand, never mind climb steps.

As soon as I stood in front of Eli's bathroom mirror, my eyes widened at the sight of the red patches on my face, arms, and neck. It wasn't until I brought my arm to my face that I realized some blotches had bumps popping up. After lifting my shirt and pulling down my pants, I discovered that pretty much everywhere the amber-colored ejaculate sprayed me had broken out in a rash. However, the spots where only the white cream blasted me were rash-free.

Then, right as I put my clothes back on, my stomach gurgled and my mouth flooded with puke. Somehow, I got the lid up before cream, bile, and the water I'd just drank sprayed out of my mouth. Unlike Piper, I only puked twice and felt okay enough to lay back down after.

Between the itching, the cramps, and the mild nausea, it was hard to sleep but, eventually, the drowsiness knocked me out. That is, until I woke up about an hour and a half ago to cramps, diarrhea-like noises coming from my vagina, and a crotch-full chunky cold stuff… Chunky cold stuff that rolled down my legs like oatmeal and splattered the floor and stairs during my run back to the upstairs bathroom.

Stuff I still have to clean up…

The cramps were horrendously painful, but I didn't think I'd die from them. And, while the fever and rash had me pretty concerned, I didn't think I might be dying until I saw and smelled the horror in my panties—until wave after wave of cramps had something resembling a blend of liquified meat and strawberry jam with streams of runny brown slime continuously erupting out of my cunt for almost an hour straight. That shit was beyond terrifying. I called out for help, but no one came to my aid. And since my phone was dead, I couldn't even call the girls or my mom.

So, I just sat there crying while having a panic attack until it finally stopped about fifteen to twenty minutes ago.

A knock at the door comes right as I'm in the middle of washing my hands. "Whitney, is that you?" Lizzy says quietly.

"Yup," I say, cutting off the water. "You okay?"

"Now I am," she says. "You?"

"Yeah…" I pull my shirt over my head. "Hey, can I borrow a pair of underwear?"

"I already brought you a pair, along with pajama bottoms. Figured you were going through what I was going through since we both let that thing cream us." She lets out a nervous giggle.

When it occurs to me that we've spent the last part of our evening naked in front of each other, I just open the door wide and flash her a smile. "It was so bad, Lizzy," I say, taking the clothes from her.

She turns around to give me privacy. "I legit thought I was dying…"

"Me too…" I say, pulling up the undies. "Alright, you can turn around now."

She does, then her grayish-blue eyes widen. "Your skin… it's all blotchy!"

"You should've seen it before… I had all these little bumps popping up after my shower, but the itching stopped when the fever broke, and I guess the rash went away around then."

"Well, that's good."

"Yeah…" I scan her mouth and neck. "I take it you didn't have a rash?"

She shakes her head. "Just fever, cramps, and globs of gross jelly gushing out of me…"

"That's probably because you didn't get do a bukkake in the brown ejaculate like I did… Sav pretty much only had the amber slime directly on her belly and thighs since she was covered in white cream from the tits up. So, if she has a rash below her boobs and nowhere else, and if Piper doesn't have a rash at all, we'll know that's what caused the bumps."

"Yeah, I was gonna check on them next."

I turn to the toilet. "I didn't flush because I wanted to take a picture after I charged my phone… You wanna see if what I *menstruated* looks like what came out of you?"

Lizzy winces. "I took a picture too… But, yeah… At this point, I doubt anything will gross me out."

I lift the lid and gag as soon as I set eyes on it.

Lizzy gags too. "Yeah… about the same as mine," she says, thumbing away at her phone. "I had more of the cottage cheese-looking globs, and there wasn't nearly as much of that brown stuff in my panties, the tub, or in the toilet."

"Hmm… Yeah, that stuff was pouring out of me like maple syrup. Super thin, kinda sticky… Pretty much looked like the ejaculate that me and Sav *showered* in…"

"I mean, some brown stuff leaked out of me right after I pulled the glizzy out of me, but not *that* much… I guess that means more of the amber slime comes out the longer the plant cums…"

"That's the conclusion I came to too…" I say, closing the lid. "Alright, let's go check on Pipes. She was puking like crazy earlier, and I saw the downstairs bathroom light was still on around 2:30 when I ran back up here…"

"Oh, shit…"

"Yeah… Oh, and fair warning… Since I wasn't wearing panties under my shorts, goo was dripping down my legs from the time I got off the couch, so watch your step in the hall and on the stairs."

She winces. "Noted. And no worries. I'll help you clean it up after we check on Piper and Savanna."

I flash her a pitiful smile. "Thanks. Also, speaking of Savanna… Let's not tell her about our uterine-vaginal *diarrhea* situation, okay?"

Lizzy's brows furrow as her face scrunches up. "Eww… *Please* don't ever call it that again. And good call. The last thing we need is Sav giving us shit and saying '*I told you so*,'" she whispers in a nasally voice to mock her.

"*Exactly*," I say, giggling after. "I'm too tired and cranky for that shit."

PIPER CUMMINGS | 18
Saturday

Light knocks against the door stir me awake, but I don't bother opening my eyes. I just groan and nestle the side of my face against the towel I'm using as a pillow, drifting back asleep a second later.

"Piper?" Lizzy calls softly from outside. "You okay?" There's a short pause, then I hear the doorknob turn ever so slowly. "We're coming in, okay?"

I groan as I roll over from my spot on the bathroom floor in front of the toilet, squinting both from the bright lights and the soreness in my abdomen from puking for damn near two hours straight.

"Holy shit, girl!" Lizzy says with concern as she and Whitney kneel beside me. "Did you blackout?"

I shake my head as I sit up. "Every time I thought I was done puking, I stood up to leave only to barf before making it to the door. Figured I was better off sleeping by the toilet."

"Not like you're not notorious falling asleep hugging toilets after a night of partying," Whitney says, smirking.

"Right?" I groan, forcing a smile as I slump against the wall across from the toilet. I look over at Whitney. "Hey, you swallowed some glizzy flower jizz, didn't you? Did you get sick?"

She nods. "I puked, like, twice and that was it."

I guess that means I was going to puke even if Jake didn't fuck my face last night…

"Good thing you didn't drink a liter of the shit like I did," I mutter. "I basically threw up on and off for, like, three or four hours."

Lizzy glances down at something besides the towel I was laying on. "Looks like you puked in your sleep too. Good thing you weren't laying on your back… You could've aspirated it and suffocated."

I glance down and find a puddle of milky slime with yellow bile mixed in. "Fuck… Yeah… Good thing I moved the floor mat…"

"Good thing," Lizzy echoes. "How are you feeling now? Any better?"

I shiver, my teeth chattering. "I still feel a little nauseous, but it's not as bad as before."

Lizzy touches the back of her hand to my neck. "Jesus, you're burning up…" She turns to Whitney. "She's still running a fever."

"Still?" I ask. "You two had fevers too?"

"Yeah," Lizzy says, turning back to me. "But our fevers broke about an hour or two ago. I'm sure yours'll pass soon too."

"It fucking better…" I mutter.

"It will. You just need some water, some rest, and some Advil or something to bring your temperature down."

"Yeah…" I groan as Lizzy helps me to my feet. As soon as I'm up, my gaze snaps over to the mirror and I stare at the dried white stuff all over my mouth, on the cheek I was sleeping on, and in my hair. "Your uterus still feeling hot and full, Lizzy?" Right as I'm turning on the faucet, I catch her and Whitney's reflections sharing a weird look. "What was that look for?" I say, bending over to rinse my face.

"Uhhhh…" Whitney hums for a long while, clearly stalling to come up with the right words. "Let's just say we had some crazy cramps then *it all came out.*"

I pump some soap into my hand and lather it up. "Why do I feel like you're leaving out some *very* important details?" I mumble while washing my mouth and chin. "Like, didn't you just gush out a bunch of white cream?"

"Yeah…" Lizzy says with a wince.

"And there was a good bit of the brown syrupy stuff that came out at the end in mine," Whit adds.

"Fucking gross," I say, scrubbing my cheek.

"You don't know the half of it…" Whitney mutters.

"Well, what's the other half?" I ask.

Whitney shakes her head. "Speaking of glizzy flower cum, do you or did you happen to have a rash?"

"Where?" I ask, pointing to my vagina. "Down there?"

"Anywhere where the jizz touched you," Whitney clarifies. "Your face looks clear. How's your tits and belly?"

I turn to the mirror and lift my shirt, flashing my friends. Aside from the dried stuff I puked out all over Jake Landau, there's no sign of a rash. "Looks like I'm good."

"Lucky," Whitney says with an eye roll. "I broke out from the brown goo…"

I scan her. "Really? I don't see anything…"

Whitney turns to the mirror. "Yeah, it cleared up pretty fast. Thankfully."

I wince. "Sorry for making you do a bukkake with that shit, Whit." My eyes flick back and forth between the both of them. "And I'm sorry for holding you both down on the cock plant while it was cumming… Drunk me was being stupid, per usual. I just… I thought it was safe…"

"It's okay," Lizzy says softly. "I thought it was safe too. I mean, I knew the lube-sap was, but I had no idea it'd cum that other stuff."

"No one could've seen that *coming*," Whitney adds. "Pun intended."

Lizzy and I shake our heads.

"That pun hurt worse than throwing up for three hours," I say, giggling after.

Lizzy giggles too. "Yeah, it hurt worse than those cramps too."

"Sheesh, that must've been a really bad joke then," Whitney says, grinning.

We all laugh quietly.

"Lizzy," Whitney says quietly, "let's clean up *that mess* before we check in on Savanna."

"Okay," Lizzy says.

"What mess?" I ask. "Wait, let me guess, plant cum gush out of you before you made it to the bathroom?"

Whitney nods. "Yeah…" She turns to Lizzy. "Since she'll probably see it out there anyway, maybe you should just show her the pictures you took."

Lizzy pulls out her phone from her sweatpants' pocket. "Fair warning… it's gross and worse than you'd expect…"

"And we plan on keeping Savanna from finding out because she's going to be annoying about us fucking the glizzy flower. So, this stays between us three, okay?" Whitney whispers.

I nod. "Secret's safe with me," I whisper back.

Lizzy holds up her phone, showing me a picture of this pile of gelatinous stuff in the crotch of her panties—a massive glob of pink slime mixed with globs of melted mozzarella cheese-looking stuff and chunks of strawberry jam. The next pic she swipes to shows even more of the gross stuff in the toilet. That's when I double over the sink and dry heave.

"That…" I say in an exasperated breath, panting for air. "That came out of *both* of you?"

They nod slowly.

"Fuck," I say. "This flower glizzy jizz sickness if no joke…"

We all laugh nervously.

"It really did a number on all of us…" Lizzy says turning to Whitney. "Alrighty, you go grab some towels from the linen closet and I'll go get some Advil for Pipes, m'kay?"

Whitney nods. "Okie dokie," she whispers back. "I'll clean the living room since that's where most of it fell out of my pants."

Hearing that makes me groan and gag.

"I'll get the second floor and the stairs then," Lizzy adds.

"I can help with the stairs," I chime in.

They both shake their heads.

"Trust me," Whitney says. "You don't want to see this shit in person, and you *definitely* don't want to smell it…"

"Yeah… Just go up to my room and rest, okay?" Lizzy says, rubbing my arm. "We got this."

SAVANNA LOCKHART | 18
Saturday, in the middle of the night…

An annoying itch on my belly, thighs, and pubic mound brings my glizzy flower-related sex dream to an abrupt end.

"Grrr…" I groan. Keeping my eyes shut, I lift my shirt and give my stomach a nice long scratch before sliding my hand into my pants and scratching my thighs. Now my hand moves up to my pubic mound. As I writhe on the couch to adjust my position, I feel a damp, stickiness between my thighs.

Am I wet from that gross sex dream or am I still lubed up from the sap I fingered into me earlier? After giving my mound a scratch, I part my thighs slightly then drag a finger past my clit. En route to my hole, my finger glides across something slicker and thicker than I've ever produced on my own. *It's sap,* I think, slipping my middle finger deep into my pussy, stirring it around inside of me. Things feel just as slick as they did when I first fingered that slick honey into me.

Feeling that slickness makes me think back to the vivid dream I just had. I dreamt I was bouncing on that plant phallus the way the girls were earlier, riding the slippery thing hard and fast until it throbbed inside of me, filling me with a bucketful of cream like it did to Lizzy. Part of me wants to sneak back outside right now so I can do what I wanted to do earlier. If they would've left me alone, I would've carried out the dare, but I just couldn't while they were around. Because I'm not comfortable doing stuff like that with people around, even if it is them.

Since there's no way I'm going back out there in the middle of the night, I settle on pumping my finger in and out of me to the fantasy. Hearing the delicious, sticky, squelching sounds coming from down below drives me wild, probably because I've been crazy horny since fingering sap into me hours ago. And, for some reason, masturbating right now feels better than it ever has, probably because being lubed up with sap makes everything super sensitive down there.

Beyond the sticky, schlicking between my legs, I hear a wooden floorboard groan. That makes me freeze in place.

"Savanna?" Whitney says.

Even though I knew someone was there, I jump, pulling my hand out of my pants. "Fucking hell, Whitney!" I shout.

She clicks on the lamp and a dim, yellowish light illuminates her grinning face. In her hand, there's a damp rag. "Were you just masturbating?" she asks during her walk over to the couch she was sleeping on.

"No! I was scratching myself!" I say in a hush, panicked voice as I sit up.

She arches her eyebrows as she squats and wipes something off the floor. "Didn't sound like *scratching*... Sounded like you were stirring mac and cheese down there..."

"Shut the fuck up..." I snarl.

"Lizzy, Sav is up!" she announces. "And she's down here fingering herself!"

"No, I wasn't!" I shout, scowling at Whit as two people come running down the stairs. Lizzy then rounds the corner into the living room with Piper at her heels. "I *wasn't* fingering myself. I was scratching my thighs because that plant jizz gave me a rash!"

Whitney turns and smirks at the exhausted-looking girls. "I heard mac and cheese being stirred..."

"You're annoying..." I snarl through clenched teeth.

She smirks. "Where's your rash? Belly down?"

I nod. "Yeah, how'd you know?"

"The brown syrup that the glizzy flower ejaculated gave me a rash," Whitney explains, "but none of us got rashes from points of contact of the white cream."

"You still itchy?" I ask, scratching my belly.

Whitney shakes her head. "Nope. My rash is gone already."

"Da-fuck?" I mutter, scratching my thighs.

Piper gestures to the trashcan I set by the couch. "Did you puke too?"

I nod. "Not nearly as much as you though..." I glance down at Whitney who's still wiping up the floor. "Did you puke in your sleep too?"

She gets this weird look on her face. "*Yup*... How much did you throw up?"

"No much," I answer.

"Same," White says.

"Did you have a fever at all?" Lizzy asks.

My mouth twists to the side. "I *think* so? I woke up in a cold sweat a few hours ago, but I feel fine now, aside from this annoying-ass itching."

Lizzy touches the back of her hand to my forehead then my neck. "Your temperature feels normal."

"Did you all have fevers?" I ask.

Whitney and Lizzy exchange a look.

"I do," Piper says, turning to the girls who are now shaking their heads no at me. "But it's going away."

I squint at Lizzy and Whitney. "You two still having cramps?"

"Nope," they say in harmony.

"Our wombs emptied themselves and now we feel normal," Lizzy adds.

"Lucky you guys," I say, using one hand to claw at my thigh while the other scratches my belly. "I'm fucking miserable!"

"Let me see your stomach," Whitney says, kneeling before me.

I lift my shirt and look down. Right around my navel, there are pink blotches, and some spots have little bumps.

"That looks pretty bad," Whitney says. "Maybe you're just allergic."

"Fuck me…" I glare at Lizzy. "So much for your glizzy flower being *safe*…" I snap.

"I mean…" Lizzy says, wincing. "The sap-lube stuff didn't do anything to us, and the white's ejaculate only gave us weird cramps because we let it fill our wombs. So… it *was* safe until the brown stuff started squirting out."

"Exactly," Piper says, smirking. "So, next time we fuck the glizzy flower—"

"Next time?" Whitney blurts out, snickering after.

Piper continues. "—all we have to do is not drink the cum, pull it out before it fills our wombs with a liter of cream, and stop messing with it after it cums for a third time because that's when the musty, brown syrup comes out."

I shake my head while scratching myself. "Fuck that… And fuck you, Piper, for making me shower in a slime we knew nothing about…" A growl rumbles in my throat as I start scratching the unbearable itch. "Do you have any hydrocortisone here, Lizzy?"

She shakes her head. "Nope."

"Well, fuck… I need something for this rash, like, now." I rise from the couch. "You know what? I'm too itchy to fall asleep. And, since my mom has anti-itch cream at the house, I'm leaving now."

"It's, like," Piper says, glancing at the clock, "nearly five in the morning."

"And your point?" I grab my phone then march to the kitchen where I left my keys. "I'm not drunk anymore, I'll be fine."

"Well, I don't feel like sneaking back into my house this time of night, and you kinda drove us here, so…" Piper says as I'm slipping on my shoes. "You coming back to pick us up later?"

I shrug as I unlock the door. "Depends how annoyed at you I still am…"

"Fair enough," Pipes mutters.

"Alrighty…" Lizzy says. "Well, text me when you're home, Sav. And feel better!"

"Will do." I storm out of the house and power walk to my car faster than I ever have in my life.

CHAPTER 8
SCIENCE BABES

LIZZY RUTHERFORD | 18
Saturday afternoon…

Just as I'm lifting the frying pan with scrambled eggs off of the stovetop, the toast pops. "Breakfast is ready!" I announce.

"It's, like, 12:30," Piper says as she walks into the kitchen dragging her feet. "Isn't this technically brunch?"

"Maybe if you and Whitney didn't sleep until noon, we could've eaten earlier," I say, portioning out the eggs onto the three plates.

"And what time did *you* wake up, Lizzy?" Whitney asks as she takes a seat at the table.

"11:45…" I mutter. After Savanna left this morning, the three of us went straight to my room and slept in my bed together, just in case one of us got sick or something again. Thankfully, nothing happened, so we slept another six hours on top of the five or six hours we got last night. Aside from me and Whitney having a few mild uterine spasms and Piper still feeling a bit nauseous, we all woke up feeling great.

"Exactly," Whitney says. "So, even if we woke up when you did, we still wouldn't be eating until noon."

"So it is brunch!" Piper chimes in, slapping a hand on the table. "Does that mean we get mimosas?

"Umm…" I hum while buttering my toast. "There's orange juice, but since my parents don't particularly drink champagne, we can have screwdrivers instead."

"Fine, I'll get the vodka," Piper says.

"Are you serious?" I say with a grin.

"After the night I had?" Pipes says with an arched brow. "Yes. I'm serious. I'm sure we could all use a drink."

"I know I could," Whitney mutters, shoveling eggs into her mouth.

"Same," I sigh, taking a seat.

"When are your parents coming home?" Piper asks.

"Sunday afternoon," I answer, chomping into my toast with a crunchy bite after.

"Will they miss the vodka?" Pipes asks.

"Considering there isn't much left? Probably," I say. "But if you want to mix the mango White Claws with orange juice, we might be able to make a knock-off mimosa."

Piper snaps her fingers and points at me. "This is why I let you come up with the ideas." She gets up and hurries to the fridge.

"Soooo…" I say, dragging the word out. "How long are you all staying over for?"

"Why, you wanna kick us out so you can be alone with your glizzy flower?" Whitney asks with a smirk, nudging my arm.

"Hey, if you're gonna ride that freaky plant dong again, count me in!" Piper says in a sultry voice.

"Seriously?" I ask.

"I kinda want it to creampie me…" Piper says, cracking open a mango White Claw.

"Even after we showed you what came out of us and told you what we went through?" Whitney asks.

"Kinda… Yeah…" Piper says shamefully.

"Well, you're gross," I say, pausing to swallow my scrambled eggs. "And the reason I asked how long you were sticking around for is because I think we should dig up the soil beneath the glizzy flower."

"Why?" Piper asks.

"*Why?*" I repeat with emphasis. "Because that thing oozed enough sap to lube up every woman in Olympia, Washington, and it came enough cream and syrup to fill two five-gallon buckets… Like, aren't you curious to know where it all came from?"

"Good point…" Whitney says. "I was so fucked up last night, I didn't even consider how that much could come from such a relatively small plant… Now I kinda wanna know…"

"See, that's where we differ," Piper says. "Because I *don't* wanna know. Like, what if we dig it up and see something really fucked up? We might get traumatized and end up having PTSD and nightmares for the rest of our lives."

"Another great point," Whitney adds. "Ignorance is bliss."

"Well, *I* wanna know," I say. "So, if you won't come with me, I'll just dig it up myself…"

Whitney winces. "If you're going to do it anyway, I'm going to want to know what you find… So, I *guess* I'll go with you."

"Hard pass for me," Piper says. "Whatever you uncover, tell me *after* I get to experience getting a one-liter cumshot pumped into me."

"You're sick," I say. "I don't wish what happened to us last night on anyone…"

"What happened to you two won't happen to me if I don't let it pressure wash me right up against my cervix," Piper says. "All I gotta do is wait for it to throb then pull it out after the first squirt. Easy-peasy!"

I shake my head. And, just as I'm opening my mouth to talk her out of it, the doorbell rings. All three of our heads snap towards the windows facing the front of the house.

"You expecting someone?" Piper asks.

I shake my head. "Maybe it's Savanna?"

"Maybe…" Whitney says, checking her phone. "She didn't text me though."

"Or me," Piper says.

"Me either," I say, quietly pushing my chair back and standing up. "I'll go take a peek. If it's the cops, I'll whistle or something."

Whitney's eyes go wide. "Why would it be the cops?"

I shrug. "I don't know. I'm just saying, if it is, I'll let you know so you can dump the White Claws."

"Oh! Good idea," she says.

"I'll go upstairs and make sure no one shady is lurking around then," Piper says, rising from her seat. "My dad said you gotta be careful because sometimes people will ring your bell while someone else hides elsewhere and waits to barge in. Apparently, it's been happening a lot in Connecticut and Boston in nice areas."

"I guess I'll keep watch from the living room…" Whitney says, looking all wide-eyed and paranoid.

I tiptoe to the door. Through the peephole, I see three girls who are maybe four years older than us. They don't look like meth heads or anything, so I open the door and peek at them through the locked glass door. The one right in front of the door is a pretty white girl with auburn hair and green eyes, the other is a brunette with big brown eyes, and the third is a very petite Indian girl with long, flowy black hair who looks like she's about 6-inches shorter than me, standing at 5-feet tall.

"Hello… May I help you?" I say, squinting at them.

The girl with auburn hair waves energetically, smiling brightly. "Hi! I'm Allie, your neighbor to the southwest. And these are my friends Priya and Catie," she says, gesturing to the Indian girl and then to the mousy brunette, respectively. "Are your parents' home by chance?"

"Are you here to see my parents?" I ask.

Allie shakes her head. "No… I just thought you looked a little young, and I was hoping to speak with an adult."

"About?" I follow up.

"Uh… about an invasive species we're investigating in the area," she replies.

I arch a brow. "An invasive species?" My mind wanders to the mysterious glizzy flower in the woods behind my house. "You scientists or something?"

Allie smiles and nods. "Actually, yeah! I'm a botanist."

Priya raises her hand. "Mycologist!" she says with a smile.

"Geneticist," Catie, the shy-looking one says.

My eyes widen. *A plant specialist, a fungus specialist, and a geneticist show up looking for an invasive species days after a dick-plant pops up in the woods behind our ranch? Can't be a coincidence…*

"Cool," I say. "You with the government or something?"

Allie shakes her head. "No. I work at a marijuana company, Priya works at a mushroom farm, and Catie is getting her master's. We're just… conducting private research on new species we sort of just discovered…"

"Oh… What is it?" I ask.

Allie looks over at the girls, and they glance at her with neutral expressions. Poker faces.

"It's okay, you can tell me, I'm 18," I say with a smile.

"Umm…" Allie says, wincing. "What I'm about to show you, you can't tell anyone about it because our research is confidential until we can present it to the university."

"No, yeah, for sure!" I say, unlocking the glass door and stepping outside. "Your top-secret research is safe with me."

The second I stand before Allie, a heavenly scent titillates my nose and gets my pulse racing. It's a familiar fragrance that smells like sugar cookies, sweet mango, and flowers—a smell that hypnotized me and my friends last night and made us do naughty things.

"Holy shit, you smell like—" I pause when I catch myself about to say *glizzy flower*. "You smell like heaven…"

Allie narrows her eyes at me like she knows what I wanted to say, then she smiles knowingly. "Thank you! You ever smelled this fragrance before?"

"Nope, but it smells amazing!" I say, trying to maintain a poker face. "What is it? Chanel?"

She giggles. "No, it's actually something I uh… extracted from the *plant* we're researching."

Holy shit… The glizzy flower has got to be the invasive species they're investigating… She did say she's my neighbor to the southwest. In that direction, there's nearly a mile of woods between here and the next community, so maybe she found one by her house too…

"Oh," I manage to say, side-eyeing her companions in an attempt to discern if they're as horny as I'm starting to feel.

"Here, let me show you a picture of the plant so you know what to look out for," Allie says, looking down at the phone in her hand. "That way, if you come across it, you can let me know."

"Okay, sure," I say.

"Fair warning: the plant looks a little… *inappropriate*," Allie says with a wince.

"Inappropriate how?" I ask.

The girls exchange a look.

"Let me just show you," Allie says, tapping at her screen.

As she lifts the phone to show me, my core spasms from this weird, tickling sensation at the top of my vagina.

"You okay?" Allie asks, lowering her phone.

I nod. "Yeah, I just had a muscle spasm, that's—" A uterine cramp comes out of nowhere, and it hurts so bad that I double over and have to grab hold of the doorframe. "Ah!"

"Oh my god!" Allie says. I catch her staring at the crotch of my sweatpants as reaches out to grab me.

Why is she staring at my crotch? I look down to see if I've peed myself or if leftover cream leaked out and soaked through my sweatpants. *Feels dry down there, and I don't see anything... Maybe she knows why I'm having cramps. Because maybe the same thing happened to her... That's why she smells like a glizzy flower.*

Just as quickly as the pain came on, it starts to fade. "I'm fine. I'm fine," I groan, standing upright.

"You sure?" Allie asks with genuine concern.

I nod. "IBS, that's all." My mom suffers from that, so it seemed like a good excuse.

"Oh, I'm sorry... IBS is no joke," Allie says.

"It's fine. Could be worse!" I say with a wince of a smile.

All three girls nod.

"Alright, so, here's the picture of the invasive plant," Allie says, holding her phone up to my face.

The picture on her screen looks exactly like the thing we fucked last night, except the phallus on this one is a bit girthier.

"Looks like a penis," I say, looking up at her with a grin.

Allie's brown-speckled, green eyes search mine intensely. "*Right?* You ever seen anything like this before?"

I shake my head. "Nope... Is that even real?"

"Oh, it's *real*..." Allie says dramatically.

"What's it called?" I ask.

"We call it the yoni flower," she answers. "It comes in two... *forms*... and this form is called the linga flower form."

"Linga?" I echo.

"It's Hindi for a man's... *you know*," Priya says.

I giggle. "Makes sense." I think about how all of us were sick last night and brainstorm a way to ask if it's dangerous to humans without arousing suspicion. "You said it's invasive… So, is it, like, harmful for the environment? Like, if my horses find it, will they get sick?"

"While this thing does parasitize nearby plants, we don't have any reason to believe it causes any harm to animals," Allie answers, slipping her phone back into her pocket.

"Oh, well that's good," I say, sighing in relief, thinking back to all the dead grass and bushes around the glizzy flower, and recalling how the tree behind it lost some leaves.

"Yeah… Listen—" Allie says, pausing for a moment as she reaches into her purse and pulls out a post-it note that has a string of numbers written on it. "I'm sorry, I didn't get your name…"

"Right… I'm Lizzy," I say.

"Okay, Lizzy… If you happen to be wandering around the woods and you come across something that looks like that linga flower, please don't touch it. Just call or text me right away, okay?" She hands me the post-it.

"Okay…" I say, staring down at the note with her first name and phone number, my heart racing. "Why shouldn't I touch it? Is it… dangerous to humans and not to animals?"

"Ummm…" Allie hums for a while, looking at her friends. "*You* wouldn't die if you touched it or anything like that. And it's not poisonous."

"Well, that's good," I say. At that exact moment, my core spams from this weird, tickling and stretching sensation deep in my vagina. It sort of feels like my cervix is gradually dilating or something.

"Yeah…" Allie says. "It's just…" A long pause follows. "Listen, Lizzy, I'm just going to be direct with you, okay?"

I nod.

Allie inhales deeply then huffs. "This may seem silly, and it probably goes without saying, but… just because it looks like a man's penis, whatever you do, do *not* put it *inside of you.*"

I try to smile but it comes off more like a wince. "Who in their right mind would stick a freaky dildo plant inside of them?"

Allie snickers, guilt flashing on her face. "Let's just say that the plant's fragrance has some kind of pheromones that basically hypnotizes people to want to do inappropriate things with it…"

"I see…" I mutter, blushing. "And what happens if a girl… you know… Puts it in her…"

"Uh… We're not at liberty to say at the moment," she says. "Just know it's something you don't want to ever experience."

Too late, I already experienced it, I think, nodding. *And, clearly, you did too. But if you're alive and healthy, it can't be all that bad.*

"And if you *do* come across it and you find yourself feeling *tempted,*" Priya pipes up, "just dig up the soil around the base of the flower and you'll be too grossed out to even think about."

"Oh… Okay then…" I say with one last nod, dread making my stomach twist into a knot. "Well, if I come across it, you'll be the first to know, Allie. And I won't do anything inappropriate with it, I promise."

The auburn-haired biologist smiles warmly. "Sounds good, Lizzy." Allie starts to walk away only to pause and twirl back around. "Oh, and sorry for just showing up like this out of the blue and then dropping such a bizarre bombshell on you. It's just *extremely* important that we locate and contain these plants ASAP. And I didn't want another day to go by without making sure you and the women in our community were informed. Because I couldn't take it if something happened to anyone and I didn't try to prevent it." She flashes another smile, a very genuine one.

"No worries," I say. "I appreciate you all stopping by and educating me on the… uh… *linga* flower, so thanks!"

"You're welcome," Allie says, giving me a wave. "Goodbye! Take care!"

"Bye! You too!" I reply, waving at the other two girls when they start waving at me on the way to their car.

When I step back inside the house, I shut the glass door and drop the window before stepping off to the side. I don't close the front door all the way though, I leave it cracked so I can listen to them through the screen.

"That was weird," Whitney says. "And why were two of those science babes so hot?"

"Shh!" I hush, leaning towards the cracked open door.

"You sure that was the right girl?" Allie says in a hushed voice, clearly unaware of how well sound travels on the wind on open land.

The right girl? How could they possibly know that—

"I swear it's the fence and same barn from the TikTok," the mousy brunette says. "And I never forget a face." That's when her car door slams.

What are the odds that the girls looking for the glizzy flower saw that TikTok before it got taken down and somehow also recognized my house? Was it even in the background?

"What the fuck was that about?" Piper says on her way downstairs. "Were they looking for the glizzy flower?"

Nodding, I fish my phone out of my pocket, pull up the copy of the video I have saved and hit play. Sure enough, I can just make out the fence and the barn in the background at the end of the video. I suppose if they knew the plants were in this area, they could've just gone on Google Maps and looked for any property with a red barn. There aren't many...

"Yeah..." I finally answer. "They showed me a picture of a similar one that had a thicker shaft. They called it a yoni flower and said it was in the linga flower stage... Or *penis* stage."

"How'd they know to look here though?" Whitney asked.

I show her the TikTok video.

"When did you make this?" Piper asks. "And since when did you have a secret TikTok account?"

"I only post cringy videos on it, so I don't share it with anyone," I answer. "And I made that Wednesday—the day I found the glizzy flower… It went viral and got taken down the next day."

"Of course a video with a dildo flower wouldn't stay up," Piper said, shaking her head.

"The important question is, why did they make it sound like fucking the flower was dangerous?" Whitney asks.

I shrug. "I dunno. But what I do know is that auburn-haired girl smelled *exactly* like the glizzy flower. Like, I got horny as soon as I opened the door."

"Seriously?" Piper and Whit say at the same time.

I nod. "And she talks like she might be the person who did something with it that she wishes she hadn't, so… maybe whatever happened to her is the same thing that happened to us. And, if that's the case, it's clearly not something *life*-threatening."

"Maybe…" Whitney says. "You still want to go back out there and see what's beneath the soil? Because now that the pretty Indian girl said that seeing what was underground would turn us off, I'm super curious."

"Me too," Piper says.

"I'll grab us some shovels and gardening gloves," I say, heading towards the back door.

CHAPTER 9
FLESH POD

LIZZY RUTHERFORD | 18
Saturday afternoon…

It doesn't take much shoveling to hit something soft and squishy…

It only takes two sets of garden glove-covered hands to uncover a one-foot-wide patch of some kind of disgusting, subterranean mass.

It takes exactly two seconds of staring at what was hidden beneath the dirt for all three of us to turn away and puke up our breakfasts onto the soil below.

"Oh, fuck!" Piper groans, hurling again as soon as she glances back at it. "It looks… fleshy and squishy… like melting skin…"

"And it smells gross as fuck!" Whitney adds. "Reminds me of that amber-colored ejaculate's odor…"

After removing my mom's gardening gloves and tossing them over to the shovels, I use the back of my hand to wipe away the regurgitated breakfast from my mouth. Looking away from the barf that just splattered on the soil before me, I rise from my haunches and reluctantly turn back to face the horrifying, flabby *mass* we've uncovered.

There's this thing called SCOBY that's used in the fermentation of Kombucha. SCOBY is an acronym for 'symbiotic culture of bacteria and yeast,' and it's usually beige to tan or even yellow in color. When I used to help my mom make Kombucha, I remember thinking that it looked like a slimy, gelatinous slab of spoiled ham steak.

That's what this glizzy flower's underground *organ* looks like.

It's lumpy, beige, slimy, and webbed with veins like the placenta they showed us in health class. And, considering I accidentally jabbed it with my shovel pretty hard and it didn't rupture, I know it's super thick and tough as a chunky cut of beef.

"How big do you think it is?" Piper asks.

"Only one way to find out," I say, grabbing the shovel.

She and I scoop away soil until we uncover the edges. Nearly 6-feet by 3-feet, that's how large the veiny flesh pod we uncover is. *It looks so… alien…*

"Hey, is it just me, or is this thing beneath the stalk a ball sac?" Piper says after using her gloved hand to brush away the last clump of soil beneath the white stalk. She quickly rubs away more dirt.

My jaw drops at the sight of it. Right where the white stalk meets the gross pod, there's a fleshy, wrinkly beige sac with the imprint of two oval lumps bulging through the *skin*. "Holy crap… Looks exactly like a scrotum with testes in it." Coincidentally, the balls also happen to be on the same side of the glizzy flower as the *underside* of the shaft where the frenulum is.

Piper removes her glove and rubs it with quick brushes of her finger. "Feels just like a guy's balls too… The skin around them is a bit leatherier though…"

"Bizarre…" Whitney mutters, using her gloved hand to brush more soil away from the left side of the pod. "Look at this," she mutters, pointing at these black, branched cords that have fused with the surrounding plant roots.

"That Allie girl did say that this plant parasitizes off neighboring plants…" I whisper back. Despite being super-grossed out, I kneel before the musty flesh pod and reach down ever so slowly, like I'm scared it's going to bite me.

"Don't tell me you're going to touch the pod," Whitney says in a strained voice.

I squint at her. "You didn't say anything when Piper tickled this thing's nuts."

"Also," Piper chimes in, "we all fucked this gross pod's *cock* last night and let it splooge in us, so does touching its horrific *body* really seem that fucked up?"

"My thoughts exactly…" I say, gagging. "As gross as it looks, I kinda wanna know what it feels like since stabbing it with the shovel didn't rupture it." I gag again when my fingers press into the squishy and hot flesh beneath the beige stalk—flesh that feels like the belly of a fat man who just got out of a hot tub.

"What's it feel like?" Piper asks.

"It's super warm…" I answer. "Warmer than the glizzy… Hot like you were last night when you were feverish…"

"Oh geez…" Whitney says. "Fuckin gross…"

My palm glides across the slippery thing. "Lumps and veins aside, it's super smooth…" I press my hand onto it and dig my fingers in, almost kneading into it like a masseuse. "It legit has the texture of raw steak—thick, firm, tough… like, you'd really have to cut into it to breach the *skin*." I give the flesh sack a quick, hard, push and the thing jiggles almost in slow motion the way a leathery sack filled with thick sludge would. "Imagine palming the belly of a slimy, boneless, legless, headless cow and that's what this feels like." When I press down again and feel something hard, I snatch my hand away.

"What happened?" Whitney says in a panic. "Did it hurt you?"

I shake my head. "Feels like I hit bone or something."

"What. The. Fuck." Piper says in awe. "Now I feel like I need to touch it… Might as well, right? I mean, I already made love to it and that's as intimate as it gets." A nervous laugh escapes her as she gives it a quick slap. After that, she palms it. "Ew… ew…" She rubs it, digs her fingers into it, then squeezes it. "Fucking, ew… Accurate description, Lizzy… It does feel like dense meat… Like a giant water bladder made of steak and filled with mud…"

"I can't believe FOMO has me about to do this," Whitney says huffing as she reaches for it. Almost as soon as her palm goes flat against it, she snatches it away and springs up from the ground. "Okay, nope! I'm done!" She gags as she walks away. "Bury it!"

"So this flesh pod or whatever is what creampied you two and came down my throat, huh?" Piper says.

"I'm afraid so…" I say, gagging as I stand. After snapping a picture of it, I grab my shovel. "You still wanna fuck it again, Pipes?"

"*Hell* no!" she says. "I want you to bury this gross as meat sack and sign us up for a group therapy session."

Whitney snickers. "So… What now?"

"I'm afraid to ask this," Piper says, "but should we, like, cut it open and find out where all the cum came from?"

I shake my head. "And risk getting sprayed with whatever gave us fevers and what gave Savanna and Whitney rashes? Hard pass," I mutter, wincing from another bout of uterine tingling accompanied by what feels like having my cervix being slowly stretched by a tiny balloon.

"Good call," Piper says.

"So…" Whitney says, "do we just bury it back up then reach out to the science babes so they can dispose of it or whatever?"

I shrug. "Yes to reburying it," I say, scooping up soil from the pile and dumping it onto the flesh pod. "But I don't know if we should have them get rid of it. Yet."

"Why?" Whitney says, picking up a shovel.

"Oh my god…" Piper says with a smirk, scrunching her nose. "You want to fuck it again, don't you, Lizzy?"

I scowl at her. "What? No!"

"It's okay, I kind of do too," Pipes says.

"Even after what you just saw?" I ask. "Even after you just said we should sign up for group therapy sessions?"

"That's gotta be the pheromones making her say that," Whit mutters.

Piper shrugs. "As you all know, I've had *a lot* of sex. And, despite how gross that fleshy thing underground looks, its glizzy *did* give me the best orgasm I've ever had, so…"

"As much as I hate to admit it, you're right…" I mutter.

"See! So you *do* wanna fuck it again?" Piper says.

I shake my head. "The sap is what made us super-sensitive and probably what caused those intense orgasms… So—"

"So," Piper interrupts. "We jar the sap and use it as lube whenever we're in the mood or about to have sex?"

I nod as I dump more soil onto the pod. "Basically, yeah…"

Whitney nods while tossing a shovelful of soil onto the bottom end. "Are you sure the sap wasn't responsible for our fevers, Lizzy?"

"Positive," I say. "I drank a good bit of it Wednesday and, considering the stuff was dripping out of me till the next morning, I'm pretty sure it was the chowder cum that had us feverish."

Whitney nods. "Okay, then we keep it around to harvest sap and nothing more, right?"

"Right," I say.

We turn to Piper.

"*Piper*…" I say sternly.

"Fine, I won't fuck it… Without a condom."

We all crack up at that.

I won't fuck it without a condom either, I think, smiling to myself.

CHAPTER 10
SEXUALLY TRANSMITTED THRUSH?

JAKE LANDAU | 18
Monday morning, July 25th, 3 days after Piper's puke-job…

The pain from having my throbbing erection pressing against my mattress yet again wakes me from my deep slumber. Wincing and groaning, I roll onto my back. As my boner drags across the sheet, my core spasms from the intense pleasure. It feels like I'm on the verge of busting a nut. That's how sensitive my cock has been since the night Piper the Cummings Dumpster puked *batter* all over my junk—batter that I couldn't scrub off no matter how many times I tried or how hard I rubbed. It doesn't even make sense that my dick is *this* sensitive because, the last I checked, it's still completely plastered with a thick layer of what looks like candle wax.

Or at least…. that's how it looked when I checked down there before bed last night. Every time I check down there, the infection always looks a little different. A little worse each time…

As sensitive as it feels, I'm scared to even see what it looks like now.

In the minutes after she puked white slime on my dick, balls, thighs, and abs, my skin quickly went from looking like it was slathered with batter to looking like it was I went balls-deep into a jar of buttercream frosting. Legit, it even had little hairlike frosting spikes sticking up all over down there, and it only got worse after I tried scrubbing it. I even tried soaking in my tub when I got home before scrubbing hard with a washrag, but that didn't help either.

Then, early the next morning, not only did I wake up with a boner and tingling in my urethra, but the stuff smeared from my tip to about halfway down the shaft had smoothed out into more of a beige candle wax. Meanwhile, the tacky frosting plastered elsewhere looked like it had spread further down my thighs and up my abs. After freaking out and trying to scratch the squishy, gummy stuff off with a fingernail to no avail, I went to the ER.

"You say this happened after a woman vomited on you during oral sex?" the lady doctor asked me.

"Yes…"

She just stood there staring at it for a moment. "I've never seen anything like this… This could be an aggressive form of penile thrush… do you remember if her tongue was coated in a yellowish-white film?"

"No. It looked normal."

"Hmm… There's a possibility it was contained to her esophagus… To be safe, we'll start you on broad-spectrum antifungals and antibiotics. In the meantime, I'll run some cultures and follow up with you when I have results. Unfortunately, it could take up to a week to hear back from the lab."

That's when she used some scalpel-thing to scrape a sample from my penis. Thankfully, I couldn't feel it then. However, if she did that now, well… I would scream bloody murder because it'd probably feel like she was trying to skin my cock like a carrot.

Not long after getting home from the ER, I started feeling a bit feverish. Midway through the day, my cock got sore from having a daylong boner. By the end of that Saturday night, the "frosting" on my erection and tingly balls had *smoothed out*, making it look like I dunked them both in candle wax. The waxy stuff took on a beige color while the patches on my legs and stomach looked more like tan, lumpy oatmeal… And where normal flesh met the horrific infection, these little white threads were stretching their way up my healthy skin like roots…

Yesterday, I woke up around noon despite going to bed crazy early. That's probably because my fever had gotten worse, along with the infection below. My dick was aching so bad from almost 48 hours straight with a boner that I had to stop tucking it into the waistband of my boxers and just remove my pants altogether. The puke icing on the shit cake? Those antifungals and antibiotics weren't doing shit because the oatmeal-looking growths had spread almost the whole way up to my sternum and up my ass crack. Last I checked, the mass on my backside had grown to the tip of my spine in a perfectly straight line…

Please don't be worse, I think, shutting my eyes as I peel the covers off of me. *Please don't be worse…*

"Fuck!" I shout the second I open my eyes, my gaze wandering from the thick string of honey-like slime stretching between the tip of my penis and the bedsheet like snot.

My dick no longer looks like it's covered in candle wax. Now it looks like it's sheathed in an almost… *leathery* skin that somehow has a few veins bulging up the shaft in the exact places where my veins used to be.

How are my veins bulging through if this stuff coating my dick is still thick as it was Friday night? I reach down and, the second my finger squishes against the mushy layer of beige stuff, I feel it. *It's like the infection isn't growing on me so much as it has become a part of me…*

When I start tracing my finger down the shaft to my balls, each second of extremely delicate stimulation makes my cock twitch and throb painfully. Like, I'm barely caressing it and I'm already on the verge of blowing my load, so much so that there's more of that yellow, thick stuff beading up from my urethra. That's how sensitive this new *flesh* layer is.

"What the fuck are those," I think, sitting up to get a better look at the disturbing sight near the base of my dick, wincing from a weird pain in my abdomen that I didn't have last night.

An inch from the bottom of my shaft, there are five, equally spaced, perfectly round bumps in a ring formation around my girth. I give them each a poke and, whatever they are, they're hard but squishy, like that time I had a cyst on my wrist…

"What the fuck… What the fuck…" I mutter, staring in horror at the nodules. My eyes then wander to my stomach which is now almost completely covered in a layer of hardened, lumpy oatmeal stuff that stops just below my pecs.

It's only now that I'm sitting up that I notice my abdomen is distended and bloated the way my uncle's stomach was when he was going through liver failure from cirrhosis. It's wild because I had a rock-hard six-pack when I went to bed last night. Not only is my abdomen bloated and hurting, but there's also a weird fizzy sensation in my intestines, the same feeling I felt in my bladder last night before bed.

What the fuck is happening to me? My body starts trembling and I can't tell if that's because of the fever or if it's because I'm having a panic attack.

I'm so weak and shaky that it takes everything in me to climb out of my bed. Every move has my dick, balls, prostate, and bladder throbbing and feeling like they're about to explode.

I'm so out of it and my head is so cloudy that I can't shuffle my feet in a straight line to my bathroom no matter how hard I try. *Drunk… I feel drunk. And high… Tranquilized…*

Upon stumbling into the bathroom, I click on the lights, pull off my hoody. Now I turn my back to the mirror and look over my shoulder.

"What. The. Fuck…" I mutter through gritted teeth, staring in horror at the oatmeal-like strip of *flesh* that's grown in a straight line along my spine up to right between my shoulder blades. Growing out from the spinal strip, there are branches of freaky strands zigzagging outwards from it towards my ribs and shoulders.

I need to get to the hospital, I think, shuffling in a waddle back to my bed. *But my parents are home... I can't let them see me like this... Not when I can't tuck away my boner in the waistband of my pants anymore.* I glance at my throbbing erection, thinking about how good it felt when I caressed it earlier. *Maybe if I jerk off, it'll finally go down.*

That's the only thing I haven't tried because I was afraid to touch it. But now that my mutated dick's all sensitive to the touch, I'm thinking I might be able to rub one out.

Yeah, I'll jerk off and then, when the boner goes down and my balls don't feel like they're about to explode anymore, I'll ask Dad to take me to the ER.

As soon as I climb in bed and lay on my back, I reach over to grab a tissue from my nightstand. Right before I grab one, my phone buzzes on the wireless charger next to the Kleenex box. Since I was planning on streaming some porn anyway, I grab the iPhone and unlock it.

The text is from Piper, and it reads: **Jake, why the fuck are guys from school texting me saying that you told them I gave you an STD?!?! WTF, dude! I don't have an STD! I'm clean! Are you just mad that I puked on your dick? Because I'm sorry, but I don't know why that puke didn't come off of you when it came off of me right away.**

Yes, I did text every guy who I know you hooked up with that you gave me sexually transmitted thrush or whatever, I think, deleting her text without responding just like I've done with the dozen or so other messages she's been spamming me with since Saturday morning. I want nothing to do with that gross-ass bitch after whatever she infected me with, and I wanted to make sure no one else ever has to suffer through what I'm going through.

It's funny how the girl of your dreams can become the person you hate the most after just one fucked up night together…

More angry texts from her come through as I'm perusing Pornhub for a good creampie video. When I finally settle on one of my favorites, I skip towards the end, pump some lotion in my hand, then start stroking my sensitive, leathery cock. Every time my hand glides up from the bumps around the base of my shaft to my crown, my cock throbs then this golden goo beads up on the tip of my cock before dribbling down my length. Whatever this stuff is, it's way more slippery than this lotion.

I'm on the edge of climax in just a few strokes. As the man onscreen pulls his cock out of the pussy he's just creamed, my dick throbs hard in my hand, and pleasure buzzes across my body. I quickly cover my crown with the tissue while stoking near the base. When glorious release finally comes, my body spasms and my ass clenches while something too chunky to be semen rushes up my urethra. In the blink of an eye, a thick rope of what looks like banana smoothie-colored mucus with red streaks blasts right through the fucking tissue like a high-pressure snot geyser. My body almost seizes as the powerful slime jet spurts two feet in the air. A beat later, the hot goo splashes onto my chest, face, pillow, and headboard with the stickiest splat I ever heard in real life.

"The fuuuuuck!" I groan, shutting my eyes as my cock throbs and erupts one mucus rope after another.

To keep any more of the filth from splattering my bed and wall, I stop stroking and cover my glans with the palm of my hand. Even though I've stopped jerking off, I continue coming hard. With each subsequent throb, insane amounts of goo squirts against my palm, each blast a little less powerful and a little less voluminous than the previous one. With each throb, the pressure in my distended belly dissipates as though the fluid in my abdomen is draining through my penis…

Eight throbs and eight ejaculations—that's how long it takes for my orgasm to stop.

Now that it's over, my balls and prostate no longer feel like they are about to pop. My cock doesn't hurt as bad either, but it doesn't feel like the erection is going down at all.

When I finally open my eyes, I gag from both the smell and from how disgusting the slime all over my body and bed looks. Never in my life have I been this disgusted by anything. If I had anything in my stomach to puke, I'd surely hurl right now.

What the fuck is this stuff? Discharge? It can't be... there's way too much of it... I glance back at my headboard only to find the yellow paste that's streaked and dotted with pink and red is dripping down my wall and *Spider-Man* poster. *Fuck...* I gag. *How am I going to clean that? Shit is definitely going to stain...*

The longer you wait, the worse it's going to be, I remind myself, forcing myself out of bed.

Sure enough, the wall is stained by the time I finish wiping it down with a damp, soapy towel. After giving up on cleaning the wall, I wipe the slimy gunk off my bed and headboard before tossing the dirty linens on the laundry pile in the corner. By the time I get around to putting on a fresh pair of sheets, I'm exhausted.

Even after all that cleaning, my erection still hasn't gone down. And as I lay here in bed working up the courage to ask my dad to take me to the hospital, as my brain feels cloudier than it did before, as it feels like it's getting harder to form cohesive thoughts, a wave of intense drowsiness from the fever has me doing that slow blink I always do before I pass out.

I can't get up if I tried, I think, shutting my eyes. *I'll just nap for a bit then I'll go to the hospital.*

The instant the thought leaves my mind, everything fades to black.

CHAPTER 11
HORSE-EATING SLIME MOLD

LIZZY RUTHERFORD | 18
Monday at noon, July 25th, 3 days after Glizzy Night…

On the walk to my bathroom, my panties feel damp and gooey against my folds. Odd because I'm not turned on in the least bit. In fact, I'm the opposite, if worried can be considered an antonym for aroused. Currently, it's impossible to get excited about anything being this stressed out over whatever's going on with Sundance. That can only mean one thing…

Not again, I think, flicking on the light.

As expected, when I tug my pajama bottoms and my panties down a little, I find strands of mucus the color of simple syrup stretched between my labia and the thick glob of the glistening stuff smeared against the crotch of my undies. Ever since Saturday night, I've been having weird discharge like this. I thought it was just leftover sap and glizzy flower ejaculate leaking out but, considering it's been almost three days since that freaky plant creampied me, I don't know what's going on, especially since I didn't get to collect sap and masturbate with it like I wanted to. My best guess? My uterus is having a hard time bouncing back from the foreign substance that the glizzy flower injected into me.

After sitting down on the toilet and wiping the stuff out of my panties, I slip a middle finger into my tight hole and it glides right in, making the stickiest of noises as sliminess gushes out around my digit.

Not as much as last time, I think while stirring my finger around in what feels like a tight flesh pocket filled with lube the consistency of pudding. *But there's still quite a bit in there…*

Probing myself like this and curling my finger against my G-spot in an attempt to scoop the mucus out of me? It's actually turning me on, despite my previous declaration of being too worried to get horny. It's arousing me so much that I can't help but slowly pump a finger in and out of me. The longer I go at it, the wetter I become and the sticker it sounds. The next thing I know, the goo diluted with my wetness starts streaming out of me, running down my hand and splashing in the toilet water like heavy raindrops.

"Oof," I moan quietly as I speed up, the squelching and splashing drowning out the throaty sound of pleasure.

"Lizzy!" my brother shouts, banging on my bathroom door like a goddamn cop.

Thinking he just caught me diddling myself, I jump like a startled rabbit and pull my finger out of me so fast that I bang my knuckles against the toilet seat. "Ow! Jesus, Eli! Why must you be so loud? I'm on the toilet, not in the shower blasting music!" I scream.

Eli chuckles menacingly. "Did I scare the *shit* out of you? If so, you're welcome because it sounded like you were straining in there."

Oh shit, he did hear me moaning… That's embarrassing…

"You're gross…" I say after a short pause. "Did you need something or are you just being a pain in the ass?"

"Both?" he laughs again. "Mom told me to get ya. The vet's here."

"Oh, shit. Okay! I'll be right down" I say as I blast the toilet water with pee.

Eli is rummaging around in the fridge when I finally make it downstairs. "Whatcha lookin' for?" I ask, squinting at him.

As I'm walking by him, he pulls out a can of Sprite and turns to me with a scowl. "What happened to all the sodas and Vitamin Water? There's barely any left."

I wince as I reach past him and grab the last dragon fruit Vitamin Water. "My bad, I've been craving sweets like crazy these last few days." I've been craving sugary stuff since the day after glizzy flower night. And it's not just me, but Whitney too…

"Do Mom and Dad know you're pregnant?" he asks with a smirk.

I swat his arm with the back of my hand. "Shut the fuck up, Eli. Girls can't get pregnant if they don't have sex, and I still have never had sex—" *With anything but a glizzy flower,* "—so…"

"Good. The last thing the world needs is little *yous* running around," he says, ruffling my hair as we walk out to the backyard.

"Ugh." I lean away and punch him in the bicep. "I'm so glad I don't have to see you again until Thanksgiving…"

"Oh, please… After a few weeks of you being at college, you're going to miss having me pop back home every other weekend."

He's right. Ever since he went off to the University of Washington Tacoma last fall, it hasn't been the same around here without him making me laugh in between getting on my nerves. Then again, he drives back home so often, sometimes it's like he never left.

Instead of turning left to head into the barn, Eli and I hang a right then go through the paddock gate, heading towards the run-in shed across the field where Mom, Dad, and the veterinarian are gathered around my stallion.

Sundance hasn't been in the stable with the other horses since I walked into his stall Saturday after we reburied the flesh pod. As soon as I found him standing there with an erection and some sort of fungus that looked like peanut butter frosting all over his tail and rump, I put on gloves and rushed him out to the run-in shed. The sight freaked me out so bad that I didn't even notice that his penis was a different color than normal until I went to close the stall gate. That's when I did a double-take, knelt beside Sundance, and saw that his massive sex organ along with his testicles were completely coated with something similar to the stuff on his hind end. Similar, except, whatever it was, it was beige instead of light brown. Also, the squishy mass coating him from his testicles down to the middle of his shaft was smooth like candle wax while everything from the middle of his reproductive organ to the wide glans was more like buttercream frosting. After the girls and I finished freaking out, I called my parents in a panic.

"Talk about a fifth leg," Eli mutters in reference to Sundance's erection as we near the two-stall, three-walled horse shed. "You said it hasn't gone down at all since you found him like that Saturday afternoon?" Since he got in late last night from his trip a few hours before Mom and Dad returned from theirs, this is his first time seeing my horse like this.

"Unless he lost wood during the night, I'm guessing so…" I mutter.

"Weird…" Eli mumbles. "And that stuff on his hind end looks more like a slime mold than ringworm or something… I've seen horses with fungal infections before, but never anything like this… never anything that gives horses permanent boners…"

"There she is," Mom says to the older woman with a long, braided, sandy-brown ponytail hanging down to her butt.

"Ah, hello, Lizzy!" Dr. Joyce Kramer says in that bubbly tone she always has.

"Hi, Doctor Kramer…" My words trail off when my gaze falls on the slimy-looking infection on my horse's back half.

Sundance's erection is now completely coated in a beige layer of waxy stuff. Actually, maybe *waxy* isn't the right word anymore… Now it looks more like leather—leather with veins bulging through. And the mass on Sundance's hide that has now spread a quarter of the way up to his belly and also in a thin, straight line along his spine no longer looks like peanut butter frosting like it did last night. Now it looks just like…

It looks just like the skin of the glizzy flower's flesh pod… But… how? I never touched him after that first time I fucked the flower… And he was fine Friday when I took him to the barn before the girls came over…

"Is everything okay?" Dr. Kramer asks.

"No…" I gasp, pulling out my phone. "That stuff on his belly wasn't there last night—it was only up to his crotch… And that tan, SCOBY-looking stuff looked more like this yesterday." I show her the pictures on my phone. "This was last night." Now I swipe to the pictures I took when I first found him like this. "And this was Saturday around two o'clock…"

"Oh my…" the veterinarian says. "It's spreading at an alarming rate then…" She stares at me with concern in her eyes. "And you said that he was fine on Friday?"

My parents and I nod as Eli takes my phone to look at the pictures.

"Nothing stood out to me before we left," Dad says.

"I washed him from top to bottom Friday morning and I didn't notice any weird patches or growths," I say.

"And all the other horses are fine?" Joyce asks.

My parents and I nod again.

"We checked them all as soon as we got back yesterday," Mom says, "and again this morning."

Dr. Joyce Kramer uses her gloved hand to poke at the gooey-looking mass on Sundance's belly. "Unless this infection was dormant for a while, whatever caused it likely happened at some point Friday. Given how quickly it's spreading, it's not unreasonable to assume that he came in contact with the infectious agent that afternoon or that evening in his stall before it got that bad overnight… What's odd to me is that the infection didn't start from his hooves or his mouth—areas that would frequently come in contact with contaminated surfaces…"

"Mm-hm," Eli hums. "From these pictures, it almost looks like this horse eating slime mold or whatever it is started spreading from the top of his tail, down to his… uh… *manhood*, then it grew across his belly and spine… It's almost like whatever started this fell onto his back…" he says, handing me my phone back.

"Precisely what I was thinking, Eli," Dr. Kramer says, nodding as she walks out of the stall. Now she scans the surrounding area. "I don't see any trees hanging over the fence surrounding the paddock…" She turns to me as I'm snapping pictures of the lumpy, flesh pod-like mass on his belly. "Lizzy, was there anything dripping on Sundance from above his stall when you put him in there Friday?"

I shrug. "Not that I remember."

"Did you notice anything strange in the stall on Saturday when you found him?" Dad asks.

I twist my mouth to the side. "Uh… honestly, I was too freaked out by what was growing on Sundance to investigate the area."

"I don't blame you," Dr. Kramer says.

"The hayloft is right above his stall," Mom says. "But I'm not sure what would've dripped down onto him from up there."

After removing her gloves, Dr. Kramer reaches into her medical bag and pulls out a few fresh pairs that she then hands out to the four of us. "While I biopsy this mass, why don't you all poke around his stall and the hayloft to see if you can find anything? I'll be with you all in a few."

When the four of us reach the stable, Mom and Dad duck into his stall while me and Eli head up to the hayloft.

"There's something white in the cracks between the floorboards," Mom says, kicking some hay out of the way. "And there are a few white spots on the hay too…"

"Marie, look at that," Dad says to Mom.

When I reach the railing of the hayloft, I look over and find Dad pointing up to where I am. "What is it?" I ask.

"Look down," Dad says. "There're white stains on the edge by your feet."

Sure enough, there's something under my sneakers that looks like yogurt poured over the edge and dried up, but everything else looks clean.

Eli squats beside me and scratches at the stuff with a gloved finger. "Feels gummy, like partially dried glue…" he mutters. "Looks like someone spilled something white then cleaned it up… I found a few spots like this over by this block of hay."

Both Mom and Dad look at me, partially scowling. "Lizzy, were your friends in here this weekend?"

"No," I say with conviction. "They were with me the whole time, and no one left the house after I put the alarm on Friday night."

Because Piper was too busy puking white sludge and Whitney was busy dealing with having clam chowder exploding out of her vagina… And Sav would never sneak out in the middle of the night. I look down at the white stuff crusted on the edge of the hayloft. *Wait… there's no way.* I squat down and scratch at the gummy white stuff caked on the edge. *This can't be glizzy flower ejaculate, could it? No… Everyone went right to bed Friday night… Piper spent all night with her head over the toilet bowl and Whitney damn sure didn't get out of bed if she was as drowsy and feeling as horrible as I was that night…*

"What is it, Lizzy?" Dad asks.

I snap out of my trance. "Oh… Nothing… I'm just trying to figure out how what could've happened."

"It's white…" Eli mutters. "Bird shit's white… Maybe a diseased owl got in and shat its brains out." He snickers and smirks.

Dad chuckles. "That thought just crossed my mind, Eli."

"Like father, like son," Mom mumbles.

"Yeah, but then who cleaned it?" I ask, rising from my haunches.

"Maybe another animal ate it up?" Eli says.

"*Eli,*" Mom says in disgust. "*Stop.*"

Eli snickers. "What? I'm being serious. Animals are always licking up crap they shouldn't. Literally. And if no one came up here to clean this mess, then something else must've."

My parents and I bobble our heads as footfalls thump against wood down near the entrance.

"You all find anything?" Dr. Kramer asks as she approaches the stall where my parents are.

"Actually, yes," Dad answers. "There are some tacky, white spots down here and something crusted on the edge of the hayloft. Seems like something spilled over the edge and dripped down here. The prevailing theory from my *brilliant* son is that a bird with a bad case of explosive diarrhea got in and crapped all over the hayloft and the horse…"

Dr. Kramer smiles and shakes her head. "At this point, anything is possible." Now she starts towards the stairs. "I'll collect some samples of the material and run it against the biopsies from Sundance. If we get a genetic match, we'll work from there."

It's about fifteen minutes after our late lunch when I crawl back in bed, put on some music, and finally get around to sending out the new pictures of the mass growing on my horse to the group text with Piper and Whitney with the caption: **What does this look like to you all?**

One song later, Whitney texts back first.

Whitney: Ummm… that looks like the skin of the glizzy flower's flesh pod….

Me: Exactly!

Piper: Oh fuck… yeah it does. But how is that possible? Did you ride him after you rode the flower?

Me: No! After I first played with the flower, I just led him back to the stable by the reigns because the sap was soaking through my panties and shorts. And I didn't ride him the rest of that week either, so I'm not sure how it could've happened if that's what it is…

Whitney: Okay… now I'm scared… Has the vet ever seen anything like that before?

Me: Nope. She agreed with Eli that it looks almost like a slime mold is growing on Sundance.

Piper: I'm freaking the fuck out… Is that going to happen to us? I thought those scientist girls said it wasn't harmful to animals!!

Me: If it was going to happen to us, it would've by now, right?

Whitney: I guess… So, like, how did he get exposed to the glizzy flower goo?

Me: Idk, but there was some gummy white stuff on the edge of the hayloft right over his stall like something spilled over the edge and splashed onto him. But you 2 didn't go in the barn at any point this weekend, right?

Piper. Nope…

Whitney: Nope. Not until you called us in there on Saturday to show us what was wrong with Sundance…

Me: Exactly. So, it can't be glizzy flower-related, right?

Piper: Yeah. Maybe Sundance's infection just happens to look like the flesh pod.

Me: That's what I was thinking. Eli thinks that an owl with a weird fungal disease crapped all over the hayloft and that's how Sundance got infected…

Piper: Well, bird shit is white… so… Could be that…

Whitney: Eli would say that… LOL.

Piper: Is Sundance going to be okay?

Me: Idk… he's running a pretty high fever and that gross, slimy goop, like, grew over his butt hole, so he can't exactly poop. Probably a good thing he hasn't been eating much these last few days… Idk… It's not looking good.

Whitney: Oh geez… I'm so sorry, Lizzy.

Piper: Oh god… Lizzy, I'm sorry… If there's anything you need, let me know!

Whitney: Same, girl!

Me: Thanks. I appreciate it. I'll keep you posted on Sundance, and I'll let you know when the lab tests of the infection and the gummy stuff from the barn come back.

CHAPTER 12
RUNAWAYS

PIPER CUMMINGS | 18
Wednesday morning, 5 days since Glizzy Night

The buzzing of my phone somewhere on my bed is a well-timed, godsend of a wake-up call because it rescues me from the reoccurring nightmare that I've been having these last few days. Even though I'm happy to escape that ordeal of a dream, I'm immediately annoyed when I peek through one eye at my clock to find that it's 8:45 in the goddamn morning...

Great, that means I barely got three hours of sleep... Who the fuck is calling me so early anyway? I groan, sniffling my partially stuffy nose as I roll over and blindly slap my bed in search of my cellphone. When I finally find it under the pillow I cuddle with, I squint at the bright screen and see a picture of Lizzy making a goofy face. *You never call this early,* I think, swiping to answer.

"Ugh... Hello," I mutter groggily.

"Hey, Pipes, sorry to call this early, but I need you," she says, sounding slightly groggy and super-upset.

"What's wrong?" I blurt out, sitting up. "Are you okay?"

"I'm fine. It's... It's Sundance... He's gone..."

My heart throttles in my chest while my stomach twists into a knot. "Oh no, when did he pass away?"

"No, he didn't *pass away*, he ran away."

"Oh…" I let out a sigh of relief that me puking on her horse didn't mean I killed it—a sigh of relief that it doesn't mean Jake Landau isn't responding to my texts because my glizzy flower jizz-vomit made him so sick that he perished. "How? Did someone leave the gate of the run-in shed unlocked or something?"

"More like Sundance kicked the wooden stall door of the run-in shed so hard that the latch broke. Then, being the show jumping horse he is, he must've leaped the fence after he got out…"

"Holy shit…"

"Holy shit as right. The shitty part is that I'm the only one who woke up to loud banging out there late last night, but I thought I dreamt it because the noise stopped as soon as I opened my eyes… Had I just gotten out of bed—"

"Don't blame yourself, Lizzy," I say. "Even if you got up, he probably would've hopped the fence before you even got outside."

"Maybe…"

"Think about it this way, if he wanted out bad enough to kick open the stall door, it probably wouldn't have been safe for you safe to be around him anyway. Like, maybe the fever has him acting all aggressive and defensive like some kind of weird rabies, you know?"

"That's possible…"

"So did you just want to talk, or do you need me to come over? Because I can get ready and be there in fifteen."

"Actually, yeah, I was going to ask you to come over. Mom and Dad are busing doing chores around the ranch, and Eli is out driving around looking for him, so I was going to ask if you could pick me up and drive me around to cover the areas Eli isn't scouting. I'll give you gas money."

"Sure thing. And don't worry about gas money, I got you, girl."

The entire drive to Lizzy's place, my heart is racing and my stomach is all queasy like I just chugged half-a-liter of glizzy flower cum again. I've been feeling this way ever since she texted us pictures of the mass resembling the glizzy pod that was growing across her horse's belly and back. That's why I've barely slept in days and why I keep having nightmares. Because there's no way that what I puked up in the hayloft while blowing Jake isn't what caused the infection that's growing on her horse, not when the mass looks *exactly* like that pod's gross, flabby flesh…

As I turn onto the long, desolate road leading to the Rutherford's Ranch, another bout of postnasal drip makes me snort, drawing thickness from my nose and sinuses to the back of my throat. After hocking the loogies into my mouth, I taste that same chalky mucus that I've been having ever since Glizzy Night, prompting me to look up at the rearview mirror and open my mouth. Just like the last few times, there's this white, creamy paste streaked across on the back of my tongue…

It's been five days since glizzy flower jizz shot out of my nose, so why is my snot still white and chalky like this? That's what I wonder as I swallow the bitterness down, sniffling my slightly stuffy nose right after. *Geez… Am I, like, just going to be congested forever now?*

Seeing that pasty mucus again triggers a wave of vivid scenes from my nightmares to flicker in my mind. Every dream begins the same way: I'm queasy and can't stop projectile vomiting something that looks like clam chowder everywhere. Eventually, the puke gets on me and splashes my friends, then we frantically try scrubbing it off in the bathroom together to no avail. The rest of the dream is me watching as the white batter stuck to us rapidly morphs into tan, lumpy biomass that looks like the glizzy pod's meaty exterior. Within minutes, all of my friends turn to flesh pods and the meaty mass is about to grow over my face to suffocate me. That's usually when I wake up.

The vivid recollection of the nightmare has me on the verge of a panic attack. *That's not going to happen to us. It can't. It won't. Because the ejaculate I puked that night got all over me, and that same stuff sprayed all over Whitney and Savanna before that happened. And it gushed out of Lizzy's coochie and splashed her thighs… So, if it was going to happen, it would've by now since we all got exposed to it before the horse did. Also, it didn't stick to us like it stuck to Sundance, so there's no way that it'll turn into that slime mold stuff growing on her horse…*

That's when the image of Jake Landau trying to scrub off the white gunk stuck to his dick and abs pops into my head.

But it did stick to Jake… And Jake did tell all the guys who I used to hook up with that I gave him an STD, which means he must've had some kind of symptoms the following day… But if he was sick like Sundance, he would've told Lizzy, and she would've said something to me… Right?

Just as I'm pulling up to the Rutherfords' garage, I catch a glimpse in the rearview of a pickup truck coming down the dirt road behind me. It's only after the vehicle parks alongside my driver's side do I realize that it's Jake's parents' truck. Both his mom and dad are in the car, but I don't see him in the back seat.

Hold up, is this a setup? Did Lizzy make up the story about a runaway horse to lure me here so Jake's parents can yell at me for giving him the same infection I somehow gave to Sundance? The thought that his parents are about to kill me has my heart thumping harder than it ever has before. Like, I'm panicking so bad that I'm starting to feel dizzy and sweaty and on the verge of blacking out.

To further add to my suspicions that they know I gave something to Jake, they have this wide-eyed, worried look in their eyes as they're staring back at me.

Shit, I think, unbuckling my seatbelt. *Something isn't right. I'm fucked, I know it…*

After taking a deep breath and exhaling slowly, I open my car door and climb out. "Hey, Mr. and Mrs. Landau… You here to help look for Sundance too?" I say, my voice cracking from nervousness.

They both share a look before turning back to me.

"Oh, we had no idea they were missing a horse…" Mr. Landau says to me. "We're here because we woke up this morning and Jake was gone."

My eyes go wide. "Like, he went for a drive without telling you?"

They both shake their heads.

"No…" Mrs. Landau croaks, looking like she's about to start bawling. "His car was still in the driveway but he was nowhere in the house."

"When we got up this morning at 7:00," Mr. Landau says, "his bedroom door was open for the first time since Saturday, so we thought he was finally feeling better and decide to come out to eat. Then, when we got downstairs, the backdoor was wide open. We figured if he didn't have his car, he maybe walked over here in the middle of the night to see Lizzy and just forgot to close the door."

My jaw drops. My heart skips a beat. "Wait… What do you mean *feeling better?* Jake's been sick?"

They both nod.

"What's been wrong with him?" I blurt out in a more high-pitched tone than usual.

"He wouldn't tell us what was wrong," Mrs. Landau says. "He just said it felt like he had the flu, so he quarantined himself and just had me leave food in front of his door the past few days. The last time I actually saw him was Saturday afternoon when he came back from wherever he went."

Hearing that makes me slip into a wide-eyed trance. *Oh shit… Oh shit! Oh shit! There's no way he has what Sundance has if me, Lizzy, Whitney, and Savanna don't… It's got to be something else… Like an allergic reaction.*

"What's wrong, Piper," Mrs. Landau says. "Do you know something?"

I snap out of it and shake my head. "No… I was just thinking that he must've been really sick because he hasn't texted me back in days."

"Oh, yeah," she says, "he's been sleeping since Saturday around six or so."

At that moment, the Rutherfords' front door opens. "Oh," Lizzy says as we turn to her. "Mister and Mises Landau… What are you doing here? My parents tell you about Sundance? Please tell me you're here because you've seen him…" There's a glimmer of hopefulness in her red, puffy eyes.

"No," Mr. Landau says, scratching his thick, brown beard. "Jake disappeared in the middle of the night and left the back door open, so we wanted to check and see if he was here since your place is the only place in walking distance that he'd go…"

Lizzy's eyes go wide and her jaw goes slack. "Oh… No… he's not here. Haven't seen him since… last week Monday when he came by to watch a movie…"

The Landaus turn to each other, looking even more worried than did when they climbed out of the truck.

"I don't understand," Jake's mom says to Mr. Landau. "Where could he have gone? Why would he just leave like that in the middle of the night and leave the backdoor wide open? He didn't even take his phone." That's when she covers her mouth with her hand and breaks down as her husband embraces her.

"I'm sure Jake is fine," Lizzy says to them. "While me and Piper are out looking for Sundance, I'll call our mutual friends and ask around for you guys, okay? And I'll get Whitney and Savanna to check out a few of his usual spots too. Don't worry, we'll find him!"

"Thank you, Lizzy," Mrs. Landau says.

She offers them a smile. "No need to thank me. You know I'd do anything for Jake"

"We know you would, Lizzy," Mr. Landau says.

"Alright, we're going to head out," Lizzy says, gesturing to the front door. "If you'd like to see my parents, Dad's out by the stable and Mom's in the garden."

"Alright, thanks, Lizzy," Jake's dad says as they head to the door.

Once they disappear into the house, Lizzy turns to me. "What the fuck… What are the odds both Jake and Sundance go missing the same night?"

"Slim to none," I mutter, nodding towards my car as I start walking towards it.

"You don't think Jake got shitfaced, stole my horse, and galloped off into the night, do you?" She lets out that nervous laugh she does when something is bothering her.

I shake my head while climbing behind the wheel. "His parents said he had the flu or something since Saturday… so… doubtful that he'd be drinking…"

"Weird…" Lizzy says, climbing into the passenger seat and slamming her door shut. "So, not only did he and Sundance go missing the same night, but they both started feeling sick the morning after riding and blowing the glizzy flower made us four all feverish? Like, that can't be a coincidence…"

"Maybe the fevers we had weren't because of the glizzy flower cum after all," I mutter, staring off into nothing. "Maybe we all just happened to get sick from something else in the area at the same time…"

"I mean, it's possible, but Jake wasn't anywhere near my house Friday night."

I shrug as I start the car. "It's not like he lives that far though. Maybe the wind carried some spores or something to his house.

And he does hike through those woods behind your property fairly often because he's outdoorsy like that… Maybe he passed through that area at some point on Friday and got exposed to whatever made us all sick."

Lizzy sighs. "I guess that's possible… If there's a freaky flesh pod with a dick flower growing out of the ground behind my house, I *suppose* there could be other weird stuff growing out there… like a slime mold that infects horses or, like, some kind of mold spores that causes flulike symptoms or some shit."

"Exactly…" I say while backing out into the grass. "So, where are we heading first?"

"Horses like open spaces, so let's just head up Yelm Highway then maybe go west to check the fields and farms out that way," she says, thumbing away at her phone. "After that, we can head out towards the Nisqually Reservation by the Washington-510, if you don't mind."

"I don't mind! Anything for you."

I don't mind because there's like a 99% chance that it's my fault…

I just really hope whatever's wrong with Jake isn't my fault too…

CHAPTER 13
DEFLOWERED

LIZZY RUTHERFORD | 18
Friday, July 29th, 1 week since Glizzy Night

Between Sundance and Jake Landau still being missing now for 48 hours, I've been an absolute mess. Like, I barely have an appetite, my racing thoughts have been keeping me up until almost 3:00 a.m. every night, and then, whenever I do fall asleep, I freaking wake up every other hour.

During my waking hours, all of my energy has been focused on trying to find Jake. But since nothing I'm doing seems to help, and since I'm just getting more worried with each passing hour that Jake isn't back safe, I'm in need of a distraction. I need something to make me feel good just for a little while. Aside from smoking weed and getting shitfaced like I've done the last few nights with Piper, the only other thing that'll truly help me forget my troubles and feel the teensiest bit happy would be to get high on glizzy flower pheromones and fuck that plant until I'm coming too hard to form a coherent thought.

The more I think about bouncing on that horrific flesh pod's phallus, the hornier I get. The hornier I get, the more restless I become. It's so bad, that I go from squirming in bed clenching my thighs to shoving a pillow between my legs and humping it nice and slow.

If my parents would just hurry up and leave for their friends' house, I can head out back, collect some sap, and get my fuck on already...

If I had time these last few days to make it out back and harvest some glizzy flower sap like I planned, I could just crack open a jar right now and schlick away with my hairbrush. Me and the girls were supposed to jar some fuck-honey after we buried the flesh pod back up, but when we went back to the house to wash our hands and grab the mason jars, I detoured to the stable to let the horses out into the paddock. That's when I saw the slime mold stuff growing on Sundance. Then, by the time Piper's older sister Harper came by to pick up her and Whit, I was panicking too bad to get my ass off the couch.

The longer I grind against my pillow, the damper my panties become. My hand slips into my panties on its own accord, then my middle finger drags past my clit before slipping between my slick folds. Just like the other day, my pussy gushes with a sticky, wet noise while my finger slides deep into my obscenely slick tightness.

Damn, how am I this wet? The crazy videos I saw online about women discussing how slimy they were after contracting those Amazonian Womb Worms pop into my head. *Did a womb worm slither into me while I was naked in the woods or something?*

After pumping my finger in and out of me a few times, I pull my hand out of my pants and look down. While my digit is glistening with a layer of this clear, pale-yellow liquid, my vaginal secretions aren't that weird yellow, milky, thick stuff.

The girls online and the news articles all said Amazonian Womb Worm slime is usually cloudy and white, so I guess I'm not this wet because of that. The question is, why is it yellowish? I rub the slick stuff against my thumb and it's slipperier than anything that's ever come from down there. *This color... the slickness of it... it's like a diluted version of the glizzy flower's sap,* I think, touching my finger to my tongue.

"Mmm!"

It's kind of sweet like it too… Weird…

While I suck my finger clean, I continue humping my pillow, grinding into it harder and faster than before. But it's not enough. Fingers won't be enough either.

I need my dad's neck massager… As the thought leaves my mind, my phone buzzes beside me. *Or…*

I grab my phone and, after swiping away the notification that has nothing to do with Jake, I navigate over to the vibrating massager app that I downloaded for those nights I couldn't borrow Dad's massager. After tapping the fast pulse option, I roll onto my back, spread my legs, then press my iPhone against my clit over my panties.

"Ugh-mmm… Oh yeah…" I moan quietly.

With each pulse, my vaginal walls flutter. With each pulse, my pleasure crescendos, gradually nudging my body to the edge of climax. In a matter of seconds, my chest is heaving. Just about a minute into vibing, my toes curl so hard that they're gripping the sheet like monkeys' feet.

KNOCK-KNOCK-KNOCK is the pattern of soft banging that comes from my door just as my eyes are rolling into the back of my head.

Fucking hell, I think, quickly yanking my phone off of my pussy.

"Lizzy, we're leaving now," Mom says.

"Okay!" say breathlessly, staring at the glistening droplets on my phone screen from the wetness that soaked through my panties. "Drive safe!"

"You alright, honey?" she asks. "Sound like you're crying or something."

"I'm fine…" I say flatly.

"You sure?"

"Yeah, I was just dozing off, so I'm just a little startled."

"Oh… I'm sorry. Get some rest, dear. We'll see you later tonight."

"Alrighty. Bye."

When her footfalls reach the squeaky stairs, I switch the vibrating app to the **random pattern** then press the phone back against the hot, damp spot between my legs.

Barely a minute later, the automatic garage opens, making the entire house vibrate. Dad's truck engine roars to life a few seconds later. That's when I pry my phone away from my crotch and tiptoe over to the window. As soon as they turn off our dirt driveway onto Evergreen Valley Road, I prance over to my closet to get ready.

Given that it's still daylight, I don't want to be completely naked in the woods, just in case. So, I put on my least favorite sundress, that way I can just bounce on the glizzy flower without any prying eyes seeing any penetration. And there might be some prying eyes out there because I believe the cops are supposed to be checking the woods for signs of Jake tonight at some point today or tomorrow. Fingers crossed they don't find the glizzy flower…

On the way out of my room, I think about turning the vibrator app back on and pressing it between my legs on the walk over to keep me on the edge. *I can't exactly walk across the field with my hand between my legs… But I could just stick my phone in my panties for some hands-free fun! How do I keep my phone from being soaked in pussy juice though?* My head turns left and right over and over until my eyes fall on the backpack containing the mason jars and the condoms that I swiped from Eli's room Friday afternoon. *Bingo!*

After setting the vibrator app to fast pulse, I open a condom, stretch it over the top of my phone, then roll it on down and tie it off at the bottom.

Perfect! Now that it's waterproofed, I think, lifting my skirt and slipping my buzzing phone into the crotch of my panties.

"Oof… yassss…" I moan, pulling my undies up to my belly button so that the phone is mashed snuggly right against me.

With my backpack slung over my shoulders, I tiptoe over to my door in a bit of a wide-legged waddle since it's a bit uncomfortable having a phone between my legs. Just as I'm palming the doorknob, my knees go weak and my core spams. "UNGH-MM," I moan.

It's going to be hard to walk like this…

Eli is in his room with some shooting game blasting on his TV, so I skedaddle down the stairs and sneak out of the house as fast as my wobbly legs will take me. Halfway through my trek across the open field to the southwest corner of the fence, my pussy goes from twitching with every quick pulse to clenching hard, rhythmically and sporadically. Thick, wetness bubbles out of my pussy with each clench. Things get so sodden down there that the phone in my panties starts sliding against me a bit with each step.

A few feet from the fence, pleasure makes my knees buckle so bad that I stumble. Somehow, stopping abruptly and clenching my thighs while touching my knees together keeps me from falling.

During my climb over the fence, I start sniffing for that delicious scent. *Hmm… normally I'd be smelling the flower by now… Maybe the wind is blowing in a different direction.*

Maybe yard or two from my pleasure plant, just as I'm rounding the big tree that's blocking my view of it, I'm blindsided by a *very* intense orgasm. My legs buckle again as my womb and vagina begin contracting pleasantly. It's so intense that it brings me to my knees and I have to plant a palm against the tree trunk ahead so I don't faceplant.

"WUGH-AH-OH!" I moan breathily.

Suddenly, contractions begin rippling from my uterus down to the opening of my vagina in rolling waves that remind me of the peristaltic movements of food moving down the esophagus, causing a thick stream of sliminess to gush out of my opening with a bubbly queef. The orgasm is so intense, I have to snatch the phone out of my panties. At that moment, I'm hit with this bizarre sensation deep in my vagina that makes me drop the slick, condom-encased phone. I don't know how to explain it other than it feels like there's a firm, slimy grape being squeezed out of my butthole—that feeling, but in what feels like my cervix.

"Oooof… What the fuuuuck…" I groan in pleasure as the grapelike object bulges its way down into my vagina.

In the next beat, it feels like my cervix just snapped shut behind the ball like a sphincter, and it makes my core spasm. That sensation doesn't make sense considering the cervix isn't a sphincter… I'm no scientist, but I did take anatomy and sex-ed, and that much I know. Although, it did feel like my cervix kept randomly stretching from Saturday until about Tuesday morning, so maybe it's dilated for some reason.

The muscles in my pussy contract in a downward wave, starting from near the cervix then rippling south to my labia, forcing the ball-like object closer to my opening with each throb. As the firm, spherical thing bulges through my hymen, I sit up, lift my skirt, and pull my panties aside. A stream of glistening, yellowish slime pours out of both my panties and straight from my pussy, drizzling onto the soil like syrup.

Why does it look like I'm gushing sap? It's been a week since I rode the glizzy flower, I think, using two fingers to spread my pussy lips open.

At that exact moment, a strong contraction makes me Kegel so hard that my pussy spurts noisily right as this white ball launches out of my vagina and splashes into the slime puddle below.

"What the actual fuck?" I say in awe while reaching down with a shaky hand for the white ball that I just birthed.

The slimy thing I pick up and squeeze between my pointer and thumb is firmer than a grape but kind of squishy like a cherry that's nowhere near ripe. It feels like if I squeeze it too hard, the gelatinous ball the size of a tiny gumball might pop, so I don't apply any more pressure.

What the fuck is this thing? Leftover, coagulated glizzy flower cum? I hope it's that because no one has ever said anything about women randomly birthing little white balls before…

I roll the ball around in my hand while I try to finger out what to do with it. Part of me wants to chuck it in a bush, but then I start wondering if maybe I should keep it to show the girls, or to show my OB/GYN should I decide to go get checked out before I leave for college.

If any more weird stuff happens down there, I'm definitely going to make an appointment, I think, reaching into my backpack and pulling out one of the four 8-ounce mason jars I brought along. The gelatinous ball I drop in hits the bottom of the glass with a little bounce. *So fucking weird…*

Still mulling over why I just birthed a white ball, I sling my backpack over my shoulder and continue around the tree and underbrush in a bit of a daze. The instant my eyes fall on the site of the glizzy flower, I snap out of the trance and my jaw drops.

"Umm… What the fuck…" I mutter to no one but myself.

My eyes dart around the area in search of a sign that I'm in the wrong spot, but I know from all the white gunk dried and crystalized sap on the surrounding soil that this is where the girls and I fucked the glizzy flower. The only problem is, there's no phallic flower rising up from the soil bulge. There isn't even a soil bulge anymore, there's just a pit where the glizzy flower used to be with mounds of dark, freshly dug-up soil piled around it.

"What the fuck…" I mutter, walking around the pit. "Where did my flower go?"

That's when I see them—footprints and a thick groove in the dirt leading away from the pit that goes off to the east in the direction of Fort Lewis Road, the road that runs right past the Landau's house…

I squat down and inspect the groove track. *Looks like a single tire mark… Like one or two people used a wheelbarrow to haul off something heavy… something heavily like the giant, fleshy pod of my glizzy flower… But who the fuck would've gone through the trouble? The girls could've come over whenever and fucked this thing… If they stole it, it's not like they have anywhere on their property to hide it, anyway… And there's no reason Jake would steal it before disappearing… The only other suspects would be…*

As I'm rising from my haunches, I'm blindsided by another sharp but pleasant uterine spasm, and I swear another round object is bulging through my cervix.

"Ugh," I groan as the rippling contractions resume. "Again?"

Right as another ball squeezes through my seemingly dilated cervix, it's quickly pushed down to the exit by waves of vaginal contractions only for a third ball to bugle in my cervix a second later.

"HNNG… Ah! AHH! Holy fuck!" I groan as my body trembles from pleasure and discomfort. "Why is this happening?"

Barely a second after I pull aside my panties, the second ball plops out of me before I even try squeezing it out, hitting the ground with a squishy thud. A few rippling contractions later, the third sphere that's a bit smaller than the first two drops out of me as I'm pulling my labia to the side.

Okay, birthing a ball after an orgasm is one thing, I think, picking up the two round objects and rolling the slimy things in my hand as I rise from the squatted position. *But randomly having another orgasm, like, a minute later and passing two more? That's kinda freaking me out…*

Considering that birthing these things is nowhere near as concerning as the fever and having thick filth blasting out of my snatch all Friday night, I'm not super concerned. The only thing on my mind right now, other than Jake, is finding out who the fuck stole my glizzy flower.

As I follow the wheelbarrow tracks that weave through the woods to the east, I mindlessly take one of the balls out of my palm and roll it between my fingers. Not long after I start, I accidentally squeeze it a little too hard then the slippery thing pops out from between my fingers and falls into a muddy patch in a depression beside a bush. A few yards later, I get tired of playing with the remaining ball and drop it into the groove made by the wheelbarrow, using my foot to bury it afterward. Now I wipe my hands off on my sundress and pull out my cell to text the girls.

Eventually, the wheelbarrow tracks end on the muddy roadside along Fort Lewis Road right where a pair of big tire marks begin, suggesting someone loaded the glizzy flower pod into a truck. Since the trail's gone cold, I just head home.

Right when I reach the top of the stairs, Eli finally emerges from his room, looking at me curiously from head to toe. "What's all that crusty, yellow stuff on your dress… There's some all over your leg too."

"Tree sap," I snap, ducking in my room and shutting the door.

Not long after changing out of my sundress and sticky panties, Piper pulls up to the house. By the time I get downstairs, Savanna comes cruising down the road with Whitney in the passenger seat.

"Talk about perfect timing," I say as the girls climb out of their respective cars.

Piper hands me an iced coffee from Evergreen Valley Espresso. "They should've beat me here since I stopped for this."

"I thought we'd be late since Whitney took forever to come downstairs," Savanna says, scowling at her. Her skin has cleared up nicely since I last saw her on Tuesday.

Smiling, I shake my head. "Well, it all worked out because I just got back a bit ago."

"From where?" Piper asks, still sounding a bit stuffy.

"Went for a little hike," I mutter.

"Uh oh," Savanna says, searching my face. "Were you out back with your *flower*?" She squints at me.

I nod towards the barn. "Eli's home, so I'll tell you once we're out of earshot," I whisper.

The girls and I chat about the Jake Landau situation until we reach the fence on the far end of the property.

"Um, where are we going?" Savanna asks.

"Where do you think?" Piper fires back.

"Please don't tell me that this emergency meeting is because you wanna play another round of sexy double dare with your cock plant..." Savanna sasses as we climb the fence. "If it is, tell me now so I can turn back. I don't want another three-day long rash..."

"Yeah..." Whitney groans. "I'd turn back too."

"Fine," Piper says, turning to them while walking backward alongside me, "then you all leave so I can play alone!"

"No one is playing with anything today?" I say, leading the way through the brush.

"Why?" Piper asks.

When we round the tree, I gesture to the muddy pit. "Because the glizzy flower is gone."

"Holy crap, you've been deflowered!" Piper says with a wince of a smirk.

"Good one, Pipes," Whitney says, laughing.

"*All* of it is gone?" Piper asks with emphasis on *all*, her way of inquiring about the pod without letting Savanna know there was more to it.

I nod slowly and dramatically. "*All* of it..."

"How?" Piper asks while she and Whitney stare at the pit.

"And why is this hole so big?" Savanna asks.

"No clue," I mutter. "And I think someone dug it up and plopped it in a wheelbarrow." I point at the footprints and the singular wheel track. "This goes all the way to Fort Lewis Road…"

"So, some stole it?" Piper says, looking at me all wide-eyed.

"Who the fuck would do that?" Whitney asks.

I shrug. "None of you told anyone about the glizzy flower, right?" I scan their faces as they all shake their heads.

"Of course not," Piper says affirmatively.

"Definitely not," Whitney says.

"And look like a crazy person with a plant kink?" Savanna says. "Hell no. Not like anyone would believe us if we did…"

"Truth," Whitney says.

"It had to be those scientist girls…" Piper says with this serious look on her face. "Other than us, they're the only ones who know that pulsating dick flowers capable of jizzing even exist…"

"That's my guess too," I mutter.

"Wait," Savanna says, looking out towards the direction of the tracks, "Fort Lewis Road is the road Jake lives on… You think this is connected to him?"

I shrug. "I have no idea… So much weird shit is happening all at the same time, it's hard to tell what's connected and what's not."

"Seriously," Piper says, scanning the surrounding woods. "So, what do we do now? Call that botanist girl and ask her if they took the flower?"

I shake my head. "We can't exactly call and accuse them of stealing my glizzy flower. If they *didn't* take it, they might come down on us for not telling them I knew about it… Then we might have a bigger problem…"

"True…" Piper says, huffing after. "Well, fuck… Then let's just go look for another one. Like, there's got to be more than one out there if those girls were looking for them…"

"I suppose it's possible," I say.

"If there *are* more, it shouldn't be too hard to find one," Piper says. "I mean, you can smell those things from a quarter-mile away, so all we gotta do is sniff around until we smell something sweet that makes us all wet!"

I giggle. "I could go for a nice hike through the woods to take my mind off things," I say.

"And while we're exploring, we can search for signs of Jake," Whitney adds.

"Exactly!" Piper says. "Two birds with one stone!"

"I'm in," Savanna says. "For Jake, not because I want to find another glizzy flower…"

Piper bumps Savanna's arm with an elbow. "Come on, you don't have to lie. I noticed how bummed you looked when you saw a pit instead of that sap-squirting plant that we all had so much fun with the other night."

"I was more confused than *bummed*," Savanna mutters. "And I didn't have fun… I don't know how any of you could call that fun when Lizzy's flower glizzy basically gave us all an STD." She shoots a look at Piper. "Speaking of *STDs*… Why is everyone saying that you gave Jake Landau an STD?"

Piper's eyes go wide and all the color leaves her face like she just saw a ghost. "I don't know who started that rumor or why, but I didn't give anyone an STD! I told you all on Friday when Lizzy was putting a condom on the flower glizzy that I've been tested and I'm clean! Fuck…"

"When did this rumor start?" I ask.

"Saturday, I think," Savanna says.

"The same day his parents said Jake started feeling sick…" I mutter, turning to Piper. "Did you hook up with Jake recently?"

"What? Me and Jake? Come on…" Piper blurts out.

"Pipes… I know you two have been hooking up for at least a year," I say in a flat tone. "I'm not that stupid…"

"Oh… Alright, fine," she says through a sigh. "Yeah, we've hooked up, and I'm sorry for that because I know how you feel about him. But we haven't hooked up in over a week. One of my sneaky links is probably just jealous that me and Jake were hanging out or something."

I scan her face. "Okay…"

Piper gets this worried look in her eyes. "We good?"

I nod. "Of course we are. Like I said, I knew for a while…"

"You sure?" Piper says to me. "Just say the word and, whenever Jake comes back home, me and him won't do anything with each other ever again."

"It's whatever, Pipes," I say. "I really don't give a shit anymore. I've given up on Jake the day he told me he was going to prom with Jenna Hanley after I hinted that we should go together. Seriously, it's fine."

"Okay…"

An awkward silence fills the area.

"Alright," I say, gesturing towards the house, "let's go grab some water and snacks, then we can go exploring."

"Good, because I was going to ask if I could get my jogging sneakers out of the car before we left," Whitney says.

"Same," Savanna adds.

As I lead the way to the fence, my mind wanders back to the STD rumor. *Why would someone start a rumor about Piper giving Jake an STD the same day he started experiencing flulike symptoms? It just doesn't make sense…* I side-eye Piper. *Either she did give him something and he told the guys so no one else hooks up with her or someone is trying to slander her…*

But she says she's clean, so I have to trust her. I have to believe her over some stupid, albeit weirdly timed rumor, right?

CHAPTER 14
NATURE'S FLESHLIGHT

ELI RUTHERFORD | 19
Saturday, August 6th, mid-afternoon
10 days since Jake Landau & Sundance disappeared…

Like clockwork, an hour after our parents left for the weekend, I hear the backdoor's hinges groan through my opened window. That's my cue to set down my Xbox controller, roll my gaming chair over to the window, and pull aside my curtains just enough to peek through without getting spotted. As expected, my sister, Whitney, and that gorgeous skank Piper are striding hurriedly across the field to the southwest corner of our property—the same spot where they keep hopping the fence and disappearing into the woods.

What the fuck are you girls up to out there?

It's not uncommon for them to hike in the woods behind our ranch once in a while, but they've never gone out there *this* frequently… Also, it seems they only venture out whenever Mom and Dad are gone, which is odd considering our parents never cared if we smoked weed. So, if that's what they're doing, there's no need to sneak around. Which means it's something worse…

This all started last week Friday, two days after Jake Landau disappeared. Around the time our parents were heading out to dinner with their friends or whatever, Lizzy told Mom that she was dozing off. Then, as soon as Mom and Dad left, I heard the back door open. When I peeked through the blinds, I found my little sister in a sundress with her hiking bag on her back, waddling hurriedly across the ranch like she had a stick up her ass. A few minutes later, she came back home with yellow, snotty-looking stains on her dress, and there was something crusty smeared across her inner thigh too. When I asked what that stuff was, she just said, '*tree sap*' before ducking into her room and slamming the door.

A few minutes later, she emerged in jeans and a T-shirt, met her friends out front, then they all went back out to the southwest corner of the property and disappeared into the woods. Ten minutes later, they came back to the house, changed, and grab water before venturing back to the woods and disappearing for hours. When they returned, I asked where they went and Lizzy just said they were trying to see if they could find Jake…

The next day, they did the same thing. All four of them went hiking around noon then came back before sundown. On Sunday, Lizzy went out there alone for a few hours. Monday and Tuesday were rainy, so she stayed in all day cooped up in her room. As soon as things cleared up on Wednesday, Piper and Whitney came over, then they ventured back out there. On Thursday, it rained again, so she went out for a drive with Piper and didn't come back till late.

Then, yesterday, Lizzy headed to the woods alone for a few minutes only to come running back to the house barely ten minutes later. Thirty minutes after that, Whitney and Piper came over once again, then the three of them rushed straight out to the woods as soon as they got out of their cars. It was weird…

I need to know what the fuck they're up to, I think, sitting back in my chair once the girls disappear into the woods. *Did they find Jake? Is he living out in the woods for some reason?*

Now I start thinking about all the reasons Jake Landau would have to run away and live in the wilderness without telling anyone but those girls.

Were his parents abusing him?

No… that can't be it. His parents are the nicest people in the world.

I've known Jake since we were toddlers. Me, him, and Lizzy grew up together, so he and I were like brothers who always confided in each other. So, if his parents were hurting him, he would've told me. Or he would've at least told Lizzy…

If their woodland adventures aren't connected to Jake, what could they possibly be doing out there so often? And why did they seem so weird when they came back yesterday? It's like they were high on something…

"Fuck it," I whisper, powering off my Xbox Series X.

I'm going out there. As soon as they return, I'm heading out to the woods and I'm going to see if their footprints will lead me to wherever they're always sneaking off to…

Lizzy, Whitney, and Piper weren't out there long today, which means wherever they went wasn't too far from the fence. Not long after they walk in the house, I hear the bathroom door downstairs slam shut followed by Lizzy and Piper speaking in hushed voices out in the hall. Lizzy's bedroom door closes softly shortly after that, my cue to head out.

My window, like Lizzy's, faces the south and has a clear view of the woods outback. To make sure she doesn't see me like how I always see her, I sneak out the front door then slip past the front side of the barn. Now I head to the east and hop the fence. From there, I slink just behind the tree line bordering our fence until I hit the southwest corner where they've been climbing over.

Sure enough, there are footprints in the soft, rain-saturated soil that leads in a pretty defined path towards the largest tree in sight that has a wall of underbrush on either side of it. As I round the lush, green foliage, I see a rather large depression in the dirt ahead. That's when I catch a whiff of something sweet and floral.

Looks like someone dug something up here and buried it back up, I think, walking around the 6 by 3-foot wide, 2-foot-deep hole… *Looks big enough to fit a body, and it looks like it was even deeper before someone tried to fill it in… That's concerning… Did they murder Jake and move the body? No way… Lizzy wouldn't do that. She couldn't've because she's been a mess ever since he went missing, and she was home the night he vanished… There's got to be another reason…*

As I stroll up to the other end of the ditch, I see what looks to be a long, thin, straight line carved in the dirt. It looks to me like something with one wheel rolled through here to the east…

What has one wheel other than a unicycle? I wonder as I follow the track deeper into the woods, sniffing like a dog when that mouthwatering fragrance starts smelling even stronger. Out of nowhere, my dick goes semi-erect, prompting me to adjust my manhood. As I do, the image of the single-wheeled cart in our shed pops into my head. *A wheelbarrow… A wheelbarrow with a body in it…*

"No way… There's no way that—Mmmm…" I moan from the heavenly odor overwhelming my nostrils. As I suck in a deep breath through my nose, my pants tighten from the full erection that's pitching a tent down below.

What the fuck is that smell? I inhale deeply again while tucking my boner in the waistband of my shorts. *And why the hell am I so fucking horny all of the sudden?*

That's when I catch a glimpse of something red and vibrant in the corner of my eye. Sprouting up beside a withered bush with browning leaves is a white, 3-inch long stalk the width of my pinky that leads up into a bulbous growth that widens into this pale, veiny pitcher plant-like sheath of a receptacle. The top third of the receptacle is bent at a 90-degree angle, situating it in such a way that these five, red, glistening petals are angled my way, facing me.

And in the center of the flower before me, there's something that makes my cock throb—a wet, slightly gaped slit that looks just like a fucking vagina.

"Yoooo," I whisper in awe as I kneel before the pussy-looking flower. That's when the vanilla, fruity, floral scent gets even stronger. "So, this is where that smell has been coming from…"

I give it a sniff, and my cock throbs hard against my waistband, forcing precum to ooze out against my stomach. *Fuck, it's got me buzzing like I'm high… Is this why the girls were acting weird when they came back yesterday? They sniffed this flower and got all loopy like I'm feeling.*

Now that I'm up close in personal with this naughty flower, I see that, towards the bottom of the slit, there's a tight little hole that looks wide enough to fit a finger. And, upon using my phone's flashlight to illuminate said hole, I see that it does straight down into that veiny, pitcher plantlike sheath beneath the petals. Also, towards the top of the slit, it even has a tiny urethra-like pinhole right underneath a little clit-looking bump too. Both are *exactly* where they should be in relation to the opening of a real vagina.

"Fucking unreal," I whisper, caressing the flower from the clit-like bump down along the fleshy curtains.

Holy shit… it's so fucking wet and soft, I think, pushing my pointer finger into the tight, little hole, driving it in as far as it'll go.

When the webbing between my digits presses into the flower's *labia,* I curl my finger and it bulges through the sheath that looks sort of like an inverted penis now that I'm looking at it this closely.

It's so warm… Why is it warm? A groan rumbles in my throat as I imagine this flower swallowing my dick instead of my finger. *Fuck me, it even feels just like pussy… No… it feels better than any pussy I've ever fingered.* When I pull my index finger out, it's glistening with this yellow sheen that's more slippery than any vaginal juices I've ever had on me. *Wait, is this the sap Lizzy had all over her dress? It's the same color. Did she finger this plant? Is that why these girls keep coming out here?*

My cock throbs hard when I slip my middle two fingers into the hole. The tight canal stretches to accommodate both of my digits, hugging them loving me like a virgin pussy, and I swear the flower's petals just flexed into a wider blossom in response.

This hole definitely goes all the way into this sheath down below, I think, wiggling my finger and watching it bulge in the middle of the natural fleshlight's tube again. *It's a bit wider this far down too… I bet I can fit my cock all the way to where the stalk meets the cockhead of a bulb at the base of the pitcher-sheath…*

When I pull my fingers out, I touch the glazed digits to my tongue and my tastebuds are greeted by the sweetest, most delicious thing I've ever tasted. As I savor the flavor, I rub the slickness against my thumb.

"Fuck it… I have to know what it'd feel like to have my cock in this flower," I whisper as my clean hand finds my belt.

Following a quick scan of the woods behind me to ensure no one's around, I tug my cargo shorts down. I bend the bright red flower down towards my crotch with one hand while the other lines up my cock with the flower's hole. The instant my tip presses into that warm, wet flower's slit, my dick throbs hard, then it starts twitching like crazy as my glans spreads those glistening pussy lips apart and glides its way past the tightest part of it.

"Oh, fuck yeah," I groan as I glide deeper into the flower.

With my penis now buried a third of the way past the opening, I grip the firm, thick sheath like I would a fleshlight, and I buck into it nice and slow, impaling the flower until the five wet petals are pressed against my thighs, scrotum, and the base of my abs.

I'm balls-deep in a flower… Fucking wild, I think, slowly pulling my sap-coated cock out. Right before the head of my dick is about to slip out of the hole, I pump back into the tight flesh pocket with a bit more speed. It feels so good that my core spasms. *This… this is nature's fleshlight…*

After boring into it two more times, I stop pelvic thrusting into it and instead start jacking off with the flower with quick shallow pumps, keeping at least three-quarters of my cock buried in the flower's sheath at all times. Masturbating with this flower in quick shallow jerks makes the stickiest, wettest noise I've ever heard. That sound along with how fucking incredible it feels is driving me absolutely wild. Legit, I'm about to blow my load and it's barely been a minute.

A few strokes later, the flower becomes a bit tighter around my cock. It also feels like the sheath my penis is buried in is swelling in my hand. Still jerking off with the flower, I tear my eyes away from the canopy above find that there's this white, creamy stuff gushing out around the base of my shaft, making a sticky mess as it mixes with the lubricative sap.

Then, out of nowhere, right as my cock is buried as deep as it'll go in the flower's sheath, the organic fleshlight throbs rhythmically around my dick, almost like a real pussy would during climax. Having it milk me like this feels so fucking good that I cum in two throbs. And, as my body goes limp from the best orgasm I've ever had in my life, white goo sprays out from the top of the slit. Then the pleasure is interrupted by a flare of pain when the flower's cavity clenches around my penis like the vice grip of a fist trying to squeeze a lemon for all its juice. At the same time, the petals of the flower clamps around my balls, against my thighs, and against the base of my stomach with the force of a rock climber's fingers.

"ARGHH!" I groan, trying to pull the pussy flower off of my dick. The flower doesn't budge. Not only is it squeezing around my cock insanely hard, but when I pull it, it feels like it's tugging my skin, almost as though it's adhered to me. And when I try prying the petals off my balls and thigh, they start pulling my skin too, and I can't peel them off. "Oh fuck… What the fuck! What the fuck!" I panic, still trying to yank the flower off.

No matter what I try, nothing works. Every attempt hurts. So, I just kneel there, staring down in disbelief and shock at the pulsating flower that my dick is buried inside of, hoping this thing will eventually relax enough so I can pull myself out of it.

I can't fucking believe this… I got my dick stuck in a flower that looks like a pussy… Now I see why flies fall for Venus flytraps… My heart skips a beat. *Wait, is this thing going to dissolve my penis? Is human cock the prey this flower needs to feed off of?*

As that thought crosses my mind, the warm flesh squeezing my cock begins to fizz like freshly poured soda is filling this thing's cavity. Despite how pleasant the tingling feels, it's alarming as fuck.

Oh shit, is it dissolving my dick? In a panic, I start tugging at that sheath, but it still doesn't budge. *It won't budge because it glued itself to me so it can eat in peace…*

"Fuck!" I scream so loud that the branches above shake as the birds I've scared take flight. "Fuck! Fuck!"

Right as I squeeze my eyes shut, there's a popping sound down below. When I open my eyes, I see that the stalk has detached from the round, bulbous base of the sheath that looks like a swollen penis head.

It looks like my dick is wearing a hollowed-out dildo as costume, I think, lifting my flower-sheathed boner as I rise to my feet.

From the tiny hole in the middle of the bulbous glans that was connected to the stalk, there's white gunk dripping out of the sheath. My gaze then wanders to the limp stalk that's currently leaking runny, brown stuff.

"What the fuck do I do?" I whisper, my unblinking eyes staring at my flower-sheathed dick.

I need to figure out a way to dissolve the glue stuff and get this flower's swelling to go down. I inhale deeply and try to brainstorm a solution. *Cold water makes swelling go down, and most things dissolve with water…*

Maybe it'll come off if I soak in the tub, I think, bending over and pulling up my cargo shorts.

Just like I do whenever I have a boner, I tuck my flower entrapped erection in the waistband of my boxers. Since I don't want to apply too much pressure to my situation down there, I don't fasten the button, I simply tighten up my belt just enough to keep my shorts up. Now I run back to the house.

Even though I don't have time to waste, I go back to the house the way I came, slinking around the barn and barging through the front door. Of course, Lizzy, Piper, and Whitney are down in the fucking kitchen when I walk in.

"Eli?" Lizzy calls from the other side of the house. "That you?"

"Yup!" I say, racing towards the stairs.

"Why the fuck are you running through the house like a maniac," she asks, stepping into the hallway right as I'm just a few feet from the steps. The girls appear behind her.

Shit, I think, angling my body away from them while hanging my arm over my crotch to obscure their view.

"Because I have to use the bathroom!" I shout while taking the stairs two at a time.

"Why were you blocking your crotch like that?" Piper shouts. "You hiding a boner from us?"

"Ew," Lizzy says, shoving her.

"Shut the fuck up, Piper!" I shout as I reach the top of the steps.

As soon as I reach my bathroom, I slam the door, lock it, and run over to my tub. With the cold water on full blast, I pull up the stopper then strip faster than I've ever stripped in my life.

"Is everything alright, Eli?" Lizzy says from outside the door. "I thought you said you have to use the bathroom, so why is the tub running? You shit yourself?"

"No!" I bark. "I don't want you and your friends listening to me shit! Now, *respectfully*, please fuck off!"

"Fine!" Lizzy says.

"What's up with your brother?" Piper asks.

"He shit himself," Lizzy says loud enough for me to hear, giggling menacingly afterward.

"She's a fucking liar!" I shout, easing down into the cold water. "Fuck off, Lizzy!"

As their giggling and footfalls begin to fade, I reach down and try tugging at the flower once more. Of course, it still doesn't come off. It doesn't budge even a little. It's seriously glued to my cock. To make matters worse, the flower is starting to feel warmer and fizzing even harder than before.

Please let this cold bath help, I think, my teeth chattering as cold-water sloshes against my nuts. *Please, please let this work…*

The Next Morning

Yeah, that cold bath I took last night didn't do shit. Even after soaking in cold water for hours and desperately trying to soap up the places where the petals are stuck to my skin, the adhesive gunk wouldn't dissolve. The flower's grip around my cock did diminish though, going from vice grip to tight hug. But even though it loosened up, it wasn't enough to pull my dick out of this flower.

After the shower, things went from horrible to beyond fucked up when I started feeling feverish shortly after crawling into bed.

Thankfully, after sleeping nearly twelve hours, I woke up in a cold sweat with no fever and no more tingling around my dick. That would be great news if my perpetual erection wasn't still stuck inside this flower's toasty flesh sleeve.

Maybe I can pull it off now, I think, sitting up in bed.

"Ouch!" I scream out the second I pinch two separate petals.

Why did it just feel like I pinched myself? I try it again, this time pinching two different leathery leaves.

"Ow! Ow!" I groan, wincing as I jump from the pain.

Dude, what the fuck… Why am I feeling that?

Using my pointer finger, I lightly touch the bulbous tip of the sheath that looks more like the head of a penis than it did last night. The second my flesh meets the plant's leathery skin, my cock twitches from the pleasure as if I'm caressing my actual crown, and it feels *way* more sensitive than it ever has.

"Dude… What the fuck…" I close my eyes and lightly trace my way down the shaft. Each second of that caress makes my dick twitch. "How… how am I feeling this…?"

Did the flower… grow onto me? Did it… fuse to my flesh?

As I inspect the areas where the flower is glued to my skin, I notice that the white gunk that's dried around the base of my cock and around the petals looks like fuzzy, tan frosting…

It looks just like the shit that was growing on Lizzy's horse… But there's no way this is the same stuff. It can't be… Sundance's junk wasn't stuck in a flower…

"Oh, fuck… this is fucked up… This is royally fucked up…" I whisper…

What the fuck am I going to do?

At that moment, I hear Lizzy and her friends laughing down the hall.

Great, they're all still here… I'm not leaving my room until they're gone—until I figure out how to get this flower off of me. There's no way I'm going to the hospital when all the doctors in town are family friends… There's no way! Those people gossip too fucking much… Maybe I should drive to Seattle and find a specialist. Yeah, that's what I'll do.

I grab my phone and start googling.

Nature's Fleshlight…

CHAPTER 15
COINCIDENCES

LIZZY RUTHERFORD | 18
Sunday near sunset, 11 days since Jake & Sundance vanished

"Um," Piper says as she and I both come to a dead stop a few feet from the spot in the woods we've been frequenting these last few days—the spot where I dropped one of the three the balls that I birthed by this very same bush nine days ago. "What the fuck happened to the vadge-star flower?"

The vadge-star flower is what Piper cleverly called the new, naughty plant that I discovered two days ago during a solo hike along the wheelbarrow track path. She called it a vadge-star because the thing that sprouted up from the egg-ball that I dropped here looks like a fleshy, wet, red starfish the size of my hand with an opening in the center of its petals that looks *exactly* like a vagina. Like, there was even a slit with two fleshy *curtains* on either side that were identical to my dangly labia minora. It even had a little clit-like bump with a *urethra* exactly where they'd be in relation to the little hole that led to a tight, sap-lubed cavity that was softer and wetter than my pussy on a good day.

And the leathery, pale tube between the flower and the stalk looked veiny and phallic, just like the glizzy flower did. Basically, the vadge-star flower looked just like the glizzy flower if someone ripped it off the stalk, flipped it upside down, and reattached the tip of the phallus's head to the stalk, making the red underside of the petals face outward…

I stand there with my mouth agape, blinking rapidly at the flower-less, white stalk beside the dead, leafless bush. "It looks like someone ripped it off or something…"

Piper squats before the semi-limp stalk. "Looks like someone fucked it before taking the floral fleshlight home with them," she whispers, pointing at the crystallized sap puddle topped with gummy white spots. The scene looks just like the dried mess we left behind after screwing the glizzy flower 16 days ago.

I kneel beside her and stare at the pale globs on the dirt, thinking about how Dr. Kramer told me and my parents last Friday that the samples of the white gunk from the barn shared DNA with the biopsy she took from Sundance. Even though they were a match, the samples didn't share DNA with any of the bacteria or fungus she tested for.

"Considering how much dried sap there is and how the flower only creamed white stuff after we fingered it for a while, I think you're right…" I say to Piper. Two days ago, after I called her and Whit over to see the new discovery, we took turns finger-blasting the vadge star. Whitney, the last to go, rubbed the thing's *clit* while pumping two digits in and out of the hole until the petals started spasming, its five meaty leaves curling inward over and over like horrific fingers. A moment later, it creamed her with the same white thickness that shot out of the glizzy. That's when we backed away.

Piper looks over at me with a naughty smile. "You don't think your brother—"

"I don't even wanna think about it…" I say through gritted teeth, my face scrunched up in disgust.

"Think about it… He *did* come back in the house yesterday looking all red in the face… And, before he ran up the stairs, he *was* hiding his crotch from us like he had a boner."

"Ewww. Stop… Seriously, Pipes."

"Or… *Or*… maybe he wasn't hiding a boner… Maybe he was hiding the vadge-star flower in his pants… because where else would he hide a flower the width of our hands that's attached to a long, thick, hollow dildo of a flesh tube?"

"You make a valid point…" I mutter. "And he did come back acting all weird and flustered…"

"Mm-hm… And he must've come back from somewhere *nearby* because his car wasn't gone when we went downstairs…"

"Yeah…" I say, nodding. "That's too many coincidences."

"You think that's why he's been locked in his room all day and wouldn't come out even when you told him you warmed up food for him?" A wicked smile stretches across his face. "You think he's been fapping with his floral fleshlight all day thinking of me?"

"Eww…" I scoff, shoving her. "Just… eww… Please stop with the visuals."

Piper laughs like a movie villain, *muwahahahaha*-style.

As I rise from my haunches shaking my head, I zone out, thinking back to how we felt after we screwed the glizzy flower. "If he *did* do something that I'd rather not think about with the vadge-star flower, there's a possibility he's in his room feeling sick like we were afterward…"

"Shit… yeah… you're right… He did say he didn't have an appetite and that we needed to '*shut the fuck up*' because he was trying to sleep at, like, three in the afternoon…"

I nod slowly, looking in her direction but staring into nothing. "We should check on him."

"Do you *really* think Eli would tell us that he's feeling feverish after getting his cock creamed by a flower with a pussy hole?

Because you know damn well that we wouldn't have told him shit if he was home the night we rode the glizzy flower… We would've just pretended like we were really hungover…"

"You're right about that…"

"Yup. And we can't really ask him if a flower made him sick because that'd raise a whole bunch of questions we don't need to be answering."

I nod. "Very true… I guess I'll just vaguely ask him if he's feeling alright and see if he needs anything…"

"Smart girl. And we can do that after we see if the other vadge-star is still there," Piper says, walking in the direction of where I dropped and buried the second white ball a few yards from here.

Before we even reach the spot, we both start inhaling deeply from the sweet, heavenly scent that's hanging over the area like a dense fog. As expected, the second vadge-star flower is still fully intact, looking just as wet and plump as yesterday.

"Looks like whoever stole the other flower didn't make it this far," Piper says, searching the ground for tracks.

"Yeah, and there's no sap or dried-up, white goo around this one's stalk," I mutter. "Guess that means no one fucked it…"

"You know what's another weird coincidence?" Piper says, glancing back over her shoulder at the path we just came from.

"What?"

"Both vadge-star flowers popped up right along the wheelbarrow tracks between where the glizzy flower used to be and the small clearing ahead…" She stares deep into my eyes, searching them for a moment in silence, the gears in her head clearly turning. "You think the glizzy flower or the pod dropped seeds or something while it was being moved?"

I exhale slowly, trying to steady my racing heart. *For a second there, I thought she was going to ask if seeds were dropping out of me.* Part of me wanted to tell her and Whitney that these vadge-star flowers sprouted from the white balls that dropped out of my uterus. But since Whitney didn't say anything weird was coming out of her when I asked yesterday, I was too embarrassed to confess it.

"You think seeds could sprout to the size of flowers as big as my hand in less than two weeks?" I ask. "Seems unlikely to me…"

She nods. "Yeah… Unless these things just happen to grow as fast as mushrooms…"

"Or maybe it's been growing underground for a while and only sprouted up after reaching a certain size," I say. "There was a lot of dirt on the petals when we first found them."

"True… Considering there's a flesh pod with a cock-shaped flower that has a body temperate and cums after you stimulate it enough, anything's possible at this point…" She smirks.

"True story," I say with a huff, shaking my head as I turn back towards where we came from. "Alright, let's head back and check on my brother."

CHAPTER 16
ZOMBIE

ELI RUTHERFORD | 19
***Wednesday… sometime after midnight, 3 days after waking
up to the flower merged to my penis***

Am… I… dreaming? The thought in my mind sounds choppy and
distant, like I'm listening to my inner voice playing on a skipping
record through a cup pressed against a wall.

My body… I'm aware of it… I can… feel it…

I can feel my bare feet slapping across the damp grass and soil
with each lumbering step…

I sense the ache from where my arm, hip, and leg crashed into
the ground after I mindlessly crawled out of my window and rolled
off the slanted roof.

I can feel my torso swaying side to side like I'm too drunk to
keep upright…

I feel the cool night air washing over my naked form during
my trek across the field.

Even though it feels like I'm dreaming, my senses… they're
sharp… like I'm awake.

I see the woods getting closer and closer.

I can smell the musty stench wafting up from my body—that
same horrible odor that's been filling my room since the other day.

The itchiness where that gross slime mold-looking stuff has been growing up my spine is itching like crazy, but I can't reach back to scratch it… because my arm won't obey my command.

When I try to scream for help, nothing comes out except one of the intermittent, ghastly groans that have been rumbling in my throat since I woke up with intense brain fog this afternoon.

When I try turning my head or looking down, my neck and head don't obey.

I just keep lumbering forward, marching right into the fence, bumping into it like a drunk, blind idiot.

I don't know why, but something in me is telling me to get over that fence—something is driving me to get to the woods, just like something told me to avoid sunlight as my body mindlessly paced my room and kept waddling past the window.

Turn. Around. Go… Back home… That's what I tell myself, but my body keeps pushing forward, butting into the fence over and over and over.

A deep growl vibrates in my throat as my first pounds down on the wooden barrier. The resulting pain beckons an angry, bestial roar from my throat.

I can feel my already racing heart pounding faster.

I feel the rage.

Just fucking… climb. Climb over…

After butting up against the fence for the tenth time, I try reaching out to climb over the wooden barrier, but my body won't cooperate. It's like watching a first-person POV movie from the perspective of a zombie. All I can do is spectate and wait for this mutated corpse I'm trapped in to figure it out, just like how I had to watch myself figure out how to open my bedroom window.

Am I… dreaming?

In a fit of rage, my body barrels forward, hitting the fence so hard and fast that my top half teeters over the wooden beam like a seesaw. Then the world spins as I go from seeing the trees ahead to seeing the ground rushing at my face.

Then… pain… Pain from my head smacking against the ground as the wooden fence scrapes against the thick, lumpy, tan mass on my legs.

As the groaning corpse on autopilot that I'm trapped inside of pushes itself up onto all fours, I can see it… the corrupted flesh that's grown over my thigs and my abdomen—the same gross, lumpy, slime mold stuff that's growing up my spine… the same mass that spread across the horse… I can see my veiny, beige erection throbbing and dripping brown syrup as the five petals sticking out around the base of my cock flex open wide like an angry starfish. These petals have been doing this since they detached from my flesh a few days ago.

Seeing the horrific thing that's happened to my body—feeling this pain and sensing the world around me as vividly as I ever have makes me realize that I am not dreaming…

I am conscious. Barely.

Trapped in an infected, mutated body that needs to…

Avoid light…

Get outside…

Go into the woods…

Dig.

Dig.

Dig under the cover of trees…

The horrific realization makes my eyes burn, and a tear rolls down my cheek as my body finally staggers back onto its feet…

My lumbering form wanders aimlessly through the woods in a mostly straight path, branches and rocks and other sharp things stabbing my bare feet along the way. The entire time, my head pans slowly from left to right and back to left like a security camera, searching for… something…

In search of the right place to rest…

The longer I wander through the woods, the harder it's getting to form thoughts.

Fear.

Frustration.

Pain.

An impending sense of dread.

That's all I feel as a montage of this infection's progression plays in my mind. It quickly spread outward from the flower fused to my cock, making me sicker and sicker with each inch of flesh it corrupted. Pretty much right around the time it started growing up my spine, the disease eroded my thoughts—it eroded them so fast that I couldn't even get to the hospital like I wanted to.

Avoid people.

Eat.

Consume sweets.

Sleep.

Avoid light.

Get to the woods.

Dig.

Dig.

My chin tilts towards the sky, then my sights set on a thick tree canopy where I can only see a few patches of the stary night sky.

Now my head angles down—down at my erect cock, down at the dirt below.

Dig…

Here…

Dig. Here…

The command is the only thing I hear in my head.

One minute I'm standing upright, the next I'm kneeling in the mud and digging my fingers into it.

Digging and scooping, over and over. Eating soil sporadically.

Consciousness erodes even more. Faster now.

My hands are burning, hurting… They're wet with… Blood?

The hole's getting deeper. Fast. Fast because my arms are in a frenzy of scooping and dirt throwing.

Sit. Lay.

My body shifts from kneeling to sitting with my bare, mutated, sphincter-less ass on the cold, wet dirt.

Scoop. Cover.

My arms reach up out of the pit I'm currently sitting in and they scoop soil down into the hole—down over my legs and abs.

I'm… burying myself?

Stop…

I… Have to… stop… myself…

Tears stream down my cheeks as I desperately try to will my body to cooperate.

The next thing I know, my legs and torso are covered.

One arm pulls itself down into the dirt while the other scoops dirt down onto my face. That's when I puke the mud I just consumed. The thick warmth spreads down my chin and flows into my nose.

Once heavy dirt covers my face, consciousness rapidly fades.

My body writhes deeper into the burial pit while my other arm pulls itself into the soil.

My hips buck upward on their own accord and I feel cool night air greet the head of my penis once it pushes through the soil.

My penis is the only part of me not underground.

It's sticking up through the dirt like…

Like. A. Flower…

My body gasps for air, sucking in a mouthful of mud in the process. A gagging sound rattles in my throat as I suffocate.

In a matter of seconds, all my senses begin to fade.

CHAPTER 17
THREE IS A PATTERN

LIZZY RUTHERFORD | 18
Wednesday, August 10th, 4 days after Eli got sick

A groan escapes me as I awake from loud knocking down the hall.

"Eli, please answer me," my mother pleads a few decibels below shouting, banging on the door again a bit harder than last time.

Why the fuck are you being so loud? I think, peeking through one eye at my clock. *It's 7 in the fucking morning…*

There's another round of loud knocking. "You've been locked up in there since Saturday and I'm worried sick, so if you don't answer me, I am going to kick this door down, sweetie!" Mom says.

The panic in her voice, Eli's unresponsiveness—it's worrisome enough to get me out of my bed.

"I found the spare key, Marissa," Dad says, stomping his way down the hall. "Hello?" Dad's voice booms. A doorknob rattles. "Eli, if you don't open this door right now, I am going to unlock it and we're coming in. You hear me son?"

That's when I open my door. Right as I peek into the hall, I see dad slipping the key into the doorknob. "What's happening?" I groan sleepily.

Mom looks at me with glassy eyes. "Eli's not answering us."

My heart races as I hurry down the hall, then my stomach twists into a knot when Dad's expression goes from worried to shocked upon opening Eli's door all the way.

"He's not in bed," Dad says, storming into the room with mother hurrying in right on his heels.

The moment I turn into his room, the moment I set my sights on his unmade bed and the clothes scattered on the floor, I'm hit with this horrible, musty stench. *It smells like… It smells like the brown slime the glizzy flower jizzed everywhere towards the end…* Just as my eyes set onto his open, screenless window, I catch a whiff of this faint, floral, sweet odor. *It smells like those flowers…*

"He's not in the bathroom either…" Dad says.

"Where the hell is he then?" Mom says, checking under his bed. "The door was locked, and I didn't hear anyone disable the alarm last night. And I would've heard it because I barely slept at all…"

Dad approaches the open window and sticks his head out. "The screen's down on the grass. Looks all bent up like someone kicked or punched it out…"

"That doesn't make any sense…." Mom mutters, pacing the middle of the room. "Why on earth would Eli push out the screen and sneak out the house through the window? That… that doesn't make any sense…"

This is just like what happened to Jake, I think, slowly dragging my feet over to my brother's bed in a wide-eyed trance. *His parents said his bed was messy, there were clothes all over the floor, and that there was a musty odor hanging in the air… It's the same smell Sundance had before he kicked his stall door open and ran away… Same smell as the flesh pod… That's too many coincidences… Two is a coincidence, three is a pattern…*

Something kind of shiny on his sheets and comforter catches my eye. Upon closer inspection, I find clear, brown streaks crusted on the fabric.

Looks like spilled maple syrup. This… this looks exactly like how that brown slime dried on Savanna's panties when I finally got around to washing them…

"Did you find something, Lizzy?" Dad asks.

I shake my head. "Just this crusty brown stuff on his sheets…" As I pull the comforter aside to see how much of the stuff there is, I uncover something I was hoping I wouldn't find. "And Eli's cellphone…"

"He never goes anywhere without that damn thing," Dad says, taking it from me and tapping at the screen. "Do you know his passcode?"

I shake my head, taking a slow deep breath to calm my heart and steady my nerves.

"Did Eli say anything strange this weekend?" Dad asks. "Do you know if maybe something personal was going on with him?"

I shake my head. "He ran into his room acting all weird on Saturday saying that he had to use the bathroom, then he wouldn't leave his room all Sunday because he said he was sick. Other than that, he barely spoke to me when I checked on him. I didn't even hear him using the bathroom these last few days…"

Should I tell them about the vadge-star flower? No… how would that do anything other than make my brother look like a pervert? Besides, plants don't make people disappear out of thin air… It's gotta be something else. It's got to be…

"I haven't heard him use the bathroom since we've been back either," Mom mutters. That's when she breaks down, wailing like a banshee.

A beat later, I begin sobbing. Because I'm a sympathetic crier who was already on the verge of tears.

Dad consoles Mom then pulls me in, wrapping an arm around me too. "We're going to find Eli. No matter what, we *will* find him."

CHAPTER 18
NEW DAY, NEW FLOWER DONG

LIZZY RUTHERFORD | 18
Thursday Morning, 1 day since Eli vanished…

It's been 15 days since Jake Landau and Sundance mysteriously disappeared after coming down with a fever, and there still have not been any leads nor has anyone found any bodies anywhere…

It's been 29 hours since my parents and I found Eli's room empty, presumably after he crawled out of his window and wandered off without his phone…

If the cops haven't found Jake's body, there's still hope, I think as I climb the fence that separates our property from the woods. *If there's hope for Jake, that means my brother is still out there somewhere. And if he's on foot, he can't be too far away.*

Just like after Jake vanished, the girls and I went driving around all Wednesday checking all the spots where Eli usually hangs out, stopping by all of his friends' houses and his favorite restaurants in town.

Now, after coming up dry on leads, I've decided to venture out to the wilderness this morning while my parents are out. They forbade me from coming out here until we figure out why my brother and Jake vanished in the middle of the night, but I don't give a shit. As freaked out as I am now that two of the three most important guys in my life disappeared after possibly being lured out of their houses and kidnapped, I feel more compelled now than ever to search the woods.

Just a few minutes ago, I found a pair of footprints the size of my brother's feet in the soil not too far away from where his window screen hit the ground—the kind with toeprints like someone shoeless headed south towards the woods instead of north towards the road. And after heading in the direction of single pair of footprints, I found a bunch of spots in the dirt where it seems like someone randomly started dragging their feet across the yard before walking normally again…

Someone definitely went this way, I think, squatting and inspecting the displaced soil inches from the woodland side of the fence. *There are handprints here… Looks like someone fell then dug their toes and fingers in the dirt while they pushed themselves up.* A foot away, there arc two, parallel grooves leading away from the fence like whoever fell here got up and began dragging their feet again before walking normally a few paces later. *If these are Eli's tracks, why would he come out here without shoes? And why was he dragging his feet? Did he get hurt after falling off the roof?*

The normal footprints abruptly blend into drag marks in the soil as though the person started shuffling again. And after wandering deeper into the woods in the general direction of the tracks near the fence, I don't find anything else. Part of me wants to call my parents right now to tell them that I found tracks leading to the woods, but on the off chance that there's something out here that's only making male humans and male horses sick, I don't want my dad anywhere near these woods…

Maybe a quarter-mile later, my body begins buzzing from that familiar, arousing scent that I know all too well. Scowling while sniffing rapidly like a bloodhound, I frantically scan the area. The stronger the fragrance gets, the more soaked my panties become.

I've pretty much been going straight south, I think, glancing at the compass dangling from the carabiner hook on my right backpack strap. *Yeah, I'm still heading south, so I'm nowhere near the vadge-star flowers, and the wind is definitely blowing from the west... so... There couldn't be another vadge-star flower or glizzy flower out there, could there be? Like, did a seed-ball somehow fall out of me when I hiked through here the other day?*

A few yards after following the only path through the brush, right as the fragrance becomes overpowering, I spot this a moss-covered Douglas Fir with a diagonal line carved through its bark—a mark that I made a few days ago on this tree and several others to remind us where we've been so we don't keep canvasing the same areas over and over.

The path of least resistance is a narrow dirt passage between this tree and the smaller one to the right of it that leads through a corridor of undergrowth. That path opens up to a narrow underpass beneath a distinct archway of soft, leafy plants—a beaten path through a tunnel of greenery that we've taken many times to go to Yelm Lake, a path we've traversed a few days ago searching for Jake. After ducking under the archway of bowed branches and looking up, my jaw drops and my eyes widen at the sight in the clearing a few feet away.

"No way..." I whisper to no one. My pussy clenches hard from a desperate need to be filled by the thing growing out of the soil ahead. "A new glizzy flower..."

Right off the bat, the first thing I notice is that the soil bulge below the flower looks darker and richer than the surrounding dirt in the area, almost like someone recently dug a hole and then planted the glizzy flower's flesh pod in the pit before burying it with the soil that was dug up from deeper in the earth.

Why would someone plant this here? As I kneel on the dirt mound before the flower, I notice there are little clumps of dirt on the glizzy's crown, shaft, and petals, much like how the recently sprouted vadge-star flowers looked when I first found them. *There wouldn't be dirt on the phallus if someone buried it here,* I think, gently brushing the soil off the glizzy. *So maybe it just sprouted?*

While the dirt specked phallus of this flower is beige and veiny like the first one, this dong is longer and girthier—somewhere between 7 and 8-inches long and maybe 5 or 6-inches in circumference. Also, the five petals dangling from the base of the shaft are smaller, about the length of my fingers and the width of a ruler whereas the original flower had petals almost as big as my hand.

These are the same size as the ones on the vadge-star flowers, I think, caressing a soft, fleshy, warm leaf.

The last major difference between this one and the one that was stolen from me is that this glizzy flower's stalk is much shorter. There are maybe 2-inches of stalk growing between the soil and the base of the phallus where the petals are dangling from. That means the total length of the flower is about 9 or 10 inches from the bottom of the stalk to the tip whereas the old one had a 5-inch stalk rising out of the dirt with a total flower length of about 12-inches.

Smaller petals and a shorter stalk suggest that this one just sprouted, I think as I curl my fingers around the shaft. My pussy Kegels over and over while I stroke it from head to petals. *If it did just sprout, then why the heck is the phallus already the size of an adult man's dick?*

Right when the flower throbs gently in my hand, my pussy clenches in response. And as sap rolls from tip to the shaft, I feel thick wetness dribbling out of my fluttering vagina.

God, I am unbearably horny, I think, sucking in a deep breath of this flower's intoxicating fragrance. *Horny and buzzing all over. And I'm buzzing so hard my mind feels cloudy.* When my pussy throbs again with the need to be filled, I clench my thighs together. *I don't have time to fuck this flower right now... I have to find Eli.*

Dizzying arousal makes my hand wander into my shorts on its own accord, then my thumb rubs my clit through my soaked panties.

As stressed as I've been since Jake and Sundance went missing—as worried sick as I am over Eli, it would be nice to feel good and escape my troubles for just a little while…

My chest heaves as I snort in more of that fragrance like it's airborne cocaine and crushed molly. With the shaft gripped tightly in my hand, I lean in and lick the sap oozing from its tip.

"Mmm…" I moan from both the taste and the pleasure from thumbing my sensitive bundle of nerves.

Fuck it, I think, pulling my hand out from between my legs and undoing my button. *I've got jars and condoms in my bag still, so I'm going to collect some lube-sap for me and the girls, then I'm going to slip a condom on this thing, slather it with sap, and fuck it until I can't cum anymore.*

With the stalk bent and angled towards me, I hold a tiny mason jar beneath the crown and start beating off the glizzy. Surprisingly, it does take long at all to fill the 8-ounce jar to the brim. Halfway through filling the second one, the unbearable need to impale my throbbing vagina on this thing makes my body tense with anxiousness. I feel exactly how I did when I watched Piper fuck the glizzy flower 3 weeks ago while eagerly awaiting my turn.

A few dozen strokes later, right as the third jar is almost topped off with golden sap, the phallus starts swelling a bit, pulsating in my hand like it's about to blow its load. That's my cue to stop. And while the glizzy is *calming down,* I take that time to take off my shorts and panties. I take that time to finger my gushing hole.

When the throbbing stops and the rod's swelling goes down a minute or so later, I suck off the plant, taking a few gulps of sap before letting the stream that follows pool on my tongue. Once my mouth is overflowing with slimy nectar, I roll on the last ultra-thin condom then spit the sap onto the glizzy while jerking it off to get it nice and slathered up. The second it's all lubed up, I waste no time positioning myself over it.

Because the stalk of this plant is so much shorter than the other one, I can't just bounce on the glizzy in a squat, I have to get on my knees and spread my legs into a sort of half-split.

"Ah… Ahhhh…" I moan as the girthy head parts my labia and bulges past my hymen. "OH! FUUUCK! YESS!" I cry out as it glides in deeper, stretching me out in way that the other glizzy flower didn't until it started swelling. It hurts so good I want to cry.

With my palms flat on the ground and my toes dug into the dirt, I grind down on it in a sort of cowgirl position. That's the only way to get it to bottom out. And I need it all the way inside of me so I can batter my cervix with that firm, yet mushy cockhead. As I bounce on this flower's phallus, as I slam and grind my cervix hard against its tip, I feel the glizzy start to push deeper than it should go—I feel my cervix stretching to accommodate it like a butthole would with a dildo.

Toying my cervix like this? It's something that shouldn't be impossible…

But I know it's possible for me… Because…

Shortly after birthing those balls two weeks ago, I ordered a speculum on Amazon, inserted it into my cavity, squatted over a mirror, and looked inside with a flashlight. That's when I saw it. The fleshy donut of a bulge separating my vagina from my womb that should only dilate during childbirth didn't have a pinhole opening like the pictures I looked up for comparison. Nope. Instead, my cervix was dilated to around the width of a skinny hotdog. But there wasn't a gaping hole leading to my uterus, there was something that looked just like a tight butthole that grew across the dilated hole—this puckered, wrinkly flesh that was a pale pink…

Since I was curious if it worked like my anal sphincter, I used a toothbrush handle to poke the hole. To my surprise, the cervical *sphincter* stretched to accommodate the handle's penetration, just like my asshole did the one time I slid a finger up there to check what anal would feel like. Surprisingly, it didn't hurt either. Toying the bizarre cervical sphincter felt really, *really* fucking good.

Before that day, I've never actually seen my cervix before, so I don't know if it was always like this or if it changed after the glizzy flower ejaculated in me. My guess? It's probably the latter because I did have those weird tingling, stretching sensations for days following that night. And, shortly after the stretching and tingling stopped, those little white egg things start coming out of my womb. It's almost like the passage *mutated* to allow those little balls to be birthed out of me. That has to be it since there's no way something the size of a grape could pass through a normal cervix…

After lowering my ass closer to the ground than before, a moan escapes me as the thick cockhead pushes through the tight ring of flesh of my cervical sphincter with a sharp, delicious popping sensation.

"Oh fuck…" I say breathily, wincing from the strange yet incredibly pleasant sensation as I grind down and drive it deeper into me. Pleasure explodes behind my bladder as the warm, throbbing phallus penetrates a part of me never before touched. "It's in… It's in my fucking womb… Oof." A shaky groan rattles in my throat as my uterus spasms pleasantly, sending waves of pleasure rippling across my body.

This flower's cock is so deep inside of me that my folds are almost touching the soil—it's so deep that, when I reach back underneath me, I discover that my vagina basically swallowed it almost to the tips of its petals.

Because of how intense it feels having a dick in my womb, I bounce on it nice and slow, riding it with shallow rises and falls to keep the head from poking my uterus.

Oh fuck… This feels… Amazing… Best sensation ever!

It doesn't take many slow bounces for my climax to peak, triggering the most intense uterine and vaginal orgasm I've ever experienced. My womb spasms violently in the best way. My vagina contracts hard and fast. My eyelids flutter as my vision blurs. My limbs go weak and I inadvertently take the glizzy deeper than I wanted to as I collapse belly-first on the ground.

That's when the phallus swells out of nowhere and starts pulsating, repeatedly stretching inside my cervical sphincter.

My limbs feel numb and noodly, so I can't get myself to rise off of the thing in time to get the wide phallus out of my womb. "AHH!" I scream from the flash of pain.

Deep inside of me, I feel the tip of the condom swell like a balloon, quickly expanding with heavy, hot liquid. A second later, it bursts, then a jet of thickness blasts right against the roof of my womb.

"OOOHH-FFFFUUUUUUGH!" I cry out as sludge fills my sacred organ.

Somehow, I find the strength to crawl forward just enough for the slimy, girthy glizzy to slip out of my cervix with a sharp pop. The sensation is so intense that my legs and arms go weak and I fall flat again with the throbbing rod still inside my pussy. With each cum jet that blasts my cervix and fills my vagina with hot muck, I wince and moan. Because it hurts, but it weirdly feels amazing. Only after the fourth jet of liquid heat do I find the strength to writhe and squirm my body far enough forward for the head of the still swelling glizzy to wedge right in the opening of my vagina. That's when I Kegel and push as hard as I can. There's a squishy *bloop* as the dong launches out of my tightness. Each contraction sends hot mud oozing out of my pussy with this gross, gushing, bubbly noise.

"Ohhh," I groan, rolling onto my back. Now I lift my head and look down at the *baby bump* at the base of my belly. "Fuck... Not again..."

Just like the first time that I got creampied by a glizzy flower, my womb feels hot and full.

Why on Earth did I think the condom would stop that pressure washer of a dick from jizzing in me? Like, what was I thinking?

You were thinking you could cum before the plant did and pull it out before it splooged in you...

It takes everything in me to sit up and maneuver into a squat. With my legs still shaking from the orgasm, I slide the two middle fingers of both hands into my cream-filled cavity and pull my labia open as wide as they'll stretch. As soon as the goo is done flowing out of me, I push as hard as I can.

"HNNGGG!" I groan as hot sludge squirts noisily out of my cervical sphincter while cream gushes out of me like a geyser of clam chowder.

Unlike last time, the stuff in my womb is pouring right out, probably because my cervix works more like a butthole than it did before the glizzy flower's jizz mutated my womb or whatever...

It only takes a few pushes for the pressure and heat in my womb to fade. While I wait for the rest of the white sludge with brown swirls to flow out of me, I stare in awe at the thick goo puddle spreading outwards on the ground between my legs.

Geez... I legit could've filled a large pot with all that cream...

When my vagina stops dripping, I finger myself to scoop out what's left, then I use the towel I brought along for cleaning up sap to wipe up my pussy and legs.

As bad as I want to stay out here for a few more hours searching for Eli, it's probably best that I get home just in case I get a fever and painful cramps again, I think, pulling up my panties and shorts.

As that thought crosses my mind, my sore cervical sphincter flutters, triggering a little spasm in my womb.

Oh, gawd… please don't let what happened last time happen again… I really don't want to go through waking up to my panties full of chunky stuff and dealing with painful cramps again…

Just in case I get deathly ill in the next few hours and die in my sleep or something, I text Piper and Whitney: **So… I found a new glizzy flower & I did that thing we said we wouldn't do again… Put a condom on it this time, but it came so hard the rubber burst inside me… I'll let you know if I get all sick again… Side note: I collected some lube-sap for you before I did the thing… Come over and pick it up tomorrow!**

The Next Morning

The first thing I feel when I wake up is this dull ache deep in my vagina that makes me groan as I stretch out across my bed. But that's it. There's no intense cramping. No tingling. My clothes aren't drenched in a cold sweat. There's nothing cold and mushy in my panties.

When I peek through one eye at the wall across from me, I'm relieved to find bands of sunlight painting stripes across the white paint. *It's a good sign that I slept till morning instead of waking up in the middle of the night this time around,* I think, rolling over and finding 8:33 A.M. displayed on my clock. *Wow, and I only slept like 8 hours this time…*

When I touch the back of my hand to my neck, I don't feel warm at all, my body temperature just feels normal.

I feel pretty great today, I think while sitting up. *Maybe I'm immune to whatever made me sick last time… If that's the case… that means I can fuck this glizzy flower to completion whenever I want, without a condom…*

After climbing out of my bed, I drag my feet towards the bathroom then, right before I reach the door, my gaze falls onto the pictures of me and Eli on the wall by my dresser. That's when last night's vivid nightmares come back to me in flashes—dreams more vivid than anything I've ever had. I dreamt my brother was suffering in some dark place. I dreamt he was being buried alive.

The wave of horrible memories triggers tears to stream down my cheeks in a matter of seconds.

I'll find you, Eli, I think, caressing the framed picture of us as kids hugging each other. *Me and Mom and Dad will find you before any of those horrible things happen to you…*

CHAPTER 19
CLAM CLAMPED, EGG WENT POP

WHITNEY EMMERICH | 18
Friday night, August 19th, 4 weeks since Glizzy Night—8 days since Lizzy texted about the second flower

"You sure you two don't want to come with us to the Sigma Chi party?" my roommate Maya asks as she rises from the edge of her bed. "Aria's cousin is a brother there, so if you're worried about Luke not getting in, don't be."

"Yeah," Aria, the girl we met earlier at our dorm's social, says from the chair on Maya's side of the room, "I already texted him that I was bringing some people from my floor and he said bring whoever."

"Thanks, but we're good," I say, turning to my boyfriend with a naughty smile.

Luke aches a brow, giving me a little smirk. "You sure, Whit? It's our first night at UW. Don't you wanna kick off our freshman year right before midterms and shit?"

"What I want," I whisper, running a hand up along his thigh, "is to relax after all that unpacking and spend some *quality time* with my boyfriend who I haven't seen since he ditched me for his family trip in July…"

"Translation?" Maya says, "She wants you to give her the D while she has the room to herself."

The girls and I giggle.

Luke just shakes his head, flashing me this wicked grin while gazing into my eyes.

"Don't worry, Luke," Aria says while rising from the chair, "unless we're super-hungover, we're going back to Sig Chi tomorrow, so you won't miss out on your first big party."

"Sounds like a win-win to me," he says.

"Alrighty," Maya says, grabbing the bottle of vodka from my desk, "if you're not coming with us, you have to do one more shot with us."

"I won't say no to that!" I say, climbing off the bed.

Maya pours the shots, then four of us cheers before throwing them back and chasing them with the Bubly sparkling water that we've been mixing with.

"Kay, we're outtie!" Maya says, tossing her empty can in the bin. "You two have fun!"

I grin. "We will! You two have fun too!"

"Oh. We *will*," Maya says on the way out the door. "If you get done early and decide you wanna join us, just call me and we'll come out and get ya, girl!"

"Sounds good!" I singsong. The second the door shuts, I push Luke to the bed, straddle him, and kiss him in that sloppy way I always do when I'm this drunk.

"You're not wasting any time, huh?" he mumbles against my lips as his erection plumps against my vagina.

I don't answer, I just slide my tongue all over his while I undo his belt.

As soon as his pants are unbuckled, I pull my shirt over my head then I help him take his off. Now I dismount and tug his jeans off, throwing them across the room after.

"Too fast, sweetheart," he says, breathing heavily. "I need the condom from my back pocket."

"Not tonight," I whisper, writhing my hips like a belly dancer while pulling down my panties and leggings. "I want you to finish in me." After having that glizzy flower splooge in me, all I could think about is finally experiencing what it feels like having a real cock spilling warmth inside of me. I've been aching for us to finally be alone ever since he came back last week, and this is the first chance we've had.

He grins like the goddamn Joker. "Wait, for real?"

"Mm-hm," I hum, naughtily biting my bottom lip as I reach into the top drawer of my nightstand to grab the mason jar of glizzy flower sap Lizzy gave me before I left.

"If this becomes a norm, we may never have a social life…" He smirks.

"Good," I whisper, straddling him and grinding my obscenely wet slit up and down the length of his dick.

Luke groans as his cock throbs against me. "Whatcha got there?" he asks, eyeing the jar of golden slime that I'm unscrewing.

"Lube."

He snickers. "Babe, you're wetter than a fish—wetter than I've ever felt you before. I don't think you need that."

When I scooch back and sit on his thighs, his dong springs up from beneath me, glistening from my wetness. "This is *special* lube. The kind that makes everything feel, like, two times better."

"Oh, fuck… It's already going to be hard enough lasting without a condom…"

"I'm sure you'll manage," I say, drizzling the thick sap all over his dick like it's a phallic stick of French toast.

Once his cock is glazed with a decent amount, I jerk him off a few times to slather him up, then I hold him in place and impale myself on him. My core spasms as he glides into my depths.

"Oh…" he groans, his body convulsing beneath me. "Oh yeah, Whit…"

It only takes about a minute of me riding him cowgirl for the sap to start working its magic—for it to make my pussy super-sensitive and have me feeling like I'm high on the best weed.

"Is this lube doing anything for you?" I whisper in a shaky, breathy voice as I bounce and grind down on his cock the way Piper told me to do to the glizzy.

"Actually, yeah," he mutters.

As the pleasure intensifies, as I edge toward climax, I start fucking him harder and faster.

"Whit…" he groans. "If you want me to last longer… you might wanna… stop. *Now*…"

I lean forward and start grinding into him harder and faster. "Cum for me, babe," I moan, kissing him after. "Fill me up."

I don't know if it's because the idea of him finishing in me drives me wild or if the way I'm grinding into him has my clit rubbing against his pubic bone but, whatever it is, it pushes me over the edge and I climax hard. It's not just my vagina that's contracting rhythmically, but also my womb. And as pleasure radiates outwards across my whole body, scrambling my thoughts and blurring my vision, I feel like another one of those weird ball thingies is bulging through my cervix.

Please don't tell me I'm laying those little eggs again… I thought that was a one-and-done thing, I think, reflecting on the night I masturbated with the sap hours after Lizzy gave it to me.

Just as the tiny ball pops through the tight passage, Luke bores up into me hard, mashing the squishy sphere right against the space between my vaginal wall and cervix. "OOOH-RUHH!" he groans like an ape, his body spasming beneath me as my orgasm milks the cum out of him.

Having his cock throbbing inside of me pales in comparison to how the glizzy flower feels, but the sensation of his warmth spurting gently against my cervix feels way better than getting my womb pressure washed with that flower's piping-hot chowder, that's for sure.

Then, out of nowhere, my *pussy* suddenly stops contracting and just cramps hard, clamping around his cock like the fist of a gorilla trying to mush an apple into sauce with all his might. That's when I feel that little egg-ball thing pop against his cock, sending thick paste spreading outward between his penis and my rigid vaginal walls.

"AH-OW! FUUUUCK!" Luke cries out.

"Ahhhh!" I scream, collapsing onto him from the intense pain.

"WHUGH—what the fuck, Whit…" he groans.

"Ah… Ah-ah… Sorry… I don't know… ah… why I'm… cramping like this. AH-HA-OW!"

"URGGH! It feels like you're about to snap my dick like a twig!"

I inhale deeply then exhale slowly. "Yelling at me isn't going to help me relax, *Luke*…." Once again, I take a deep breath then exhale nice and slow.

"Sorry, babe," he says, stroking my head lovingly. "Just breathe. Clear your mind and breathe."

For what feels like three minutes, we lay with our genitals conjoined, me doing yoga breathwork while he massages my scalp and sweeps the other hand up and down my back. Then, just as suddenly as the vaginal clenching came on, my pussy relaxes out of nowhere.

"Oh, thank God," I sigh out breathily, pulling his flaccid cock out of me before rolling onto my back.

Luke lets out a tired chuckle as he reaches down to massage his penis. "What even just happened, Whit?"

I snicker. "I have no fucking idea. That's *literally* never happened before…"

"Maybe your pussy had an allergic reaction to semen or something…" he says, sitting up a bit and staring curiously down at his hand and crotch.

"Maybe…"

"What is this gummy white stuff? Did I make you cum so hard that you grooled all over my cock?"

I snicker. "What are you even—" As soon as I sit up and look down at his junk, my eyes widen in horror.

There's this thick, white paste that looks like wet cookie dough smeared all over his tip and on the underside of the first inch of his shaft. As he pulls his hand away slimy strings stretch between the cream on his penis and his fingers like gum.

That white stuff… it's all over the part of his dick where I felt him pop the ball thing inside of me…

"That must just be discharge…" I mutter. Obviously, there's no way I'm telling him that little white balls started plopping down into my vagina a week after I *cheated* on him with a weird plant. Hell, I didn't even tell the girls about it because I was too embarrassed, especially because Lizzy got creamed by the glizzy flower and didn't say it was happening to her too…

"Is discharge usually *this* thick?" he asks, reaching over and grabbing a tissue from my nightstand.

"Not usually…" I say, fingering creamy paste and semen out of me. "Whatever it is, it's not sticking inside of me…"

"What the fuck…" Luke hunches over and starts scrubbing his dick with the tissue. "Uh… it's not wiping off… The tissue is just sticking to it like it's glue or some shit…"

"Oh… Sit tight, babe, I'll get you a damp, soapy rag," I say, climbing over him. After grabbing a washrag from my dresser, I squeeze out a glob of body wash onto it then I dampen it with a little cold water from my insulated bottle. "Here you go!"

"Thanks." He gets to scrubbing with a bit of vigor. A few seconds later, he wipes away the soap with the dry end of the cloth only to reveal that the white, gluey stuff is not only still there but now it's even more smeared across his shaft. "Um…" he says, turning to me with the most worried look I've ever seen on his face. "Whitney, why won't this come off?"

My eyes go wide. My jaw drops. My heart begins pounding as I slip into a trance.

"Whitney?" he says somewhat sternly.

"I don't know… but we'll find a way to get it off, okay?" I grab my panties and pull them up. "Uh… Get dressed, go to the shower, then just stand under the hot water for a while. Like, maybe soaking might help… In the meantime, I'll try googling some answers…"

"Uh… yeah, okay…" he mumbles, scrambling out of bed while staring down at his cottage cheese-coated cock.

The instant he leaves the room, I call up Lizzy.

"Hey, Whit," she answers on the first ring, still sounding super-depressed over her brother still being missing.

"Hey, Lizzy," I whisper. "How're you doing?"

"Well, I managed to get out of bed to shower today. And I had more than just one meal, so… better than the last few days."

"Aww. Hey, that's progress… You just gotta take it one day at a time."

"Mm-hm… Please don't tell me you called me at 10:05 on your first Friday at UW just to check up on me again. Like, I appreciate it, but you should be out having fun, not worrying about me…"

"Lizzy, you're basically my sister. Even when I'm having fun, I'm worried about you. You should know that. But, if it makes you feel any better, I didn't just call to check in on you. I have a bit of a problem."

"Oh… You okay?"

"Uh… yes? I think I am… But Luke… uh…"

"Whitney, what's wrong?"

"This might be kind of a weird question, but since we got creampied by the glizzy flower, have you ever… umm… have you ever had little white balls—"

"Pop out of my cervix and fall out of my vagina after random contractions or after an orgasm?" she finishes in a hushed voice. "Because yes."

"Oh my gawd! I thought it was just me it was happening to!"

"Me too! I was kind of embarrassed when it happened and didn't want to freak you out, so when you didn't bring it up, I decided to keep it under wraps."

I giggle nervously. "Same… When did it first happen to you?"

"Seven days after Glizzy Night. While I was out hiking. I was just walking then *boom,* my womb spasmed and then I birthed three little, squishy balls in the middle of the woods. You?"

"Oh, wow! It happened to me the night you gave me that sap. Three of them shot out of me mid-orgasm."

She giggles. "Yeah, it happened to me again a few days after I uh… rode the new glizzy flower I told you about."

"Did you ever pop one or have one pop in you?"

"Nope, why?"

"Well… The reason Luke and I didn't go out tonight is because I knew I'd have the room to myself and I thought it'd be nice for us to stay in and… *you know…*"

"Make up for the time he was gone this summer," she finishes.

"Mm-hm! And after having that glizzy flower creampie me," I whisper, "I told Luke to finish in me this time so I could see what it was like."

"*Oh.* And how was that?"

"Super-hot, especially because we came at the same time. Well, it was hot for, like, a second because my uterus laid one of those egg-thingies mid-orgasm again, then my *clam* clamped around his dick like a vice and the egg went *pop* right against his cock."

"Oh, shit…"

"Yeah, and it gets worse."

"Uh-oh… How so?"

"Well, after my vagina clamped around him, it didn't relax for a few minutes, so his cock was stuck getting crushed inside me…"

"Sort of like how our vaginas seized up when the glizzy flower came in us…" Lizzy whispers.

"*Exactly* like that… And then, when my love muscle finally relaxed, he pulled his dick out and there was white paste smeared all over it."

"Shit… That must've been embarrassing."

"Oh… It was… But that's not even the worse part…"

"How could it get worse?"

"Well, he tried wiping off the creamy stuff with a soapy, dampened washcloth, but it wouldn't fucking come off no matter how long or hard he rubbed… So, now he's in the shower trying…"

"Um… what?"

"Yeah… And here's the weirdest part. Not only was I able to finger the *egg's* goo out of me with no problem, but I also used the same washcloth he did to wipe off my hands before I called you and it came right off. It came off my hands but it didn't come off his hands or his dick…"

"I don't…" Lizzy starts to say until her words trail off. A long pause follows

"Lizzy? You still there?"

"Yeah… sorry… I'm just trying to make sense of that… Like, why would it stick to him like glue but come right off of you? That… that doesn't make sense…"

"Now you see why I'm freaking out…"

"I'm sorry, Whitney, but I don't have any answers or solutions for you…"

I sigh. "I was afraid you'd say that…"

"There is one more thing about those *eggs* that I didn't mention earlier…"

"And what's that? Is it something bad or good?"

"Neither?" she says. "Those white balls that I birthed in the middle of the woods?"

"Yeah…"

"Well… I dropped one in the mud next to a bush by accident, then I buried the other in the middle of the wheelbarrow track a few yards later. And then… when I went back out there 5 days later… I found a vadge-star flower growing in both of those same spots…"

"No fucking way…" I mutter… "You're shitting me…"

"I wish I was…"

"So… we're *not* laying *eggs*, we're… birthing *seeds*?"

"Unless someone saw where I dropped those ball-thingies and decided to play a cruel joke on me by planting vadge-star flowers in their place, then yeah… they're seeds… Seeds that are filled with white glue…"

"A glue that only sticks to men apparently…"

"Yeah…"

"Alright, now I'm kinda freaking out."

"Me too… Because I've had this theory for the last few weeks that there's something that's only making males sick before they mysteriously disappear…"

"Shit… yeah… Sundance… Jake Landau… then your brother… Meanwhile, we all got sick after glizzy flower night and recovered within 12-hours or whatever…"

"Mm-hmmmm," Lizzy hums.

"Does that mean… Does that mean Luke is going to get sick now?"

"I don't know… I hope not. I mean, as you know, Eli is the only person who we suspect interacted with a vadge-star since he walked in hiding his crotch the day before we found the flowerless stalk with a dried mess around it."

"Yeah… But Jake went missing before the vadge-star flowers popped up, right?"

"Right. And Sundance didn't go near the glizzy flower, the vadge-star flower, or any of their secretions, so… it could be something unrelated. But if Luke gets sick in the next 12 to 24 hours—"

"We'll know if the glizzy flower and its *offspring* are making guys sick…"

"Yup… so… just keep a close eye on Luke. If he gets feverish, take him right to the hospital and don't let him out of your sight."

"Okay… yeah…" I say as the bedroom door opens.

Luke just stares at me from the doorway with wide, worried eyes, then he shakes his head no.

"Alright," I say to Lizzy. "Luke's back. I gotta go."

"Okay," she says. "Good luck. Keep me posted."

"I will. Bye."

"Bye."

The call ends.

"Who was that?" Luke asks with frustration in his tone.

"Lizzy. I called to ask if she ever had her vagina clamp up like that before…" I point to his crotch. "No luck?"

"Still there…"

"You wanna go to the ER or something?"

He scowls. "No… I'm just going to go to bed and see if I can peel it off in the morning."

"Okay, yeah… Um… Luke?"

"Yes?" he says, sitting on the bed beside me.

"I'm sorry that whatever happened to you happened…"

"It's whatever…" he grumbles. "I mean, it's not like you have an STD or anything, right?"

"Uh, of course not… You're the only guy I've ever been with, so if I have something, I obviously got it from you…"

He searches my eyes with this intensity that makes my stomach sour. "Mm-hm…" He rises from the bed. "I gonna head back to my room…"

"What?" I blurt out, springing up from the mattress. "Why?"

"I'm frustrated, my dick is sore from scrubbing it, and I just don't feel like sharing a bed while I'm in a bad mood, that's all." He heads for the door.

"Babe, you're not mad at me, are you?"

"No," he says flatly.

"You don't think I cheated on you, do you? Because you know I'd never do that to you."

"Whitney, I told you, I'm ticked off and I want to sleep in a bed by myself, okay?"

"Okay," I mutter, my eyes burning.

"I'll see you tomorrow."

"Good night, babe."

He leaves the room without looking at me, slamming the door behind him.

Fuck… I feel so bad about what happened that I'm sick to my stomach…

Also, so much for not letting Luke out of my sight…

CHAPTER 20
CALL THE BOTANIST!

LIZZY RUTHERFORD| 18
*Monday, August 22ⁿᵈ, late afternoon, 3 days since Whitney
called about an egg popping on Luke's wiener—31 days since
Glizzy Night*

I should be in the middle of my first day of college classes like the
rest of my friends…

I should be walking across the University of Portland campus
on my way to my third and final class of the day…

But I'm not…

Instead, I'm at home, laying in my bed staring up at the ceiling
in a trance with tears running down my cheeks. Thanks to the
crippling depression over the fear that I'll never see my brother or
Jake ever again, this is basically how I've been all day every day
since the Saturday after finding that second glizzy flower—ever
since we hit the 3-day mark of Eli's disappearance.

That's when I started losing hope…

The only time I've gotten out of bed to socialize in the 12 days
since Eli vanished was the Friday afternoon that Piper and Whitney
came by to pick up the sap that I collected for them. Oh, and then
again last Wednesday morning when those two and Savanna came
over to say goodbye before leaving for their respective colleges.
Other than that, I've barely even spoken to my parents, who seem

equally as depressed as I've been. Hell, the only time I leave my room is to eat while my parents are out doing work around the ranch.

I was supposed to hit the road for Portland last Friday, but I woke up that morning feeling so low that I decided last minute to defer my first semester to spring next year so I could be home with my parents. Like, there was no way I could go off to college while my brother is still missing… That'd just be fucked up. And there's no way I could focus or even take care of myself while I'm like this. Also, like, what if the cops showed up saying they found his body or something? I'd be so devastated and distraught that I'd just end up flunking out anyway. So, I figured I might as well save my GPA the irreparable damage by starting up classes in the spring after Eli comes home safe…

As I roll onto my side and curl up into fetal position with a body pillow clutched to my chest, my phone starts buzzing under the covers beside me. "Ugh," I groan, feeling around for my Galaxy.

The only reason I'm even checking is to see if someone is calling with news about Eli or to see if Savanna is finally calling me back after going ghost on all of us the day she left for the University of Southern California. The only reason I pick up is because it's a group facetime call with Whitney and Piper.

"Hey, girls!" Piper answers cheerily without looking down at the phone. Her camera is pointing up at her from a low angle as she's walking through a building of some kind. "Good timing, I'm legit just walking into my dorm."

"Hey," I answer, my voice low and devoid of emotion. "How's the first day at UConn?" I set my phone down as I reach over to grab my water bottle from the nightstand.

"About what you'd expect for the first day," Piper says with a lack of enthusiasm. Her first pick was to go to the University of

Southern California with Savanna, but since her dad's a professor at the University of Connecticut, she chose to go there because a perk of his employment at UConn allows her to attend there for free. "Just went over syllabuses. Professors seem chill so far. Oh! Remember that girl I told you about? The one who I partied with this weekend who out-skanked me?"

"Mm-hm," I mumble, still chugging water.

"I asked her why she always seemed like she's rolling on molly and she confided in me today that she legit has an Amazonian Womb Worm!" Piper says. "Then she starts bragging how she's been getting barebacked all weekend because, *apparently*, womb worm slime makes you immune to STDs or some shit. Now I'm, like, totally jealous of her and strongly considering finding a way to get one." She cackles.

I gulp down some more water then set my bottle back on the nightstand. "That's wild. And please don't go contracting a womb worm. I read that the narcotics those worms secret messes up your brain chemistry," I say, finally looking back to the screen. My eyes widen and my heart starts racing when I see Whitney looking super-distraught with red, puffy eyes like she's been crying. "Whit… what's wrong? Did you finally see Luke? Is he okay?" The last I heard from her, Luke told her on Saturday that he was feeling feverish, and he has refused to see her since. That's when we facetimed Piper and told her about the *egg*-balls we've been *laying* and what happened with Luke Friday night.

Piper urgently lifts the phone to her face. "Shit, sorry for rambling on! My dumbass would've realized you were upset if I took the time to actually look down at my fucking phone. What happened, Whit?"

Whitney sniffles. "It's fine. I was trying to get myself to calm down the whole time anyway… Are you both alone?"

"Yeah," I say, putting in my headphones.

"Yup, my roommate won't be back for a bit," Piper says.

Whitney takes a deep breath then blows out slowly. "Alright, so… I got Luke's roommate to let me in their room as he was on his way to class. And, when I walked in, Luke was… I don't know… Luke was, like, out of it… just lying down with the covers pulled up over him. So, I asked him if he got that white gunk off of his dick yet and he just said no. So, I said, *'what do you mean no?'* And then he said, *'not only is it still there, but my dick, balls, and my ass are covered in the stuff. Oh, and my fucking abs and palms.'*"

"Wait… what do you mean?" I mutter. "Like, *how* did it spread?"

Whitney shrugs. "I have no fucking idea!"

"What does it look like? Did he show you?" Piper asks.

Whitney nods slowly and dramatically. "Yeah… he showed me. After I fucking begged him to. And…" Her eyes go wide and she shakes her head. "It looks *exactly* like the slime mold stuff that was growing on Sundance…"

My jaw drops. "No fucking way… Do you have a picture?"

"No, he wouldn't let me take one, but I promise it was *identical* to what was growing on your horse. Like, the top half of his dick was covered in this leathery-looking skin that had veins bulging up along the shaft. And everything from the bottom half down to his testicles is covered in something like squishy candle wax. Some spots look sort of like off-white frosting… Oh, also, an inch from the bottom of his shaft, there were five round bumps in a ring formation…"

"No way…" I say in awe. "And what about the stuff on his belly? The same as—"

"It looks *exactly* like the flesh of the glizzy flower's pod—exactly like what was on Sundance's belly and back. Tan, lumpy, shiny, squishy, oatmeal-looking crap with something similar to buttercream frosting on the edges where healthy skin meets the gross flesh, like the frosting stuff turns into the pod-flesh stuff…"

"Oh fuck…" I gasp. "Oh fuck. Oh fuck…"

"What doesn't make sense is…" Whitney says, her words trailing off for a moment. "What doesn't make sense is that I had the egg's goo in me and on my thighs and hands, but nothing happened to me… And I legit checked inside my vagina with a mirror and a flashlight, and everything looked normal…"

"Guys…" Piper says, staring at the camera all wide-eyed with tears pooling in her eyes.

"What is it, Pipes?" I manage to say despite how badly I'm hyperventilating from the revelation.

"There's something I need to tell you," Piper mutters in a daze. "Something I should've told you weeks ago…"

"What?" I ask.

"Promise me you won't be mad?" Piper says, wincing.

"I promise I won't be mad. Just tell me! We've literally never kept anything from you this whole time."

"Alright," Piper says, sighing dramatically after. "So… that night we fucked the glizzy flower? I uh… I sort of snuck out of the house to meet up with Jake in the hayloft of the stable."

"Wait…" I mutter. "So… the white goo we found was from you?"

"Yeah…" Piper says, looking away from the camera. "I uhh… I deepthroated Jake and, right in the middle of it, all the glizzy jizz in my stomach made me so sick that I threw up all over his cock… I threw up *so* much that it spilled over the edge and rained down on Sundance's rear-end." She hesitantly glances back at the camera, tears spilling down from the corners of her eyes. "Lizzy, I'm so sorry but, if what's happening to Luke is what happened to Sundance, that means me puking glizzy cum is the reason your horse got sick… I just… I wasn't sure until now…"

"Fucking hell, Piper!" I say, still in a trance, shaking my head slowly. "If the glizzy flower's white ejaculate does the same thing as the goo from the egg-thingies, that means Jake *did* get sick because of you. That means the rumors of the *STD* were true…"

"I didn't know!" Piper sobs. "I couldn't have known because, like Whitney said, I had that white stuff all over me and it came off easy. And you *both* had it on your skin and in your vaginas, but nothing happened to you two either, so I didn't know Sundance and Jake got sick because of me until literally *just* now!"

"You should've told us…" I mutter through gritted teeth. "That could've been the missing piece of information we needed to help us figure out that glizzy flower secretions were making males sick… I could've warned Eli to stay away from the vadge-star flowers…"

"Guys," Whitney says.

"Um," Piper says, wiping the tears from her eyes. "Did you or did you *not* fail to tell us right away that the white balls that dropped out of your cunt grew into vadge-star flowers because you were too embarrassed?"

"Guys!" Whitney says again.

I just nod.

"Exactly!" Piper snaps. "We all keep secrets when we're scared and embarrassed… Again, I didn't know any of that was my fault until Whitney told us about Luke just now. Had I known, I would've said something. I swear. But I'm saying something now, and I'm sorry I didn't confess sooner. I wish I did, Lizzy. I really do…"

"You're right," I nod. "I forgive you, Piper"

"Alright!" Whitney blurts out. "Now that we're done playing the blame game, we need to hurry up and figure out why the fuck Sundance, Luke, and Eli all disappeared after getting sick…"

"Yeah, that part doesn't make sense," I mutter. "Like, if we found a puddle of goo Sundance's stall or Eli's room, then we'd know the infection liquifies males or something. But there was nothing left behind in his room, the run-in shed stall, or in Jake's room."

"Lizzy," Piper says, "those scientist girls who came by the house looking for the glizzy flower, do you still have the botanist's number?"

I nod. "Yeah, I saved it in my phone just in case we all got ill again."

"Then you need to call the botanist right the fuck now and tell her everything that's been happening," Piper pleads. "If you tell her the truth, maybe she'll tell us why only guys are getting sick and mysteriously disappearing afterward. Like, the way she was talking about containing those plants *ASAP*, she has to know something."

"Yeah," Whitney chimes in, "and she must know a way to reverse whatever is happening to Luke."

I nod. "I'll call her right now and get back to you all. Whitney, get Luke to the ER ASAP, and don't let him out of your sight until I hear back from the botanist girl, okay?"

"Okay, yeah!" Whitney says. "I'm heading back to his room right now!"

"Alright," I say. "Call you two back in a few." As soon as I end the call with them, I open my contacts and swipe up until I see **Allie (Botanist)**, then I tap the call icon. She doesn't pick up the first time, so I redial her. And when she doesn't answer the second time, I call right back.

"Hello?" a young-sounding woman answers hesitantly.

"Hi, Allie?" I greet.

"Speaking. Who may I ask is calling?"

"It'ss Lizzy Rutherford, the girl you came to see about the glizzy flower—I mean, the linga flower or whatever you called it."

"Oh, hey! What's up, did you find one?"

"I think you know that I lied about finding one, don't you?"

"I had a strong hunch you were lying…"

"And does that mean you and your friends stole it from behind my house?"

There's a long bout of silence.

"We may have retrieved one from near your property a day or two after we stopped by…" she finally says in a bit of a whisper.

"I knew it…"

"Is that why you're calling? You're looking for it because you want it back? If you are, trust me when I say that you're *much* better off having that thing as far away from you as possible."

"No… that's not why I'm calling."

"Oh… Is everything okay, Lizzy?" she asks in a serious tone.

"No… Everything is far from okay…"

"What happened… do you… do you have a flower between your legs?"

"Hm? No… What does that even mean?"

"Oh… never mind… Just tell me what's wrong."

"Uh… I didn't just lie about knowing where the glizzy flower was, I also sort of *did things* with it… and my friends did too… Literally the night before you showed up."

"And *none* of you have flowers between your legs?"

"Umm… I'm still not sure what you're asking, Allie, but no?"

"Okay… Did the flower uh… I don't know how to say this without sounding like a freak, but… did the flower *finish* inside of you all?"

"If by *finish* you mean did it throb and swell and fill our wombs with hot white cream, then yes… It finished in me and my friend Whitney, and now we have weird white balls coming out of us and we're freaking out about it—"

"Shit," she blurts out. "Where are you right now?"

"Home…"

"Are your parents home?"

"Yes… Why?"

"Because we need to talk. In-person. Privately."

"Oh god… Why? Is something wrong? Because—"

"Listen, I'll tell you everything when we meet up, okay. Would you be okay coming over to my house? I don't live far."

"Uh, sure… Yeah…"

"Okay, I'll text you my address. Or would you like me to pick you up?"

I almost say yes, and then I remember that my car is finally back from the shop. "Um, no, I can just drive over."

"Okay. Texting you my address now. If you get lost, just call me, okay?"

"Okay…"

"Alrighty, see you in a few. And try not to freak out. Everything is going to be fine, okay, Lizzy?"

"Okay…"

"Alright, see ya."

"Bye."

As soon as the call ends, I get a text from her.

Allie (Botanist): 9901 93rd Ln SE in Olympia, WA.

When I tap the address and bring up Google Maps, I find out that Allie's house is literally three-quarters of a mile away from my house if I just walk straight through the woods to the southwest. Hiking there would probably take me about ten minutes. However, if I drive, it's about 3.2 miles away because I'd have to go all the way up and around Evergreen Valley, turn left down Meridian Road, then take 86th Avenue to Tucker Road and follow that until her house at the end of the road. Since I'm in a rush to get there, I decide to drive over.

CHAPTER 21
SECRET OF THE GLIZZY FLOWER

LIZZY RUTHERFORD| 18
Monday, 12 minutes after talking to Allie on the phone…

Right after parking at the end of her driveway, I text Allie that I'm here. Before I'm even halfway to the welcome mat, she opens the door and waves.

"Hey, Lizzy," she says, flashing me a sad smile as her eyes glance down at my crotch for a quick second.

"Hi, Allie," I say, flashing a worried smile back before looking down at the tight, black leggings I'm wearing. "Is there something on my pants?"

"No… Sorry… I was just checking to see if you had a flower between your legs, which you clearly don't if you're able to wear tight pants."

I scrunch my face as I squint at her. "Are you ever going to explain what you mean by that?"

"I will," she says, stepping aside so I can enter. "After we talk."

"Okay…" As soon as I step through the doorway, I'm hit with the arousing, delicious scent of the glizzy flower. "Wow…" I pause to inhale deeply. "Do you always just wear that flower's fragrance?"

"All day, every day…" she mutters, gesturing for me to follow her into the living room.

"Oh, why? Do you just enjoy making everyone horny all the time?" A nervous giggle escapes me.

"When I said that I extracted the yoni flower's fragrance and wear it as a perfume, I lied. It's more like…" She flops down onto the couch and sighs. "It's more like I permanently smell this way after I let the flower finish in me."

I sit beside her. "What, so I ride the flower and I end up randomly laying little seed-ball-thingies that grow into vadge-star flowers and you get to smell like a sex goddess all the time?" I smirk.

"Vadge-star flower… I like that name…" she says with a smile. "And, while smelling like this might be a gift, I promise you the curses I've been left with immensely outnumber that one benefit…"

My eyes go wide. "What else did the flower do to you?"

"I'll tell you as soon as we're done talking, okay."

"Great… Now I'm even more worried…"

"Don't be…" she says, giving my shoulder a friendly rub. "You're going to be okay…"

"I hope so…"

"You will… Now, tell me what happened after the linga flower *finished* inside of you and your friend. Did you just *pull it out* and that was it, or did you have a hard time getting it out? Like, was it *stuck* inside of you as though it was covered in crazy glue instead of lube?"

"Um… well… My vagina sort of cramped around the swollen thing, so it definitely didn't come out as easy as it went in, but it slid right out when my friends helped me up. But Whitney—"

"Wait, friends? How many of you were there doing stuff with the flower?"

"Four of us."

"Oh… Could you tell me what fluids got on or in who?"

"Only me and Whitney let it *finish* in us. My friend Piper rode it for a little bit then, after I got *creamed*, she took off the condom and blew it until it splooged. After she drank a bunch of the white ejaculate, Whitney rode it while it was still spurting. And after it shot, like, two jets into her, she climbed off of it, then she and our other friend Savanna basically showered in the ejaculate… I know, we all sound like a bunch of depraved freaks, but we were drunk and the things we did were all dares—dares that our wild friend Piper came up with."

"I see… Don't worry, no judgment here… I've done many things I'm not proud of with that flower… Also, did you say you had a condom on the spadix—I mean, the uh… phallus while you rode it?"

"Yeah. Our friend Piper is a bit *promiscuous*, so I had her put a condom on before she rode it, then I put a new one on before I went. Also, we both bit holes in the tip of the rubbers so the flower could keep lubing itself up… Whitney's the only one who didn't use a condom because Piper dared her to fuck it while it was still *coming* after her blowjob…"

"I see… And did the spadix get stuck in Whitney at all?"

"Um, no? I mean, she said something about how it felt kinda sticky and pulled her inner flesh while she rose off of it, but it didn't get, like, *stuck* inside of her… It came right out…"

"Hmm… sounds like the condom prevented it from sticking in you, and it sounds like Whitney pulled it out before it glued itself to her."

"Wait… what?"

"I'll explain in a bit. What happened to you all later that night? Did you and Whitney get a fever and weird, painful cramps in the middle of the night?"

"*Oh yeah*… And this gross stuff gushed out of us with each cramp…"

She nods. "I've been there. Scary as hell, wasn't it?"

"Absolutely terrifying. Thought I was dying…"

"Me too. And then I woke up the next day feeling normal."

"Yup. Same. Woke up in a cold sweat and that was it."

"What about the other girl? The one who guzzled the ejaculate?"

"Oh, she got feverish too and spent all night puking up white stuff. But she was fine in the morning."

"Okay, good… Forgive me asking you this but, you and Whitney, have either of you had sex with anyone since you've been birthing the white egg-things?"

"I'm still a virgin… But Whitney had unprotected sex with her boyfriend this past Friday. That's actually why I called you…"

Allie's eyes go wide. "Uh-oh… What happened? Don't tell me that one of the spore-eggs popped against his penis?"

"Actually, yeah… After her vagina clamped shut on his wiener… And she just told us today that his penis and scrotum are covered in weird, leathery, beige flesh and that there's stuff that resembles the glizzy flower's flesh pod growing up his abdomen, spine, and butt cheeks…"

"Oh shit… Shit. Shit. Shit," she mutters.

"Yeah… I know it's got to be bad because it sounds like what's happening to him is what happened to my horse before he kicked open the stall door and ran away," I say.

"Wait… Hold on… What? Your horse? How did your horse get exposed to the spore-eggs? Do I even want to know?"

"He didn't… That night we did stuff with the glizzy flower, Piper blew my neighbor Jake in the hayloft of my stable, then she puked the flower's ejaculate all over his junk. Some of her vomit splashed down on my horse when she turned her head away."

"Wait… *Jake*… Jake *Landau*?"

I squint at her. "Yeah… Do you know him?"

"No… some lady from the FBI came asking about disappearances in the area. She mentioned him and an Eli Rutherford. Did Eli happen to live with you?"

My eyes go wide. "Yeah… he's my brother, and he was home for the summer… He disappeared almost two weeks ago—three days after me and Piper discovered someone ripped a vadge-star flower off the stalk a day after we last saw it."

Allie gets this glazed-over look of horror in her eyes as her face goes blank. "Oh god… no… no…"

"Uh-oh… You know why Jake, Eli, and my stallion all mysteriously disappeared after they got sick, don't you?"

Allie takes a deep breath then sighs as she reaches for the laptop on the coffee table. "Before I show you what I'm about to show you—before I tell you a bunch of things you wish you didn't know, I need to ask you one thing. Have you come across any other linga—glizzy flowers since we took the one from your backyard?"

"Actually, yeah…"

"When and where?"

"Two weeks ago—a day after my brother went missing. I followed a pair of tracks from my house south to the fence, then I kept heading south for almost a mile towards Yelm Lake until I smelled it. Didn't take long to sniff my way to it. The weird part is, I had passed *right* through that same area a few days prior during my search for Jake. There was nothing there then, not even a bulge in the soil…"

Allie huffs. "Did the soil look like someone just buried a pod there?"

"Yeah…"

"Were the petals the size of fingers instead of the size of hands?"

"Actually, yeah… Same size as the vadge-star's petals."

"And was the stalk between the soil and the spadix shorter than the first flower you found."

"Mm-hm… Why are you asking all of that?"

With a huff, she logs into her laptop and clicks around before turning her screen to me. "This is Matty Barlow, the guy who got a spore-egg popped on his penis after my *vagina* clenched around him mid-orgasm." Now she clicks the **next** arrow, bringing up a photo of Matty where most of his body is covered in the same gross biomass that makes up the flower's flesh pod—the same mass that grew all over my horse. "This is him four days after being infected." She clicks again, bringing up a picture of a gross flesh pod in a wheelbarrow with its erect glizzy flower sticking up out of it. "And *this* is him after we dug him up from the woods behind your house the day after I met you."

"Wait…" My stomach churns. My heart throttles so hard that my vision is pulsing. "I don't understand what you're saying right now."

Allie clicks to another picture, one of a handsome white guy who's naked from the waist down with his dick buried balls-deep in a vadge-star flower. The petals are curled inward and stuck to his flesh like large fingers are trying to squeeze his crotch, and it looks horrific.

"This is my friend Brandon Harris minutes after he stuck his penis in a yoni flower, or vadge-star as you call it," she says.

Allie clicks through more pictures of Brandon. In each subsequent photo, more and more of his flesh is covered by the SCOBY-looking mass. The last picture she shows me is of Brandon standing in front of her patio's slide door completely naked and covered in corrupted flesh, a long strip of pod-mass meat running up the middle of his back.

"And this is Brandon in what we call the podling stage. This is right before he mindlessly walked out of the house in the middle of the night."

"Wait, why would he just wander outside like that?" I ask.

"You see this gross stuff growing up his spine?"

"Mm-hm. That's how it grew on my horse too. Right along the spine in a straight line…"

"Well, we think it does to men what Ophiocordyceps unilateralis does to ants. The fungus hijacks the brain of ants and makes them leave the hive and cling to a leaf with their jaw so it can spread spores down onto other ants. The yoni flower makes men do this…"

Now she closes out of the slideshow and double clicks on an mp4 file. The video that pops up shows the mutated Brandon guy using his bare hands to dig a hole at the foot of a Duncan Cedar tree. Allie then fast forwards to the 40-minute mark. A few seconds later, Brandon stops digging then climbs into the pit that's about 6 by 3-feet and about 3-feet-deep. Without paying the girls above him any mind, he lays flat on his back then simply begins burying himself alive with the soil he just dug up. And he keeps on burying himself until he's completely covered. That's when he pulls his arms down into the soil until his hands disappear below ground…

"There's no way that's real," I say, my unblinking eyes still staring blankly at the screen.

"I wish it wasn't, but it is, Lizzy…" she says, double-clicking another video. This clip shows her and the Indian girl named Priya cutting open a pod in the middle of the woods. Moments after they peel back the large, rectangular flap that they cut out, bones, a spine, and a skull with a freaky-looking brain in it appear suspended beneath the flesh door.

"Oh gawd… Is that… Brandon or Matty?"

She shakes her head. "Neither. This is us dissecting the very first linga flower pod I ever found before what happened to them happened… I'm not sure how old this one is, but we think it was hidden deep in Olympic Nation Forest for decades or possibly centuries…"

"So… Jake… Eli… They… *That* happened to them?" I sigh out a shaky breath. "They buried themselves alive with their wieners sticking out of the soil like a flower and… *died?*"

"Unfortunately, yes… And I'm so sorry to be the one to drop this bombshell on you, but… every guy who has *sex* with a yoni flower or who gets a spore-ball popped on their penises during sex or who apparently also get the linga flower's ejaculate on them turns into a zombie-like drone who buries themselves alive. And, once they do, their body rapidly finishes transforming into the pod while a stalk grows between the pod and their penises to make it sprout above the ground…"

I go from sitting there silently to sobbing in the blink of an eye. "So… you're telling me that the last glizzy flower I found a few weeks ago…"

Allie nods. "If you found days after Eli vanished in a spot that you recently checked before he went missing, there's no doubt in my mind that the new linga flower and the pod beneath the soil was likely your brother… Especially if the petals were the same size as the ones on the yoni flower that went missing."

I retch hard, slapping my palm against my mouth to keep myself from puking. "No…HURRP…" I retch again, swallowing hard to keep from puking on Allie's couch and floor. "Oh God no…"

She consoles me as my body begins trembling. "I'm so, so sorry, Lizzy."

I shake my head against her. "Please tell me you're wrong, Allie… Please?"

"I wish I could," she mutters. "But, based on what you've told me, I'm 99% sure that new one was your brother and that the linga flower belonging to Jake is somewhere else in those woods…"

"No… you have to be wrong, Allie… You have to be! Because I did things with that new glizzy ten minutes after I found it…"

Her jaw drops. "Oh no…"

"So, if you're not wrong, that means the last plant I rode until it creamed me was—" The instant I feel vomit rushing up my throat, I slap my hand over my lips again and rise from the couch.

It was my dead brother's mutated penis, I think as my mouth floods with puke that I somehow keep from spewing all over the place.

Allie grabs my arm and urgently leads me towards the hallway. "Bathroom's right there, honey!"

The toilet seat lid is already up when I race into the bathroom. Perfect because, as I'm kneeling, the taste of vomit and memory of what I did with Eli's *glizzy* makes me so sick that I retch again. Somehow, only a little bit of it splashes the edge of the toilet.

"It's okay, Lizzy," Allie says, pulling my hair back. "Just… try to remember that the last flower you found wasn't really your brother anymore by the time you found it… It was a just fungoid plant that consumed him…"

More puke splashes loudly against the toilet water. "No… if I found it *a day* after he disappeared, that thing was *still* mostly my brother…" I barf again, groaning as slimy strings drip off my chin.

"You're wrong, Lizzy," she says, sweeping a hand up and down my back in that nurturing way my mom used to when I was sick as a kid. "By the time he walked out into the night, he was no longer your brother. His mind was gone. His body from the neck down and the knees up were no longer human, it was all linga flower and pod flesh. I promise."

I just nod, staring in a trance at the little food I had today that's floating around the water. After that, I go catatonic…

I don't know how long I was kneeling there with my head over the toilet bowl but, by the time I finally pull myself together and get over to the sink to wash my mouth, my body is aching from sitting on the hard floor the way I was.

There's a knock at the bathroom door that snaps me out of my trance. "Hey, you okay?" Allie says from the doorway just as I'm cutting off the water.

"I don't know if I'll ever be okay again…"

She nods. "I totally understand that… Well, I made you some tea and toast to help settle your stomach."

"Thank you," I mutter, still half in a trance, my eyes refusing to blink even though they're dry as hell.

"No problem," she says, placing a hand on my back and guiding me to the living room.

As I shuffle my feet behind her, that delicious fragrance excites me in a way that I should be too depressed to feel. "Allie, you never told me what else the flower did to you…" I mutter.

"I already dropped a lot on you today, maybe I'll let you know another day."

"No…" I say as I ease down onto the couch. "I want to know… I need to know what other horrible things are going to happen to me or what horrible things have already happened that we don't know about yet."

Allie huffs as she sits beside me. "Well, aside from the fact that you'll probably be birthing those spore-eggs for the foreseeable future, the other major change that you may or may not be aware of is that your cervix was likely transformed into a sphincter."

I nod as I sip some tea. "That I figured out a few weeks ago when I used a speculum and a mirror to see why my cervix felt wide enough to pass those balls."

"Figured you would've after feeling gumball-sized egg-seeds passing through a hole that they shouldn't be able to fit through…"

"Is there anything else? Other than the fact that I'm always leaking this clear, pale-yellow sap stuff?"

She makes a face like she wants to say something but she just shakes her head. "So long as neither of you rides the linga flower to completion without a condom, I don't think anything else will happen to you."

"Wait, what would've happened if I didn't wear a condom?"

She searches my eyes in silence for a moment. "I'm going to show you something, okay?"

"Okay…"

"FYI, what I have to show you is between my legs…"

"Um… oh… *kay*…"

When she reaches down and grabs her skirt, something bulges between her legs.

My eyes go wide. "Hold on… Do you have—"

"A penis? No." She snickers as she lifts her skirt.

As she spreads her legs, I marvel at the sight of these five bright-red, glistening petals blossoming like an opening hand between her legs, revealing a tight little hole that's dripping with golden sap.

It looks like a vadge-star flower is growing out of her vagina…

Like, two of the hand-sized petals are growing from where her labia should be, one is growing straight out just under her urethra and clit like a penis, and the other two are down between her legs running down the length of her thighs.

"Holy fucking shit!" I scream, scurrying back from the sight that I'm unable to process. "Is that—"

"Growing out of me? Yes…" Suddenly, the hand-sized petals close up like a banana peel then unfurl back into a blossom before curling inward like mutant fingers.

"Are you… controlling those or is it doing that on its own?"

"*I'm* controlling them…"

"No way…" I gasp. "How did this happen?"

"What we know so far is that something in the white ejaculate mixes with the sap and the brown slime, creating some sort of powerful adhesive that also makes the phallus all mushy and tacky. Then, after it swells inside of a vagina that's cramping around it, it rapidly fuses to your flesh and you can't pull it out no matter how hard you try. After that, the stalk pops out of the center of the flower then the inside of the birth canal gets all hot and fizzy as it fuses to the vaginal walls. A few hours after I endured all of that, I woke up to womb cramps and the flower was throbbing on its own, gushing out the slime and flesh it didn't need. I couldn't sense what the flower was doing or touching then though. It wasn't until ten hours later that I woke up and was somehow able to feel everything that touched or penetrated the flower. That's when I figured out that I could control it…"

"Are you serious? Like, how is that possible?"

Allie shrugs. "We've discovered that these flowers have neurons. That's how they're able to throb and whatnot. So, at some point when it was merging with my vagina while I was asleep, its neurons connected to mine…"

"And… do things feel *the same* when you… you know…"

She nods slowly and dramatically. "Better actually…"

"Fucking wild…"

"It's been months and I still don't believe it," she says, pulling her skirt back down.

"So… the vadge-star flowers turn men into new pods and turns their penises into glizzy flowers, which then turns the women who fuck them into walking vadge-star flowers who drop seeds, starting the cycle all over again."

"Precisely."

"So… Whitney's boyfriend Luke… Is there any way to keep what happened to Eli and Jake from happening to him?"

Allie twists her mouth to the side while shaking her head. "We've been trying to come up with a way to stop the progression, but antifungals and antibiotics don't work. And there's not a lot we can do without tests subjects to try different drugs on…"

"So… he's going to die too?" My eyes well with tears.

She nods. "I'm afraid so…"

"Shit… Shit! This is all my fault… Had I just told you about the flower when you came by—"

"Hey, if this is anyone's fault, it's mine, Lizzy. Because these things wouldn't be spreading and making men sick if I didn't screw that Matty guy. What's happening to you wouldn't have happened if I just stopped him from leaving my house that night. These horrible things wouldn't be happening if I took that flower from behind your house just a few days earlier. All this shit wouldn't have happened to you and your brother and your friends if I just called your bluff and told you all the bad things that'd happen if you fucked that linga flower. And, for that, I'm sorry."

"It's okay, Allie… I invited my friends over to be depraved with that glizzy flower, and I'm the one that dropped the seed-ball-thing that sprouted into the flower that my brother found. None of what's happening would've happened if I didn't do any of that…"

"Listen, Lizzy. I've been beating myself up over all this crap for almost three months and it's not doing any good. All we can do now to protect others from going through what me, you, your brother, and your friends have gone through is to track down all the linga and yoni flowers, then contain them. But before that, we have to sit down with Whitney and catch her up to speed so she doesn't spread any more seeds or accidentally infect anyone else. Then we need to deal with Luke before he goes full podling and buries himself. Can you help me with all of that?"

I nod. "I can and I will. I have to since I'm partly responsible. And since I dropped this semester to deal with my brother being missing, I've got nothing but free time."

She flashes me a pitiful look. "Okay then… So, where are Whitney and Luke right now?"

"They're up at the University of Washington."

"Perfect! My OB/GYN is in Seattle and she's become sort of an expert on my situation, so we can get her to examine you and Whitney while we're there. Free of charge."

"Oh, wow. Yeah, it'd be good to get checked out by someone who knows what's going on!"

"Mm-hm!" She rises from the couch. "Do you need to go home and get ready or anything?"

I stand too. "Nope. I can leave right now if you want."

"Okay, then we can head out as soon as Priya gets home in a few minutes." She extends her hand to me. "Welcome to the Yoni Flower Squad, Lizzy Rutherford," she says with a sad smile.

I offer her a pitiful smile as I give her hand a shake. "Thanks?" A nervous giggle escapes me. "It'll be nice to be distracted for a while, that's for sure… Hopefully, I can help you *save* the world."

She smirks. "Considering you tracked down a linga flower barely a day after it appeared, and since you know your way around those woods, I'm sure you're going to be a huge help to the cause!"

LIZZY, WHITNEY, & PIPER WILL JOIN ALLIE IN **THE YONI FLOWER BOOK 2: BLIGHT OF THE YONI FLOWER**

FIND OUT WHY SAVANNA LOCKHART HASN'T BEEN RESPONDING TO LIZZY & THE GIRLS IN THE TIE-IN SHORT STORY: **Flesh Forest: Origins**

Great… I'm rolling so hard on this molly that I can't taste the most delicious burger I've ever had…

Wait, we're leaving soon? Already? And you're telling me I left my burger sitting outside for over two hours? No way… I must be losing time from drinking so much while on MDMA…

Whatever. Since I can't eat it now, I'll just take it home. Umm… what do you mean we can't take certain foods back into the US? Crap! What am I gonna do, smuggle it across the border the way I brought our party favors down to Tijuana?

Actually… that's genius! Who says Alicia 'Trouble' Romano doesn't come up with good ideas while drunk and high out of her mind?

But 5 ounces of beef though? That's a lot of meat for a girl to handle… Whatever, I'll make it work. Considering I don't remember the last 2 hours, I better get to it before I forget.

Sometime later…

Ugh… Why do I have a fever? And why am I so delirious? And… are those… maggots all over my bed—all over me? What sort of horror movie did I wake up in?

Author's Note:

I just wanted to take the time to thank all of you readers out there who have been reading my works on Literotica and sexstories this past year or so. Your comments, emails, and votes keep me going and inspire me to keep writing these deliciously messed up tales.

A special thanks to everyone who has purchased a copy of this book and the previous books in the series. Seriously, knowing you all love these stories enough to purchase them with your hard-earned money during these trying times warms my heart! I love and appreciate you all so much that there are no words to describe it. I hope that I can keep showing you how much I love you all by writing more of these tails that you love. And if you'd like to reach out to me on Twitter @BLOverman99 or email (BLOverman99@gmail.com) to chat, feel free to message me! We can talk book stuff, you can send me story suggestions, or if there's a freaky story that doesn't exist and you want it written, please feel free to follow me and private message me and maybe I can write something for ya and post free for you on my publisher's site or Literotica! If you follow me on Twitter, I follow back all of my readers, so I will respond!

For those of you who don't know, authors who write erotica books are unable to promote their books with ads and such, which means that word of mouth and user reviews are the only way to make our works visible on sights like Amazon. So, if you have enjoyed *The Yoni Flower* books and *The Amazonian Uteroboscis*, if you could be so kind as to leave a review wherever you purchased this book, that would mean the world to me! Also, if you'd like to keep up with the rest of the series, please head on over to my publisher's website [here at: https://www.scirotic.com/bl-overman] and sign up to the email list. I promise there won't be any spam. There will just be routine updates on my books and similar books to these, messages from me, and treats such as **FREE** epubs/PDFs of samples/short stories/bonus tie-ins that'll be sent out throughout the year.

Thanks again!
With love and appreciation,
B.L. Overman

About the Author:
B.L. Overman

Horror/Sci-Fi Erotica author who writes steamy, graphic, deliciously disturbing tales with unique twists.
Get ready for my next books in the series!

My books so far:

Signup here (https://www.scirotic.com/bl-overman) for release date updates & to get the first few chapters of each book early along with exclusive bonus chapters like Savanna's and Piper's bonus chapters from *Lizzy's Glizzy Flower*

Visit my Amazon Author Page to view my catalog:
https://www.amazon.com/author/bl_overman

Follow me @BLOverman99 on Twitter to keep up with updates & come chat with me so we can talk about these books or whatever else you want to chat about!
https://twitter.com/BLOverman99

Or email me if you wanna say hi, talk about ideas, or discuss my books!
BLOverman99@gmail.com